PE

I W

Kingsley Amis, who was born in South London in 1922, was educated at the City of London School and St John's College, Oxford. At one time he was a university lecturer, a keen reader of science fiction and a jazz enthusiast. His novels include *Lucky Jim* (1954), *Take A Girl Like You* (1960), *The Anti-Death League* (1966), *The Alteration* (1976, winner of the John W. Campbell Memorial Award), *Jake's Thing* (1978), *Russian Hide-and-Seek* (1980), *Stanley and the Women* (1984) and *The Old Devils*, winner of the 1986 Booker Prize. Among his other publications are *New Maps of Hell*, a survey of science fiction (1960), *The James Bond Dossier* (1965), *Colonel Sun*, a James Bond adventure (1968, under the pseudonym of Robert Markham), *Rudyard Kipling and his World* (1975) and *The Golden Age of Science Fiction* (1981). He published his *Collected Poems* in 1979 and his *Collected Short Stories* in 1980. Many of his books are published in Penguin. He has written ephemerally on politics, education, language, films, television and drink. Kingsley Amis was awarded the CBE in 1981.

By the same author

Fiction

Lucky Jim
That Uncertain Feeling
I Like It Here
Take a Girl Like You
One Fat Englishman
The Anti-Death League
The Green Man
Girl, 20
The Riverside Villas Murder
Ending Up
The Alteration
Jake's Thing
Russian Hide-and-Seek
Stanley and the Women
The Golden Age of Science Fiction (editor)
Collected Short Stories
The Old Devils

Verse

A Case of Samples
A Look Round the Estate
Collected Poems 1944–79
The New Oxford Book of Light Verse (editor)
The Faber Popular Reciter (editor)

Non-fiction

New Maps of Hell: A Survey of Science Fiction
The James Bond Dossier
What Became of Jane Austen? and other questions
On Drink
Rudyard Kipling and His World
Harold's Years (editor)
Every Day Drinking
How's Your Glass?

With Robert Conquest

Spectrum I, II, III, IV, V (editor)
The Egyptologists

I WANT IT NOW

KINGSLEY AMIS

PENGUIN BOOKS

Penguin Books Ltd, 27 Wrights Lane, London W8 5TZ (Publishing and Editorial)
and Harmondsworth, Middlesex, England (Distribution and Warehouse)
Viking Penguin Inc., 40 West 23rd Street, New York, New York 10010, USA
Penguin Books Australia Ltd, Ringwood, Victoria, Australia
Penguin Books Canada Ltd, 2801 John Street, Markham, Ontario, Canada L3R 1B4
Penguin Books (NZ) Ltd, 182–190 Wairau Road, Auckland 10, New Zealand

First published by Jonathan Cape 1968
Published in Penguin Books 1988

Made and printed in Great Britain by
Richard Clay Ltd, Bungay, Suffolk
Set in Baskerville

CONTENTS

TO

TOM MASCHLER

One

LONDON

'Now if I may bring the two of you to a final point,' said Ronnie Appleyard, with an air of genuinely asking permission, 'what about the more long-term future? Wouldn't you agree that the present Government proposals' – he turned suddenly to the junior Minister on his left – 'do no more than nibble at this vital human – '

The Minister got as far as 'Not for a – ' before Ronnie rode over him.

'Old people are not a nuisance that we're being forced to do something about against our will; they've given their working lives to build our prosperity, they deserve their full share of it and it's up to all of us, up to *you* ... '

Ronnie's abrupt pause took the Minister off guard. He had not done a great deal of television, and he had been thoroughly daunted five minutes earlier, when Ronnie had contradicted him on a factual point about National Health prescriptions. He had been right and Ronnie wrong, but a negligible percentage of the three million viewers would know that, and he was fully aware that Ronnie's way of apologizing for the lapse in the next programme would only endear him further to that vast majority who would already have forgotten about the matter at issue. The Minister made a jerky movement with his hand and said with controlled exasperation, 'Look – I and all my colleagues are bearing that in mind all the time, Ronnie. This thing is a top priority with us. You go on as if we're doing nothing about it. I've just been telling you – '

'Not nothing, Mr Gibson.' Ronnie sat motionless on his raised stool, a tall fair-haired figure, thinnish but greedy-looking. 'Not nothing. Just a good deal less than ordinary common decency requires. That's all.'

Conscious of what the use of his surname after his own christian-naming had made him seem, the Minister opened his mouth as if he meant to bite Ronnie, but Ronnie had already turned to the other participant, an elderly Opposition back-bencher whose bleating voice and perpetually puzzled expression, plus the combination of white hair and a black moustache, put him much in demand for programmes of this sort.

'Would you agree with that, sir?'

'Oh yes. Yes. Very strongly. Agree very strongly.'

'Though the record of your own Party when in office, if I may say so with all respect, doesn't exactly fill one with confidence as to its intentions towards old people.'

'Oh. Contest that. Contest that very strongly.'

But Ronnie, whose timing was never off, had seen the floor manager, crouched before him like a suppliant, extend his crossed index-fingers in the half-minute signal.

'Thank you, gentlemen. I'm afraid that's all we have time for.'

A bleat and a discontented mutter came from right and left. The red light of the camera facing Ronnie flashed on. He spoke into it, half-closing his left eye and pushing his lips forward slightly in one of his sincerity faces.

'Well, what do you think? I'll tell you what I think. I think we as a nation have got our values all back to front. What sane and responsible society would pour its money away on useless, unproductive things like our overseas military presence or the H-bomb—a bit worse than useless, that—while we're keeping our old people on or around subsistence level? Let's not forget that when we talk glibly about priorities. Anyway, no more talk, glib or not, from us. *Insight* will be back with more news and views on Wednesday, usual time. Night.'

To be fair to Ronnie Appleyard, he had no feelings for old people as such beyond a mild dislike, never wasted his time sweating about the H-bomb, and would not have cared a curse if the British army were to set about re-occupying the Indian sub-continent, provided they did so without calling on him for assistance. He even wondered momentarily whether his show of concern for the old might not tell slightly against him with the group he would have said he spoke to and for: the intelligent and independent-minded young. Then he cheered up again at the reflection that it was their parents the little bastards were against, rather than their grandparents. As the jangling and thumping of the title music filled the huge lofty room, he glanced to his flanks and did a different sincerity routine, the one with raised eyebrows and a lot of nodding. It looked unpoised into camera, but worked, he thought, at a moment like this.

Doing the routine, he said eagerly, 'That was really damn good. One of the best discussions we've ever had on this programme.' (Ronnie always said that: they had to go away liking you, or at least not hating you as much as they reasonably might.) 'Really got to the guts of the thing.'

'I thought so. I thought so,' came from his right, but the Minister spoke with some irritation. 'Look, the prescription charges went on in –'

'I know, Phil, I'm desperately sorry, I can't think what in hell possessed me. I'll put it right on Wednesday, of course. I did realize it, but too late to go back. Threw me off for a moment, actually – I hope it didn't show?' Ronnie divided an anxious glance between the two of them.

'It would take a bloody sight more than that to get anything to show where you're concerned,' said the Minister, smiling very slightly.

'Right, thank you, studio,' called the floor manager in a boxing-M.C. voice, after the last jangle and thump had faded. The clamour of packing-up began. The two wizened men in brown overalls who had operated the end-titles – the only members of the crew over about thirty – made a loud military fuss of gathering together the black cardboard oblongs. A camera wheeled away into the middle distance like a noiseless mobile crane. The producer, bearded and corduroy-jacketed, emerged from a jungle of gantries and cables by the doorway and came striding across. Ronnie reached over and patted the Minister's knee.

'Sorry, Phil, honestly.'

'Forget it, Mr Appleyard.'

The producer halted in front of the group and raised his arms above shoulder height, like Dracula.

'Lovely,' he said on a rising note. 'Absolutely lovely. Whether they'll get it in Wigan is anybody's guess, but what do we care? Vigorous and forthright. There's a lot of trendy stuff going about about why has every discussion got to turn into a disagreement, but to me, to me, conflict is the essence of good television. And after all I gather the Parties are supposed to be still divided on some issues? Thank you, Sir Thomas,'—he lunged forward and shook the Opposition member's hand, once but violently, then did the same to the Minister—'and you, Mr Gibson. Nice job, Ronnie. Just a moment.'

He caught a passing technician by the upper arm and spoke in a fast monotone. 'Fred, the next time anybody working for me gives me mike shadow and is told about it and then in his next shot gives me mike shadow he doesn't work for me any more and he finds it very hard to work for anybody else, okay? Sorry about that,' he went on instantly to the three, 'but you have to get that type of material off your chest while it's still fresh or it may go sour. Start to rankle. Anyway, who cares? It's only the telly, after all. Only the old telly. Now if you'd all like to go up to Hospitality I'll just have a quick word with the lads here and follow you along, okay?'

'I wish I could, Eric,' said Ronnie, 'but I have to dash. Long way to go.'

'It'll keep, love, whatever it is. You've got time for one.'

'Sorry, but the party's begun already and the best stuff tends to go early.'

'Oh, listen to him, isn't it awful? To think of what's in store for some poor bird on a gorgeous evening like this. Run along, then. Look, uh, that Amsterdam clip we had for Wednesday's no good. Too much Dutch. We may have to use that bloody boring Wolverhampton road-widening scheme thing after all. Or the witchcraft society.

Have a lovely big think about it, will you, Ron? If you can find the time, you horrible man. See you tomorrow.'

After promising the Minister that the prescription-charges apology would be an absolutely crawling one, making sincere farewells to both politicians (who had been watching him and the producer with smiling incomprehension and unaffectionate weariness respectively), and patting his superior on the shoulder, Ronnie left. Not that that bearded buffoon of a minimally glorified vision-mixer, he thought to himself, was superior to anyone much. Still, if it kept him amused, let him work away at his smirk-to-snarl quick-change routine on the floor and his even less compelling single act up in the box, where throughout transmission he would gesture for his cues and camera-changes like a seated Toscanini. What mattered to Ronnie was that he and his two commentator-interviewer colleagues, and increasingly himself, had the real say in what the programme did, the real power. Not that, to be fair to Ronnie Appleyard a second time, he had the least interest in power as such. Fame and money, with a giant's helping of sex thrown in, were all he was after.

He hurried now through windowless corridors lined with blown-up photographs of all-too-familiar faces, took the lift and emerged in Reception. Here, evening sunlight slanted in through glass doors, and dark-uniformed ex-warrant-officers lumbered about getting everything wrong. Here, too, the short fat shape of Bill Hamer was to be seen in three-quarter rear view, a gamboge antelope-hide jacket thrown across the shoulders, evidently with a careless or negligent intention. This habitual trick of Hamer's would have been enough, even in the absence of all the abundant other evidence, to suggest to Ronnie that Hamer was a man who really was interested in power. But, or rather and, Bill Hamer was the star and chairman of the Bill Hamer Programme, a run-through of which he had no doubt been attending. Ronnie crossed the pink marble floor towards him.

Hamer turned and lit up his face in one of his charming smiles, the one with the slight frown and the lips the same distance apart all the way along. At fifty-three he was too old and shagged-looking to do sincerity any more. He saw in Ronnie someone near the spearhead of a general threat to his position as the best-known and highest-paid performer of his type on any network, and also disliked him as a person. But, unequivocally but, Ronnie had a lot to do with deciding who was going to appear in *Insight*, and appearing in *Insight* would give a valuable boost to Hamer's claim to be more than a mere entertainer, to be a serious and responsible voice in the affairs of the nation. In the light baritone that went so well with his habitual pretence of humility, Hamer said,

'Hallo, Ronnie, you old scoundrel, where are you off to in such a hurry?'

Before Ronnie could reply, in other words instantaneously, one of the warrant-officers appeared and said in thick tones, but with nearly unmistakable satisfaction, 'I'm afraid there's no trace of your car, Mr Hamer.'

'Oh, but I can see a quite substantial one. It's just pulled up outside. Thank you so much. Can I give you a lift, Ronnie?'

While the fellow in uniform slowly mimed his way from incredulity to apology, Ronnie said, 'Jolly kind of you, Bill. You could drop me off somewhere central if you would. I'm actually going to Little Venice.'

'Not the Reichenbergers' party, by any chance?'

'*Yes. How* extraordinary.'

As they came out on to the spacious portico, designed after somebody's rough idea of a Greek temple, two identical girls, of an age somewhere in that mysterious tract between twelve or so and twenty-two or so, suddenly grew alert. They were physically, as well as sartorially, characteristic of their tribe: small, small-headed beyond proportion, with long dark lank hair, wearing pastel-coloured dresses that ended perhaps a centimetre below the crotch, tights of similar shades and pale shiny shoes. Further, they both carried autograph albums. After an exchange of whispers they scuttled up to Ronnie.

'Excuse me, are you Ronnie Appleyard?'

'Yes.'

'Can I have your autograph, please?'

'Certainly.'

While the other girl pronounced a similar formula to Hamer, Ronnie settled down to a great display on the pink page with the felt-tipped pen handed him, asking for and filling in his devotee's full name, adding the place and date, elaborating on best wishes and other dispensables. He was simultaneously savouring and trying to master his emotion, an emotion that would take weeks to fade, at the milestone-type, major fact of his having been asked for his autograph *before Bill Hamer*. Though well aware that all this unnecessary scribbling would strike Hamer as a rubbing-in—with sandpaper—of that event, Ronnie was enjoying himself too much to stop at once. He did, however, reject the idea of rounding off his inscription with 'Fight for Free Universities *Now*', which might anyway not stand to his credit in six months' time if the new swing kept up, and, on being presented with the second album, confined himself to the 'Cheers Rwww Affuywcl' he gave people when he was in a hurry.

'Thank you very much,' the mites piped in unison.

'Not at *all*,' said Hamer, and Ronnie simultaneously said, 'Thank *you* for *asking*.'

Not looking at each other, the two men crossed the pavement towards the waiting car. The sky above the Underground station, the bowling alley, the Indian restaurant was still bright blue at a quarter past seven, with a single puny white cloud near the sun. Hamer emphatically opened the rear door of the black Humber Hawk for Ronnie, beating the heavily breathing driver to it.

'I don't see why I should use my own car and driver if the firm's prepared to cough up, do you, Ronnie? How do you get over here, by the way?'

'Minicab mostly.'

'Ah.'

Realizing that it was too late now to go into why he left his car at home, Ronnie let Hamer have that one with a good grace. They settled themselves in the back of the Humber, which drove away through streets lined with hoardings and the dusty fronts of small shops. Most of the highway appeared to be under repair, or rather the traffic was denied the use of large stretches of vacant and what looked like perfectly serviceable road—no worse, at any rate, than the humped and pocked surfaces on which travel was permitted. Hamer gave Ronnie a Gauloise, took one himself, and said,

'*Insight* go off all right?'

'Nothing to it.'

'You know, I envy you chaps who get shot of the thing when the evening's still young and can just forget about it. I'll have to be on my way back in a couple of hours.'

Because Genius's show goes out during peak hours and Junior's doesn't, Ronnie supplied for him. Aloud, first swearing as the car descended a three-inch step in the roadway, Ronnie said, 'I hope the Reichenbergers' do makes it worth your while.'

'Oh, it will. I don't think I've seen you at one of their thrashes before, have I?'

'No, this is my first time.'

'You're coming up in the world, my lad. Turning into a celebrity.'

This, Ronnie saw before the words were fairly out of Hamer's mouth, was the opening move in the latest round of their mutual campaign, now in its third week, to be asked to make an appearance on the other man's show while still retaining the power of not returning the favour. At its outset, Ronnie had assured his integrity most seriously that nothing would induce him to debase the standards of *Insight* by allowing this self-infatuated talking-machine into his studio, but he had been unable to do much towards redressing Hamer's obvious advantages. Perhaps he would do better to hang back until the prestige gap had narrowed a bit. Or perhaps his integrity was going to have to sit this one out. He mumbled some insincerities as Hamer went on,

'Mind you, you deserve it. I'd say so, anyway. I know how hard you've kept at it. Still doing your column in the *Sunday Sketch*?'

'*Sunday Sun*. Yes, can't afford to weaken.'

'Sorry: of course. We don't take it at home. Don't get time to read half the stuff we do take, colour supplements and business sections and the rest of the bloody rubbish. Are you working on another book?'

'Coming out in the spring.'

'Good God! You certainly don't let up, do you, Ron? What's this one about?'

'The dental profession.'

'Ow! I'm afraid you won't be numbering me among your readers on dentists. Scared stiff of the buggers.'

The driver, the fuzz from whose ears gleamed gently in

the sunlight, said, 'My dentist gives you tranquillizers. Makes his work less tiring by fifty per cent, he says.'

'Look, just try to keep your mouth shut, will you, old chap?' asked Hamer melodiously. 'I had enough of your pissy comments on the way down. Still, you should do well with it,' he continued to Ronnie. 'What did the psychiatry one sell?'

'About eighteen thousand.'

'Hey, that's bloody *good.*' Hamer made his eyes bulge to help him seem severely shaken by this news. Struggling to take it in, he nodded to himself several times. Then he said, consideringly, 'How old are you, Ronnie?'

'Thirty-six.'

Hamer breathed in noisily through his nose. 'Mm,' he said.

It was clearly time to take the service. 'Who have you got on the show tonight, Bill?'

'Not such a very interesting lot, I'm afraid. In certain fields you might say we're getting near the bottom of the barrel.' Hamer followed up this neat buyer's-market stroke by naming a habitually protesting actress, a highly respectable music critic, a woman reporter who had won an international award and a Liberal M.P., all of them fully well enough known to have been better than appropriate TV company for Ronnie, however offensive or boring they might be. Hamer ended by saying that on the form shown earlier that evening they would not be 'anything like as relevant or penetrating' as last week's lot.

'Who did you have then?' asked Ronnie, though of course he knew full well. 'I'm afraid I didn't get back in time. Got hung up at the studio.'

'Pity you missed it, my old Ron.' Hamer used his eyes again, this time to show that he saw through this move, but without hard feelings. 'We had one of the best discussions I've ever done. Or seen.' He now named the female couturier, the pop artist and the wrestling champion who, he said, had contributed most tellingly to this discussion.

Ronnie looked impressed. 'What were you talking about? Marijuana, wasn't it? I seem to remember—'

'No, marijuana was the week before. This was *apartheid*.'

'Ng.' Ronnie hoped very much that he and Hamer were not going to have their own discussion of this now. He could get all that at home, indeed in every home he ever visited and back at the studio as well. He passed for political, and Left political, because politics, and Left politics, were the trend, and therefore the route of advancement. When the trend changed—he gave it between six months and two years—he would be ready to follow while seeming to lead. He was secretly working on a novel about a kindly magistrate in Angola, which he had visited for ten days the previous year, and had contracted with a very reputable publisher that an early and totally forgotten book of poems of his (poems that rhymed, scanned and made some sort of sense) should appear as a camouflaged reprint on the same day as the novel. He was going to choose that day himself. He was also working on his personal appearance, toning down the floral shirts, narrowing the ties, abandoning the candy-striped jackets, watching for the moment to start shortening his hair. As Hamer had said, Ronnie Appleyard deserved to get on.

He now acted in a way not calculated to help him do so. What he regarded as a failing of his, a tendency to let his personal feelings override the interests of pure ambition, came to the fore. Hamer was saying that all of us here in

Britain bore a share of the guilt for what was happening to the blacks and coloureds in South Africa. Suddenly, without bothering to ask himself whether or not he agreed with this, Ronnie realized that he just could not bear Hamer going on another second, that he would rather have been attending a play by Arnold Wesker than chatting yet again about *apartheid*.

So, resolved not to allow the other so much as a fifth of a second's counter-interruption time, he said as one word, 'That's perfectly true but Bill if I may go off the track before we get there what sort of people turn up at the Reichenbergers' he's a barrister isn't he?'

A less well-drilled face than Hamer's might have shown some surprise and annoyance at this diversion. In his heart of hearts, a small region not in close touch with the rest of him, he was perfectly indifferent to what went on in South Africa, as in all those considerable parts of the world that lay beyond the orbit of British TV and newspapers. With even the places these did reach his concern was selective. Even so, it was very inept to make this violent conversational switch instead of an attack on the British role in the Boer War, say, or a comparison with Buchenwald and Auschwitz—any of the obvious ways of preparing for the next move. Possibly he had misjudged Appleyard. He wondered what motive the hypocritical affected vain little shit had had for deciding to call off their mutual manœuvrings, for it was inconceivable that the creeping climbing trend-mad little turd was not as well up as anyone in London on who went to the Reichenbergers' parties. Anyway, what was so grand about *Insight*? Cheap journalism. Magazine stuff.

These thoughts coursed along their well-worn channels in Hamer's mind while he was saying tolerantly, 'Yes, first-class advocate, Adrian Reichenberger, I understand, company law chiefly. But in fact they're really Antonia's parties. You must have heard that, Ronnie.'

'I think I remember being told something of the sort, yes.'

'Mm.' Hamer glanced out of the window, his eye lighting on a white person here and there among the strolling or standing groups of West Indians and Pakistanis. 'Well, Antonia has this incredible faculty for spotting people. Quite uncanny. You get established chaps there, naturally. The last time I went there were a couple of that pop group – what the hell are they called? – the Passing Clouds. Not passing half quickly enough for my liking, to be quite frank with you. Posturing little queens. Still. But what I was going to say, Antonia has this flair for getting hold of the up-and-coming material. You'd be surprised if I told you how many people I've had on the programme whom I first ran into at her place. Together with a lot of frightful shits, I need hardly say.'

Hamer did the laugh Ronnie had more than once admired on the TV screen, the one that showed that he and the other fellow were now absolutely *thoroughly* at ease together. Moved partly by a disadvantageous desire to negate this effect, and partly by the hope of getting his adversary to underestimate him as naively boyish, but partly too by a real wish to know, Ronnie said, 'What's the bird situation?'

'The ... Oh yes.' The last remnants of Hamer's smile vanished. He himself was a furious adulterer, but there were ways one talked about these things and ways one did not. 'I imagine somebody like you might well find something to interest him at Antonia's.'

And Ronnie did, though not immediately. With no chance for more moves in their reciprocal confidence-game, the car had pulled up alongside a row of dreary but quite rich-looking stucco houses that faced the Regent's Canal, Hamer had given his instructions (backed up with a smiling threat) about being collected, and the two had been admitted into a large square hall by a yellow-skinned person in a white jacket. Before finding a drink and plumping into one or other of the loud-voiced groups that evidently filled the house, Ronnie had had time to tell himself that he had won the recent round on points after all. Hamer's annoyance at being bluffly interrupted would before long change into misgiving that he might be becoming someone quite suitable for being bluffly interrupted.

Do the bastard good, said Ronnie to himself as, gin and bitter lemon in hand, he moved in to the job. Hostess first. He soon found her, a brawny brunette in a purple seersucker dress, standing in a corner among a kind of copse of dyed pampas grasses. She was being talked to about stage design as seen at the Royal Court Theatre by a bearded unknown wearing knee-boots—real Bill Hamer Programme timber, thought Ronnie. When Mrs Reichenberger saw him come up she gripped the man in boots by the back of the neck and twisted him round to point in the right direction. At the same time she rolled her eyes and threw her shoulders back to an alarming degree.

'Look who's here, as they say,' she said, shaking the man in boots a little. 'Mister Heart-throb in person. TV's Young Lochinvar. Nice of you to come, Mr Appleyard.'

The possible satirical edge of these words was absent from her tone and manner. Actually she could have done with a bit of it in her manner; it was disturbing to think that all of that breast-work might be for real. But, of course, Ronnie was overjoyed at this reception. Now that the need to gain her attention and fill her with a proper sense of his importance had been met in advance, all he need bother about was showing her that he was much too amusing and unspoiled by success not to be asked again very soon. Ten minutes' work at the most, after which he could get down to the more challenging tasks of (1) closing with and exploiting some of the other significant people here and (2) homing in on some unattended or incompetently escorted bird.

In the event it took nearer twenty minutes than ten, but promised proportionate gains. After the man in boots had been sent packing – not, Ronnie noted approvingly, without just the right amount of how fascinating it had been and how a proper get-together simply must be fixed up when everybody was back after the holidays—there was suddenly talk of an art-student son whose difficulties Ronnie might be the very man to understand. As described, the difficulties turned out to be nothing that being less of a talentless loafer would not cure, but he gave a full demonstration of himself being the said very man without having to offer the smallest help. As prelude, he had done some hypocritical surprise about any child of Mrs Reichenberger's being of an age to have difficulties. Now, by way of epilogue, he did some eyes and tone of voice to suggest that he would not mind going to bed with Mrs Reichenberger. The risk of being taken up on this total falsehood was as nothing compared with the certainty of being asked to more of the old bag's parties.

Ronnie took himself off when a tiny painter and his rather larger bird moved in among the pampas. The chap was up-and-coming all right, but he had been it for nearly a decade. It was time he either came or went down again; anyway, he was not for Ronnie. Nor was his bird, who wore rococo spectacles and appeared to have whitewashed her face before coming out.

Near by, Hamer, who had left Ronnie's side within seconds of arrival, was trying to back a female Sunday-paper columnist up against the wall. The size of her nostrils alone was enough to make it morally certain that he wanted her for his show rather than his bed. And yet, even to read her column, let alone to hear what people said about it ... Ronnie went in the other direction, past an actor in a shiny green suit, a woman who was absolutely terrible at talking to the kiddies on TV, a disc-jockey carrying in his arms a wriggling toy poodle, some young crap or other in Victorian army officer's uniform, some little bitch or other dressed as a Spanish lady, a food-and-drink pundit who was vigorously keeping up with both his subjects on the spot. None of these was any use to Ronnie. He left them behind him and went into the hall to the drinks table.

Ronnie Appleyard was not much interested in alcohol, had hitherto rather disapproved of it indeed as likely to impair efficiency in the two spheres of self-advancement and sex. But both demanded a show of conviviality and a certain knowledgeableness about the stuff. And at affairs like this one, which his instinct was beginning to tell him was not going to be what Hamer had predicted, a shot of it certainly came in handy. He switched to vodka and bitter lemon, as a drink that tasted even less like a drink, and continued his visual search for something worth his while.

It could not be true that all those within earshot were talking without stopping; presumably it just seemed like it. Then, oddly, at the very next instant, most of those around him did stop. And, in the second or so before they all roared on again, Ronnie caught a man's voice raised in unmistakable and extreme anger.

Nobody else seemed to have noticed. Moved for once by

pure curiosity, Ronnie strolled up the hall towards an alcove partly partitioned off from it, once, perhaps, a small ante-room. He paused in front of a portrait of some geezer in bishop's regalia—evidently not a forebear of either Reichenberger—and looked sidelong in through the moulded archway. Yes, this was it.

Standing with its back to him was a figure that, at first glance, might have been either boy or girl: short haircut, narrow hips, tattered green sweater, faded blue jeans. But the first slight shifting of that stance announced femininity. Facing the girl, a man of about forty with a red face and an expensive suit talked urgently. He must have quietened down a good deal since his recent outburst: as then, no words were audible. However, he was being quite adequately visual with his eyes, his mouth, and his near-Shakespearean gestures. A final, furious one of these, as it might be Hamlet telling Ophelia to get her to a nunnery, came almost as soon as Ronnie had fully taken in the scene, and the man was off. He stalked out through the archway and, with a hostile stare at Ronnie, made for the front door. It banged behind him. Ronnie turned back from watching this and found that the girl had turned too and was looking at him.

Girl? For another moment he wondered whether this might not be a boy. The corrugations of the thick sweater hid whatever there might or might not be in the way of breasts, and there was no discernible make-up. But the face itself countered the least suggestion of maleness, even in its least manly form. He thought it might be the most attractive face he had ever seen, but he could not be anywhere near sure because it was so much unlike all other faces. He had not known before that a human complexion could be as sallow as that, or that there was a kind of lion's-mane-coloured straight hair to go with it, or that moles and freckles could be the same colour as someone's eyes. After all that the features, straight and severe, seemed hardly to matter. She was tall for a girl. As she stepped forward Ronnie noticed rather muzzily that her feet were bare and streaked with dirt. She spoke in a husky undertone.

'Hallo, will you get me a drink?'

'What? Uh ... what would you like?'

'Scotch and water. No ice.'

'Right.'

While he saw to this, Ronnie was wondering who the hell she was. And what she was. Not that that really mattered. He would forgive somebody who looked like that anything in the world. Even if she turned out to be a folk singer he was going to screw her.

He forced the whisky out of the butler as quickly as was consistent with bad manners, but by the time he got back to the girl with the face two other men had zeroed in on her: a television don and a little bastard in a four-button denim jacket and very-queer-film-producer's trousers.

'Sorry, chaps,' said Ronnie, putting his arm through the girl's and walking her away, 'I'm afraid something's come up ... nothing I can do about it ... sorry ... pity it's turned out like this ... '

Not having three hands he had had to carry his own drink in the one at the end of the arm he had done the piloting with, and by now there was as much gin and bitter lemon on the thigh of the girl's jeans as in his glass but, also by now, they were in the alcove where he had first seen her and he was standing in the middle of the archway in such a position that anybody wanting to get past would have had to ask him to move, or rather smite him to the floor.

'How are you?' he said. 'I'm Ronnie Appleyard.' He did the unaffectedly modest one on this, making himself sound mildly surprised that anybody at all, not just he himself, should be of that name.

'Uh,' she said. 'I'm called Simon.'

'What Simon?' He spoke rather sharply.

'No, Simon what. Simon Quick.'

For the third time, and with a touch of the eerie, he doubted her sex for an instant. Then he said, still sharply, 'Simon's a boy's name. What were you christened?'

'Never mind. I'm called Simon.'

The voice was the same husky undertone. At this stage he registered its accent as upper-crust British with an American vowel or two. Its tone was flat and weary. Her demeanour was entirely listless. He looked into her eyes. What colour were they? Very dark brown was the best he could do – a puny bloody description. But, anyway, they seemed dulled, and it occurred to him that she might be under some drug, which would be very pissy of her. He said, more sharply,

'What's the matter with you? Are you ill?'

She looked into her drink. 'I'm all right. I'm always all right. Don't ask me questions all the time.'

Oh dear: no plain sailing with this one. Not so sharply, he said, 'I'll stop in a minute. But I couldn't help noticing just now that you seemed to be having some sort of row with that chap who left. Anything needing to be done about that?'

'No. He just got mad. I told him I didn't want to do something he wanted me to do and he got mad. People always get mad at me. They ... always do.'

I bet they do, Ronnie thought to himself. 'He's not your husband?'

'No. I haven't got a husband.'

'Well, you don't need one, do you, at your age? What are you, twenty-one?'

'No. I'm twenty-six.'

'You don't look it.' And she did not. One could not trace the beginning of a line on that freckled sandy skin.

'I don't know whether I need one. A husband. People are always telling me I do.'

'What people?'

'Oh, people. You know. Have you got a wife?'

'No.'

'Have you got a girl-friend?'

'I've got some girl-friends.'

'Uh.'

Ronnie felt a curious lassitude, as if the girl were infecting him with her own. He said briskly, 'This thing this chap wanted you to do and you didn't. What was it?'

'Go away with him to Sardinia. Not sex. Just go and stay there and go on the beach and go out all the time.'

'You're well out of Sardinia, I'd say, what with the Armstrong-Joneses and Onassis and Rainier and Grace.'

'Yes, I think they're there. Do you do work?'

'Yes, I do do work. I'm a writer and a broadcaster.'

'Is that giving talks on the radio?'

'In my case it's television. I run a show called –'

'Television.' For the first time, something approaching animation entered Simon Quick's manner. 'Do you know Bill Hamer?'

'Slightly, yes,' said Ronnie in a completely steady voice.

'Don't you think he's marvellous? All that charm.'

'Well ... '

'Well, I think he's super.' Apathy retook possession of her.

Ronnie had decided to strike at once. Any moment Hamer's presence might become known, and it had to be admitted that the fat sod was a formidable bird-getter, as a little clash of wills over a red-haired production assistant had suggested last Christmas at a studio party; and the production assistant had shown no early signs of thinking Hamer was super. All considerations, including the one about Hamer not being allowed to get any sort of one-up at the present stage of the confidence-game, pointed to an immediate change of scene. Ronnie put sincerity, plus the merest dash of intimacy, into his gaze at Simon Whatsername. The ... snuff-coloured? ... eyes looked opaquely back at him. He said quietly,

'What about just skipping out of here? Going and having dinner somewhere?'

'I'd rather go to bed,' she said in her habitual monotone.

'If you're tired some food'll perk you up.'

'I don't mean that. I don't feel tired. I mean sex.'

This was exactly the sort of thing that Ronnie, in his role as a graduate student of Britain's youth, was supposed to know all about. But, for the moment, his reaction was a simple though uncomfortable mixture of lust and alarm, with alarm slightly to the fore. 'Okay,' he said reliably. 'Fine. Nothing I'd like better, love. We'll grab a taxi and go to my flat.'

'I can't wait,' the girl droned. 'I want it now.'

'But you can't have it *now*, for Christ's sake.'

'Of course I can. There are plenty of rooms in this house. I'll speak with Antonia Reichenberger. She's an old friend of my mother's.'

With a speed and agility he would have thought her incapable of, the girl dived past him and was away across the hall. It was all over in a moment. Mrs Reichenberger was only a few yards off, heavily engaged with two Frenchmen who had something to do with clothes. Ronnie lost a couple of seconds getting round the unsteady bulk of the food-and-drink expert, who was now clearly an even better-qualified expert than when he had arrived, and he reached the group to find the Frenchmen being very British, talking French with much mutual interest, the girl gone zombie again, and the Reichenberger woman gazing at him with incredulous loathing.

'How dare you?' she asked him.

'I haven't done a bloody thing, honestly. All I did was ask this ... out to dinner. Is that a crime? And then she—'

'You couldn't even do it yourself, you had to send her.'

'Look, what the hell does she say happened?'

The incredulity departed from Mrs Reichenberger's eyes; the loathing continued unabated. She took them off Ronnie finally and said, 'What was George doing while this was going on? Where is George?'

'George left. He got mad at me.'

'Hardly surprising when—'

'No, before *he* came along.' She moved her head at Ronnie without looking at him.

Mrs Reichenberger put her hand on the shoulder of one of the Frenchmen. 'David, will you bring Adrian here immediately? You'll find him by the drinks table.'

David went. The remaining Frenchman gave a sudden gasp of astonishment, muttered something and hurried after his compatriot. Mrs Reichenberger started up her stare again. Ronnie reflected that it would take a place like hell to have a fury like a woman who felt herself in any sense passed over for another. He was getting his face ready for a fresh and more measured protestation of innocence when Simon Quick said to him,

'Look, you did say you wanted to, you know.'

Ronnie did not hesitate. He said very kindly, 'I'm

sorry. You must have misunderstood me. I'm ... so sorry.'

'But ... '

'That'll do,' said Mrs Reichenberger. 'I'll talk to Mr Appleyard when you've gone, Mona.'

'That's not my name. I'm called Simon. And I'm not going.'

'Yes you are, my girl, under any name. Adrian will put you in a taxi and send you home.'

'I won't go. I'll fight. Kick you. Bite and scratch.' Even now she sounded as if she were dropping off to sleep.

'Nonsense. Just try to think for one minute. Do you want me to upset your mother about this?'

'No. Please don't do that, Antonia.'

'Behave yourself, then. Ah, Adrian ... '

The Q.C.'s distinguished face held the expression of a man who, to his surprise, finds it possible to wish even more heartily than a minute ago that he were sitting in the bar at White's.

'Yes, darling?'

'Adrian, put Mona in a taxi and send her home.'

The girl turned her dark-brown gaze on Ronnie. 'Sorry,' she said in even more of a husky undertone than usual, and went off quite meekly with Reichenberger's hand on her arm.

Ronnie's TV training helped him to get in ahead of Mrs Reichenberger, but it was a near thing. 'I really feel quite dreadful and I'd apologize like a shot and most humbly if I didn't feel absolutely certain I've done not the least thing that requires an apology and may I ask what in fact did she *say*?'

'That you and she wanted to go to bed together and could you have a room upstairs for half an hour.'

'Mm. I see. Oh dear. Well. Actually I thought she looked upset, had a row or something as I now gather she did, and I simply wondered if I could cheer her up. Next time I'll keep my charity to myself.'

'Yes, I should if I were you, if you happen to run into her again ever. Surely you can see she's unbalanced?'

A variety of retorts occurred to Ronnie, but he only put on some concern and said, 'You mean ... seriously?'

'I don't mean she's actually been in hospital, but she's been completely out of hand for years. Her mother can't control her. This kind of behaviour is nothing out of the way at all, I assure you.'

Ronnie said he was sorry to hear that, and they went on in this sort of way until it was proper for him to say he had to be getting along. By putting Mrs Reichenberger in the position of having to call him a liar if she wanted to go on having a row with him, he had staved off ignominy, but there was no point in wasting time. Whatever he might say or do he would be lucky to receive his next invitation here before the year 2000. His hostess amply confirmed this by her demeanour as she acknowledged his thanks for a perfectly terrific party.

He got away without seeing Bill Hamer, which was little enough to set against the left hook and right cross he had taken in the last hour: an important minor avenue of ambition closed to him and what would surely have been a corking screw fallen through the mesh. Not that it had been his fault in any way. And it would be most imprudent to touch a potty little bitch like that with a barge-pole, let alone with anything more personal. And there was always fat Susan.

After Ronnie had turned away from the canal towards a cab-rank, and was working away quite happily on how best to get fat Susan round to his flat without having to give her dinner, he heard a shout from behind him. He turned to see someone he thought at first was amazingly like Simon Quick running up to him. Then he saw that it actually was Simon Quick. He stopped and let her finish running up to him, which she did silently because she had nothing on her feet. These were sunburned, he noticed, as well as dirty.

'Where are your shoes?'

'I don't have shoes.'

'How silly and affected of you. Anyway, what do you want?'

'Adrian had me with him in the passage while he telephoned and I just happened to look up and see you at the other end of the hall just going out. So I waited till Adrian stopped watching me for a moment because he was talking to the taxi and then I ran after you and just saw you turning the corner.'

'What a bit of luck. But what do you want?'

'Well, just ... ' She looked up at him from under her eyelids, making him think what a non-defenceless creature she was. Then she came up with something. 'It was jolly rotten of you to say you didn't say you wanted to have sex with me. Made me look an awful liar.'

'Well I'm sorry, but you must see I had no alternative.'

'No alternative? How do you mean?'

'I'm not going to start explaining here in the street. And you wouldn't understand anyway. Now I'm off home. You can please yourself what you do.'

She slouched across and leant against the planking fence of somebody's garden. 'Are you cross with me?'

'Merely bored. Stop draping yourself there like that and get moving. Mrs Reichenberger will be on to your mother by now.'

'Don't care. You go if you want. I'll stay here for a bit.'

'Oh, God. Get into a taxi and bugger off somewhere. You can't just hang around like that.'

'Why not? Haven't got any money anyway.'

'Oh, God. Look ... here's ten bob. Where are you going?'

'Doesn't matter. Don't want it.' She came away from the fence and stood in front of him. Her eyes were only a couple of inches below his. There was a small circular mole in the exact centre of her chin and a line of still smaller ones along the angle of her left jaw. 'What's your name,' she said without interrogation.

'Christ, I told you. Ronnie Appleyard.'

'I know, I forgot. Ronnie ... '

'*Yes?*' said Ronnie in an upward glissando stretching over about an octave and a half.

'Ronnie, can't I come home with you?'

'No.'

In a quieter monotone than before, she said, 'I know I'm not beautiful at all.'

Two passing Negresses, elegant girls with straightened hair, heard this and looked drily at Ronnie. This did not prevent the momentary stirring in him of what might have been some mouldering fragment of chivalry or even, not inconceivably at a time when nobody powerful was listening, of respect for truth. He said almost involuntarily, 'Yes you are.' The Negresses, now in rear view, did not look back, but their shoulders hunched and unhunched in unison.

'Then why don't you take me home with you? I'd do anything you wanted me to and I'd be very quiet and I'd go the moment you told me to. Why don't you take me home with you?'

Ronnie opened his mouth to start reciting a few of the more obvious reasons, and then found he had forgotten them all, as well as all the less obvious ones. He knew now why he had been standing about in the street flapping his chops like this instead of shooting off home to fat Susan like a sensible man. 'All right,' he said.

'Super. There's a taxi.'

It was a bit thick in the taxi. The wheels had hardly begun to turn before she was on him, tense and trembling at the same time, open-mouthed, breathing in widely separated gasps, generally moving about with a freedom that would have been more flattering if he had had the opportunity to contribute something of his own in advance. But never mind any of that. He pressed his hand against that part of the green sweater which might be expected to lie over her left breast. Nothing seemed to be there but rather greasy wool and an expanse of rib-cage. Nevertheless, Simon Quick swung her narrow hips to and fro on the seat and moaned loudly. Ronnie leant forward and slid shut the small glass panel that gave communication with the driver. He noticed that he released her only partly in order to do this, as if to guard against her running away. Habit died hard. He also noticed that, by a rather happy verbal coincidence, they were just then bowling down Exhibition Road.

A couple of minutes later, as the taxi pulled up at a light by South Kensington tube station, Ronnie had reason to bless that ordinance of the Metropolitan Police which interdicts, under penalty, the installation of a mirror in such a way as to allow a cab-driver a view of the passenger compartment of his vehicle. Hauling Miss Quick's hand away, he said,

'That'll see us through for now, ducks. What about a cigarette?'

'Why, weren't you enjoying it?'

'Of course I was enjoying it, but there are limits.'

'How do you mean?'

'Well,'—Ronnie lit himself a Gitane—'you can't start having a full-dress screw in a taxi, can you?'

'Why not?'

'Oh, don't be a bloody fool, whatever your name is, Simon. Bloody silly name, too. What are you really called?'

'I'm called Simon. I've had a screw in a taxi.'

'Oh, don't talk cock. In broad daylight?'

'Of course not. Do you think I'm out of my mind?'

On the whole Ronnie did, but he did not want to antagonize the girl. Yet. The time would come for an elephant's dose of antagonizing, or whatever else might be needed in order to get her out of his bed, flat and life. That, however, was looking a couple of hours ahead. He muttered conciliatingly,

'Well, it's not dark enough yet for anything on that scale.'

'Of course it is.'

Ronnie looked out of the window. They were passing among a series of buildings in which afflictions of various parts of the human frame received treatment, and here lights were to be seen on various levels, but his purpose was not to make a careful, or even a hasty, appraisal of the degree to which dusk had advanced. He was simply trying to discontinue a conversation which might at any moment produce some quite irreversibly detumescing piece of silliness from this girl. And nothing like that must be allowed to happen at this stage. After what he had had to put up with for most of the last hour and more, he was going to have to poke her whether he wanted to or not.

The taxi turned left and took them along a row of shops. Here, among climbing plants, lumps of driftwood, and heaps of pebbles, pairs of velvet trousers were displayed on dummies that finished abruptly just above the waist; faceless busts in what looked a bit like bronze wore shirts of ribbed corduroy, flashed gigantic wristwatches, had their necks encircled by flowing scarves evidently made out of somebody's auntie's summer dress. Five minutes to go. With fully as much seeming incuriosity as usual, Simon Quick said from her corner,

'Ronnie, didn't you say you hadn't got a wife?'

'Yes, I did. I haven't.'

'Why not?'

'I don't know.'

But Ronnie, of course, did know. Very thoroughly. Not that it was at all a difficult problem to grasp. He had not got a wife because he had not yet found a sufficiently rich girl of sufficiently powerful family who was willing to marry him. Well, almost not yet found. There had, almost five years ago now, been one such girl who had rapidly become more than willing. Everything had seemed fine. Then, just as the engagement had been going to be announced, Ronnie had noticed that she looked like a horse, or perhaps a donkey. Whichever it had been, he had decided he could not go through with the project. Even now, he would still bitterly reproach himself for this attack of weakness, and sometimes, waking early, perhaps, on a rainy morning, and reviewing the comparative smallness of his income, his comparative lack of fame, the absolute non-luxuriousness of his flat, he would fall into something near despair at the deficiencies of his character.

'Why do people have wives and husbands?'

'I don't know that, either.'

This was truer; at any rate, Ronnie spoke it with increased warmth, with an air of actually regretting ignorance. His was not a mind that interested itself much in abstract questions of human motive, but a spot of discussion would, he felt, come in handy just at the moment.

It would help to hold off little hot-pants, and might distract him from the thought of what he was so very soon going to be doing to her, an event he had started to look forward to rather too tangibly. Something must be done if he was not to have to pay the taxi-driver with his back turned.

He went on, 'I suppose it's a mixture. Desire for security and companionship, ordinary straightforward wanting to start a family: one can't overlook the basic—' But before he could mention 'money' in the special disparaging, almost incredulous tone he had got ready for it, the girl's hoarse groan cut in on him.

'My mother's got a husband.'

'No doubt she has. Most people's mothers have.'

'No, I mean, you know, just a husband.'

'Oh, you mean a step-husband, I mean a stepfather, your stepfather.'

'That's right. He's called Chummy. He's mean. He hates me. He keeps trying to make me do things.'

'Really? What sort of things?'

'All sorts of things. Going to stay with people. Having people to stay. Going to parties. Going abroad to places. Going to concerts and races and things. All things like that.'

'They don't sound very terrible things to me.'

'They are.'

Ronnie threw his Gitane away. 'What's terrible about them?'

'They're just terrible. Boring. Always the same things. Horrible people. Talking to you all the time about boring things.'

'Can't you just not turn up?'

'I do not turn up as much as I can. But Chummy keeps on at me. And then Mummy gets upset.'

'I see.'

The taxi-driver began to struggle in his seat, as though some dreadful presence had appeared in the middle distance, something from which he would have given much to avert his gaze, but that a strange fascination prevented him. Ronnie could read the signs. He opened the communicating panel and said,

'Turn right. Southern end of the terrace.'

'Okay, Gilbert.'

The last hundred yards of the journey passed in silence. The taxi drew up double-parked outside a long line of undistinguished houses of the early Victorian period. Ronnie was in medium shape when he got out, so that he was able to pay the driver in a sort of sidelong mode parallel with his chest, rather than actually over his shoulder. He steered the girl round the bumper of an S-type Jaguar.

'What a super car. Is it yours?'

'No.'

'Is it this one?'

'No, it's this one. Down the steps. I'll lead the way.'

Ronnie shoved a plastic dustbin firmly aside with his hip, unlocked his front door and stepped in over a charity appeal that had clearly come to the wrong place. Simon Quick followed slowly. He turned the light on. The flat was really all one not very large room with a door at one side leading upstairs and a lavatory and bath opening off at the far end. Ronnie could not yet afford the style he wanted, and had resolved not to fool around with half-measures in the meantime. He kept his style for outside entertaining, his clothes and his car, a bitter-chocolate and white Porsche now sitting in a lock-up garage round the corner.

He shut the door and took hold of the girl. She was so

slender that his arms seemed to go round her nearly twice. Immediately she got going with her tense-trembling thing and her gasping, while she pressed her crotch against him so hard that he nearly fell over backwards. Her tongue was leaping about his mouth like a landed fish.

'Let's get undressed,' he said the first chance he got.

'Put the light out first.'

'No, I want to see you.'

'Please put the light out. For now.'

'All right. See you later.'

He did as he was asked. A little light still came through the window from the street above: not much.

'And draw thc curtains.'

'Oh, for Christ's sake, I'll blindfold myself if you like.'

'Please, Ronnie.'

Appendix scar, he thought to himself as he again complied, then, undressing, ceased to have thoughts in any full sense. He was fast but she was faster: a light-coloured shape flitted away through the gloom, again like a fish, while he dragged his loosened tie over his head, and he soon heard the twang of a bed-spring.

Although it was a warm evening, she was cold when he slipped in beside her; the thin upper arms were goose-flesh and the trembling seemed like shivering. In no time at all she was trying to pull him on top of her. He was all for that. Then he encountered a difficulty that was not of his making. It took some overcoming, but after perhaps a minute he overcame it, and in less than that again it was like taking the Porsche up the M1. Not for long, though. She was whispering something. It was 'Soon. Please soon.'

At once Ronnie understood a good deal. His desire and its physical manifestation subsided totally, the one almost as quickly as the other. If he had been able to go on, even now, he would have, but he could not. He got out of bed and felt his way into the bathroom. When he came out he said harshly,

'I'm going to put the light on, so see you're covered up if that's what you're afraid of not being.'

'You're mad at me.' Her voice was muffled.

'I might well be, yes, but I'm not.'

He pressed the switch down and the room appeared. He noticed the neat pile of letters on the desk, dictated to his by-the-hour secretary that morning and typed during his absence in the afternoon. In the bed, the top of a brown head of hair was to be seen on the pillow. Ronnie hesitated. Then he went on,

'I'm merely disappointed. I thought you were bloody attractive. Never mind. I don't know whether it's me you don't like, or men, or sex, and I'm not bothered which it is. That's your problem, love. Now in a minute I'm going round to the pub to get some cigarettes, and when I come back I'll expect to find you gone. You can pick up that ten bob here on the desk. Have you got that?'

The girl had pulled the sheet down a few inches, to about yashmak height. Ronnie thought that perhaps her eyes were the colour of sultanas, or of black coffee with the light through it. She croaked,

'What's the matter with you? I was having a lovely time when you suddenly stopped. What was I doing wrong?'

'We won't argue, sweetheart. I know when I'm not wanted. I'd advise you to take things a bit slower next time, but see how you feel.'

'I don't know what you're talking about.'

'Let it go, then.'

During these exchanges, Ronnie had been rapidly dressing. He now ran a comb through his hair, standing before a mirror of uncertain antiquity. Into its frame were stuck a number of invitation cards, a couple of them bearing national crests. The mirror itself was cracked and foxed in one corner, showing that it was not meant to be smart.

'Why are you being like this to me?'

Ronnie did not reply. He buttoned his jacket and made for the door.

'Well, just give me a kiss.'

'No point in that. Bang the door to when you go out.'

The street was almost dark. Ronnie crossed it and went into the saloon of the White Lion, where it was all hunting horns and models of vintage cars, plus soft nasty music. Everything went well. The landlord, who wore a maroon velvet smoking-jacket with lime-green frogging and had an unreconstructed R.A.F. moustache, greeted Ronnie heartily and congratulated him on clobbering that charlie on the box earlier. A bearded lefty in the corner by the fruit-machine nudged his white-clad bird and they both stared furtively at Ronnie. Every little helped. He bought himself a half of bitter and twenty Gitanes and asked to use the telephone.

He had almost no trouble getting through, just a single example each of dead silence after dialling, wrong number, number-unobtainable signal after first two digits and crossed line, this last providing a snatch of talk in some relatively unexpected language like Basque or Finnish. Then he got the Canadian flat-mate and finally fat Susan herself. No trouble; better yet, in fact. The producer of this week's *Monday Playhouse* on B.B.C. 1 had asked her to run an eye over it and slip him the word on whether this new boy looked good enough for it not to matter that he made with his shoulders all the time and talked half-smothered Birmingham camp. Nine ten to ten twenty-five, which meant Ronnie could not have given her dinner even if he had wanted to. He told her he would expect her at about a quarter to eleven and to bring a toothbrush, rang off, and ordered a half-bottle of Moet & Chandon and two rounds of smoked salmon on wholemeal. While the piped music bleated and tinkled in the background, he ate and drank and brooded briefly on the Simon Quick thing. No harm done this time, but he really must not allow his heart, as it were, to make a habit of running away with his head. Nobody, obviously, who had been as oncoming as that could be expected to be normal or satisfactory when it came to the point. Nobody? Obviously? Why not? Well, anyway, that was how things had turned out in this case. The only consolation was that he had got rid of her smartly, before having her round the place to be looked at could lead him to have another and equally fruitless go at her.

He was wrong about that, a common experience in dealing with Miss Quick, as he came to recognize when he knew her better. Seeing the light still burning in his flat did not throw him at all. To turn it off when leaving would not enter the head of that sort of girl: what would be in it for her? (Here at least he was right in principle.) But he was very disconcerted when he went in and saw the top of the close-cut dark-sandy head still occupying the pillow.

'What the bloody hell do you think you're doing?'

No answer or movement.

'Look, get out of that bed and out of here before I lose my temper.'

When she still neither spoke nor stirred, he seized the top of the sheet and threw it back. His intention was the strictly platonic one of shoving her anyhow on to the floor, but this entirely vanished from his mind at the sight of the long, narrow, rather hairy body and limbs, ungainly and graceful, the skin that palely but precisely mirrored the colour of the hair and that seemed only more lightly tanned over the childish breasts and what the bottom half of a bikini had covered, the jagged birthmark like a sepia ink-splash near the navel and the thin archipelago of moles than ran in a crescent over to the top of the thigh. Her eyes opened. Just in time, after a full second and a half, Ronnie got the sheet back over her, took a tin of Worthington from the refrigerator and went and sat down on the dark-green leather office chair at his desk.

'What have I got to do to make you go?' he asked.

'I'm not going. I want to stay the night.'

'What for?'

'I just want to. Why don't you want me to?'

'I'll throw you out, by force if necessary.'

'You can't throw me into the street with nothing on and I won't dress and you can't make me. Try it and see.'

Lethargically, Ronnie opened his packet of Gitanes and lit one. This girl reminded him of somebody or some nationality or race or regional group or age-group or group. If he had been able to decide which of these classes was relevant he could have named the relevant member of that class. Still lethargically, he said,

'How long are you thinking of staying?'

'Oh, just till tomorrow morning. I'll make us breakfast and then I'll take off.'

'You don't want to go home, is that it?'

'That's part of it.'

'Why not?'

'I just don't want to.'

With a slight reluctance he could not have accounted for, Ronnie said, 'I've got someone else coming round in a few minutes.'

'You mean a girl?'

'Yes.'

'Oh. Oh, well you should have said so before.' Moving faster than he wanted, she got out of bed, picked up a bundle of clothing from the floor and held it in front of her. 'Is there a bathroom or something?'

'Down there.'

'I'll only be a second.'

Ronnie turned away and picked up the letter at the top of the pile now before him. It invited a prominent trade unionist to discuss, over an elaborate lunch, the possibility of his appearing on *Insight* with reference to some momentarily burning issue or other. With all its author's efficiency, the letter laid the foundations of the impression Ronnie virtually never failed to give you up until the time he actually got you in front of the cameras: that although he had been a bastard to plenty of people in the past and doubtless would be again any day, he was not going to be a bastard to you. He read the text through slowly, trying to find a phrase to alter in his own hand and thus subtly advertise his conscientiousness, indifference to the mere look of the thing, etc. But this small task, one which he would normally have enjoyed as fully as any of the innumerable nuances of his trade, proved beyond him. Only as his pen touched paper did he remember that this was a place for the boyish-scrawl signature rather than the sober-clarity one. Folding the letter, sealing the envelope were tasks. His real attention was on the forthcoming ordeal of seeing Simon Quick walk out of his front door and on nerving himself not to impede this necessary event. He did not look round when the bathroom door opened.

'All right, I'm going now,' said the husky uninflected voice over his shoulder. 'I still don't know why you're making me.'

Ronnie said unwillingly, 'How are you going to get home?'

'Oh, I can walk. It's only just up the road from here.'

'Whereabouts?'

'Eaton Square. Mummy has this penthouse.'

The words rang in the silence like the sound of a great cash register. So Mummy had not less than eight thousand a year net, probably more. Of course. He knew now what sort of group Miss Quick belonged to. And he had been on the point of letting a sweet girl like that walk out of his life just for being an unstable child-monster of egotism simultaneously suffering from sexual compulsiveness and frigidity! Without a tremor, without hurry or delay, Ronnie got up and said quite casually,

'I'll walk up there with you.'

'Ooh, will you?' She smiled, revealing strong square teeth with an upper molar missing, then at once went doleful again. 'But you said you'd got this girl coming.'

'She won't be here for a bit yet.'

'Super. Let's go, then.'

'Where's your handbag?' This question too had been bothering Ronnie from time to time.

'I don't have one.'

'Where do you keep your stuff?'

'Stuff?'

'Christ, your ... bloody make-up, your money, your ... I don't know, your driving licence and things. Your keys.'

'I don't use make-up and somebody else always has all the other sorts of things, money and tickets and things like that.'

A child-monster with very refreshing and pissy attitudes, amended Ronnie as he shooed her out and banged the door after them. At the top of the steps she took his arm in an old-fashioned way. Normally he would have refused to be thus encumbered, but the thought of Mummy's penthouse, or rather of the kind of bank statement that must go with it, had made him strangely tolerant. He kept the annoyance the thought aroused in him out of his voice when he asked,

'Why don't you use make-up?'

'Oh, honestly, Ronnie, can you see me with make-up on? I'm all the wrong colours. Mummy's had a Paris man and a New York man on to me, but they just made me look terrible. The Paris man made me look like a Red Indian and the New York man made me look like an Arab. Nasty Red Indian and nasty Arab. I'm the wrong colours, that's all.'

Ronnie disagreed with this as stated, but he only said, 'By the way, Simon ... '

She turned towards him so eagerly that he nearly fell over her. 'Yes?'

'Who is Mummy?'

While she pondered this conundrum, they walked in step (her legs were long enough to make joint progress almost inoffensive) along the deserted lamplit pavement. Somebody drove his car across an intersection just ahead, the noise of his exhaust conveying to everyone within earshot how independent and how trendy he was. Then she said,

'Mummy's called Lady Baldock now. Before that she was called Mrs Aristophánou, and before that she must have been called Mrs Quick, but I don't remember her being called that. I can hardly even remember Daddy. He was an American. Stavros was a Greek. And Chummy's English, of course. He's called Lord Baldock. He's very horrible to me all the time, Chummy is. You'll hate him.'

The more purely historical parts of this were familiar to

Ronnie, as to any committed reader of the gossip columns of the popular Press. In fact, he knew a good deal more: for instance, that Mr Quick had been not only an American, but an American steer-and-hog millionaire; that Mr Aristophánou had been not only a Greek, but a Greek shipping millionaire, the next but one or two in the line after Onassis and Nearchos: and that with all that water under the bridge Lord Baldock would not have needed anything more than what he stood up in and his title in order to become the third Mister Juliette—what had her maiden name been? Something Frenchie, old Creole family, Louisiana, Southern belle, plantation, fried chicken, you-all brand of rubbish. Anyway, nobody needed to remember that name now; it was Baldock, Baldock all the way. *Baldock* ... With the force of a childhood nightmare, Ronnie recalled seeing, not more than a couple of years back, a newspaper photograph of the newly-married pair outside the Chapel Royal (where else?) with Lord Baldock's uncontrollably aristocratic face caught in a smirk of fanatical vapidity. And yet, in his just-attained state of universal benevolence, Ronnie could foresee no difficulty in pretending not to loathe Baldock whenever Baldock's stepdaughter's requirements might allow this. Before continuing the conversation, Ronnie considered reprimanding himself for not having much earlier pieced together the names of Quick and Chummy and other clues, but, on an evening when the future seemed to lie bathed in the radiance of an immense dollar-sign, he could not find it in his heart to do so.

'Baldock,' he said consideringly. 'Of course. Wasn't there something in the papers just the other day? Last week?'

'Mummy gave a big party for this Brazilian sculptor.'

'That's right. It sounded awfully grand. I'm afraid I

don't really move in those circles.' (*Yet.*) 'What was it like?'

'Oh, it was kind of fun.' Not a very uproarious kind, evidently. He would really have to start doing something about this voice of Simon's. If he was going to spend a lot of time in her company (which he bloody well was) he could not afford to have her sounding like somebody reading out the telephone directory whenever she spoke. Not that voice production was the only, or even the major, sphere in which she stood in need of reconstruction. That old major sphere came up with a flourish in less than a minute, after they had reached the King's Road, turned in the direction of Sloane Square, and started to move towards a hefty pillared entrance. Disengaging herself from his arm, Simon went across and leant against some area railings in much the same spirit as she had behaved with the garden fence a couple of hours earlier. Traffic boomed and snarled a few yards away.

'Ronnie.'

'*Yes?*'

'What did I do wrong in bed?'

There was a case for pretending that it had all been a misunderstanding or all his fault or all something else, but he had better start as he meant to go on. Coping with her oddities while behaving as if he were just having a high old time would take too much out of him. He was a man, a man on the make in all senses, not a sodding sexual psychology therapy unit. He said matter-of-factly,

'You're a virgin, aren't you?'

'If you're going to get all aggressive I'm off home.'

'Now, Simon, we can't have you being silly and childish. Just answer my questions in a sensible way. All right, we'll take it you're not a virgin. How many men have you slept with?'

'Hundreds.'

'How many, Simon?'

'Forty-four. I always keep count.'

'Christ Almighty. Is that counting me?'

'No. But that's not so many. It works out at about four a year since I started. I bet you figure it's been a pretty lean year for you if you haven't managed to do four new girls. That's only one every three months, you see.'

'Yes, I see. Do you always ask the chaps like you did me tonight?'

'No.' This was a petulant grunt.

'What made you ask me?'

'Thought you looked nice.'

'But why couldn't you have waited for things to take their natural course? If you've had four men, let alone forty-four, you must have been able to tell you were going to get a pass thrown at you sooner rather than later, surely? Well then, why that ludicrous business of asking Mrs Reichenberger for a bed? What the hell did you expect her to say?'

'Good evening, Whitaker.'

Ronnie's eyes grew momentarily fixed, but they unfixed again at the sight of a wizened fellow in porter's uniform, who made some cordial though unintelligible rejoinder before hobbling up the steps of the near-by entrance.

'Listen to me, Simon: why did you act up like that at the Reichenbergers'? Come on, why?'

'Don't know. Wanted you.'

'No you didn't: that was very—'

'*Did.*'

'Look, I could tell absolutely back in the flat that all you wanted was for it to be over. If you admit that we can start getting somewhere; otherwise—'

She started to speak with some appearance of emotion,

but at that moment a horrible roaring noise abruptly swelled in the roadway, rattling the windows near them and drowning every particle of what she was saying. A large open lorry was accelerating towards the centre of the city. Seen under the street-lamps, its load seemed to consist of no more than half a dozen seatless lavatory bowls, no doubt the residue of some much larger number already distributed at selected points of emergency within the metropolitan area. Well before it had receded appreciably Simon had finished whatever she was saying.

'What? What was that?'

She shook her head violently.

'What did you say?'

'Doesn't matter. Can't say it all again.'

'But you've got to ... ' He stopped when he saw how hard she was staring at him. 'What?'

'You're not to just ... Can I see you again, Ronnie?'

He pretended to consider. 'If you really want to.'

'Of course I really want to.' For her it was a frenzy of affirmation. 'Come on up and say hallo to Mummy now. Oh ... but you've got this girl coming.'

Ronnie had already done his homework on both halves of that one. The minor half was no problem. It was now ten twenty. Fat Susan was very fully used to finding him not at home when he had arranged to be and going over to wait for him in the White Lion, where he of the smoking-jacket and moustache would regale her with prurient gallantry as long as might be necessary, certainly until eleven thirty or so. The major half took a bit more facing. On limited data, it was computable that the chances of Mrs Reichenberger's not having had a little telephonic chat with Mummy—who was presumably at home—fell rather below twenty per cent. Lady Baldock could not reasonably be expected to be hearty to the part-author of the reported disturbance. But that particular strain of the music must be faced without delay. It would be a costly mistake to remain even momentarily a sinister unrevealed presence on the distant fringes of his future mother-in-law's world. He was really quite looking forward to throwing at her all his vast untapped reserves of sincerity.

'There isn't any girl,' he said. 'I told you there was just to get you out of the place. I'm afraid I got cross with you.'

'What made you change your mind?'

He was ready for that one too. 'Just a little thing, really. The way you started getting ready to leave the moment I told you I had someone else coming round. I thought that was so ... fair and decent. I can't put it any better than that, I'm afraid. Sounds awfully—'

'Oh, Ronnie.' She sprang forward and gave him an explosive nursery kiss near the ear. 'Come on up now and meet Mummy. She's terribly nice. You'll love her.'

When Ronnie and Simon entered the Baldocks' hall, it had nobody in it except the small red-haired butler who admitted them, but an instant later it began filling up with middle-aged men in dinner-jackets smoking cigars and talking loudly. They all had the air of being somebody in particular, and Ronnie recognized several who were: the proprietor of a football pool, the financial editor of a Sunday newspaper, a man who made a lot of different kinds of sauces and relishes, a man who (rather slowly) put up buildings and fly-overs. Most of them looked at Ronnie to see if they ought to be looking at him and then seemed never to have looked at him. He turned to ask Simon the next move and found that she had gone, was just turning the corner of a corridor in advance of the leaders of the black-clad horde. Bringing up the eventual rear of this came Lord Baldock, easily recognizable from his photographs, and a red-faced man of about forty whom Ronnie recognized even more easily from having seen him stalk out of the Reichenbergers' party earlier. This bit of recognition was mutual. Ronnie got an amplified repeat of the hostile stare he had had before and, while it continued, heard a voice blare out in some unidentifiable transatlantic dialect. Baldock, though clearly no older than his companion, went all senile at this, frowning as if near despair, showing most of his many top teeth and further hunching his already stooped shoulders to bring his unnaturally small ear closer to the other's exclaiming mouth. These contortions had at any rate the effect of inducing the red-faced man to continue on his way instead of doing what he gave signs of wanting to do, striding over and grappling with Ronnie physically. That moment passed: with Baldock still in the grip of bafflement, the pair reached the corner and passed from view. Ronnie relaxed a little. Running into the red-faced man was one he had not been ready for. The fellow must have moved like a helicopter to have got to wherever he put on his dinner-jacket, put it on, and arrive in time to sit down to dinner with the mother of the girl who had just refused to go to Sardinia with him. Perhaps he was mad.

It was a big square hall with lots of cut glass and ordinary glass, but before he could start assessing it Simon was back with Mummy, who started talking when she was still some distance off.

'Mr Appleyard, how nice of you to bring my problem child home. I had a most curious and slightly disturbing telephone call about her earlier this evening. I could make very little of it, but it wasn't altogether reassuring. Still, let's not bother about it now. Mr Appleyard, it's a pleasure to have you here. I watch you so often on television when

I'm in London that I feel I know you. What an excellent show that is of yours. We have nothing half so good in the United States. We could learn such a lot from you. I'm afraid I have a lot of dreadfully dull people here tonight whom it would just bore you to death to meet. But I refuse to turn down the chance of talking with you for a little while now that it's come up so unexpectedly. What would you like to drink, Mr Appleyard? If you care for whisky I can offer you a glass of my husband's favourite Scotch. Mona, find Burke-Smith and tell him to bring a bottle of the Laphroaig and some Malvern water and glasses and ice up to the small parlour. I want them immediately. See that he understands that. Then tell Chummy to slip away as soon as he can and join us; he can leave Bill Sussex in charge. And he's to make sure George doesn't come along too. George is being very pompous tonight.'

Recollecting that George was the red-faced man, Ronnie approved heartily of this last part, but had to keep this to himself, as he had had to do with his equally hearty approval of earlier parts. It was already plain that he would need every particle of his expertness in order to interrupt Lady Baldock, should such a step ever appear desirable. The effect of there being so inexhaustibly much more where that came from was what chiefly did it; the voice itself, in accent and quality, was almost a replica of Simon's – or the other way round – though it went up and down quite a lot now and again. Here, too, Simon could have got her tallness and most of her thinness, but the late Quick had probably supplied her colouring. At any rate, her mother went in for blue-veined pallor and blackbird hair in ascending coils, each the product of maintenance computable in terms of not a few dollars per square inch per week. There was a kilogram or so of jewellery and a heavy dry white silk dress, the bodice of which had evidently been sprayed with glue and then fiercely bombarded with diamonds. Poor Ronnie felt quite faint at the sight.

Manfully enough, however, he mastered this reaction, scored minor points for sincerity with eyelids and brows and chin at every turn of Lady Baldock's discourse, smiled in an indulgent manner when Simon went mutely off like an attendant in Elizabethan drama, offered no resistance to the ring-barnacled fingers laid on his forearm and the progress towards the foot of the stairs.

'I meant what I said just now, Mr Appleyard, about being grateful to you for rescuing my little Mona. She is just the sweetest child in the world, but she does have this unfortunate way of getting into silly scrapes. How fortunate that you happened to come along. You know, I think you might be good for her, if only you can manage to put up with all her ... ' Lady Baldock hesitated for the first time, then spliced in an alternative take with pro-standard smoothness. 'She has this completely disastrous taste in people. My husband and I do as much as most mothers and stepfathers, I think I can say, but an only child ... '

(A relay tripped in Ronnie's mind, sending all the figures there clicking up to twice and three times their earlier totals.)

' ... does have special problems. I do hope that any little difficulties tonight won't discourage you from seeing some more of her. She does very much need what you maybe can give her.'

There was a firm pause on this (perhaps) unintentionally loaded ambiguity. Ronnie's mind continued to click away. It came up with a strip of irrelevance about how soon could they get off him being eighty to Simon's three and a half, switched to an internal instruction that all circuits be tuned to maximum efficiency at once to meet the unusually heavy load constituted by the present situation, and fed out the following for immediate use:

'I, I do appreciate very much, Lady Baldock, your, how kind you've been in, uh, to ask me up for a drink on a, when you're busy with all these, uh, people, but, um, I think I can see why you're so, so concerned about, uh, Mona because there's obviously such marvellous basic material there perfectly sound training and everything one can see that straight away and yet, uhm, there is this, uh, unpredictability and impulse and all the, she seems, well, this is just based on a, a first impression, so it's not like to be very, um, necessarily altogether sound but it seems to me that the root of the trouble if one can call it that is simply that she has her work cut out keeping up with you.'

They had sat down somewhere but Ronnie had no time at the moment for where. He was watching Lady Baldock, who said in a sharp tone, 'Keeping up with me? In what way?'

Ronnie looked quickly away, then slowly back at her, raising his chin at the same slow pace and allowing his eyelids to fall a very short distance. He shrugged one shoulder. 'Well ... ' he said, looking away again. 'You know ... just ... the whole ... '

It came like the response in some age-old ritual, all the more deeply moving and meaningful for being entirely expected, entirely *right*: 'Well, Mr Appleyard, I must say you're not in the least the way you seem on television.' Ronnie had his beach-head now.

'Oh ... television,' he said, flinging out a hand. 'It's fun—if you can stand it. Curious half-world of fakes and hangers-on and committee men and ... just a few, a very few people with something to say. The great thing about it is that it's ... so interesting.' He looked so interested for a moment before plunging sincerely on. 'But let's forget about all that—we're talking about Mona.'

Yes indeed they bloody well were, he thought to himself when they immediately stopped doing so at the entry of the small red-haired butler with a loaded tray. Ronnie could easily see that anybody with any share of responsibility for Miss Quick might want to talk about her to any sentient being; but he and her mother had got off the mark with remarkable unanimity. He would watch that one. For now, he watched what Lady Baldock was watching, though not as intently as she: the unloading of bottles and glasses on to a circular silver table. Before this was properly under way, Simon came in, followed by Lord Baldock. She made a snarling face at Ronnie, rolling her eyes back into the corners to show it was not aimed at him. He wondered how the Baldocks liked her dirty feet running all over their Axminsters and what-have-you; rather better, no doubt, than they liked the rest of her in its present state bursting into their heavily-populated drawing-room. Perhaps Chummy had already been mean to her about it.

'Chummy, this is Ronnie Appleyard,' she said in her most bored tone, and added over her shoulder as she crossed the room, 'My stepfather, Lord Baldock.'

'Ah. *Ah*,' said Baldock, not shaking hands. 'I've heard that name, haven't I?'

'You may have done.'

'Is it your professional name?'

'Yes.'

He stared at Ronnie for a time with his mouth open. Then, with great curiosity, he asked, 'What do you blow?'

'Blow?'

'Yes. Blow.' Baldock held his hands up near his mouth, one in front of the other, and waggled the fingers. 'Like trumpet, man. Or perhaps you blow drums. I was talking to somebody the other evening who told me he blew them.'

'Oh, I see. You mean which jazz instrument do I play.'

'That's it exactly.'

'I don't play any. Not one.'

'You don't? But I thought only jazz musicians had names like that. Oh, wait a minute. Sorry. These nuclear physicists and dircctors of education and heads of art schools who keep getting together to write letters to the papers are all called Stan and Alfie and Reg, aren't they? Perhaps you're one of them.'

'No.' Ronnie shook his head firmly. 'I'm not one of them.'

'Then what *do* you do?' asked Baldock, who knew perfectly well, and knew Ronnie knew he knew.

Lady Baldock, who had just finished chiding the butler for some omission, called across, 'Chummy, bring Mr Appleyard over here. You're not to monopolize him, darling. Burke-Smith, ask Mr Appleyard what he'd like to drink.'

Ronnie saw that his choice was restricted to whether he wanted water or soda and ice or no ice with his malt whisky, but he took a long time over it while he swore a horrible revenge on Chummy Baldock, to take place as soon as convenient after the marriage register was signed. By about then the House of Lords would be due for another abusive documentary report, and, oh, what a wonderful hatchet-job he would do on Chummy in a special number of *Insight*.

'Nothing for me, thank you, Burke-Smith,' Baldock was saying.

'What about something for me?' asked Simon, who was sitting on the floor with her arms round her knees by her mother's chair.

'I wouldn't advise it, you know.' Her stepfather spoke in a wheedling tone. 'Have you had anything to eat?'

'I want a whisky. Why can't I have a whisky?'

'Simon, you know it keeps you awake.'

'Oh, Chummy, don't be so stuffy, let the child have a whisky if she wants one. A small one, Burke-Smith.'

'No ice,' said Simon, staring defiantly at Baldock, who turned away from her to face Ronnie. First revealing his upper teeth for a few moments, he said,

'I'm afraid I'm a bit of a one for following things up. Sticking to the point, you know. I was asking you what you did for a living.'

'Yes, that's right, of course you were.'

'Oh, *Chummy* ... You know as well as I do that Mr Appleyard does that marvellous programme on television. We were watching it together only the other evening. You know, about the docks.'

'If you say so, darling.' Baldock's voice, normally, it appeared, a high tenor, went up half an octave. 'But how fascinating. The good old goggle-box. Tell me, do you know Bill Hamer?'

Those of his acquaintances who cared at all for Ronnie Appleyard, and some of that larger number who did not, would have admired the way he went into action now. Sipping his whisky, which tasted oddly weak, he said in a flat voice, 'Yes, I do. Not well, but a bit. He's one of the very few people in television who have (a) really worked for their success and (b) stayed a human being after they've achieved it. He's just ... got a point of view, something to say, as we were'—nod to Lady Baldock—'discussing just now. Oh, I know it's easy to sneer at him' — nod to Lord Baldock as an especially ready sneerer — 'but by and large that show of his does a first-class job. He's very experienced, very tough, all that, but he's also very—' real? Could he risk real? Could he *stand* real? — 'very reasonable and approachable. I think he's ... I've got a lot of time for old Bill.'

Being really good at sincerity, like Ronnie, means that you can take in how they react to it. Simon, after muttering, 'That's not the way you—' glanced at her stepfather and fell silent. Lady Baldock sent a glance in the same direction, this one laced with mild reproach, and smiled warmly at Ronnie. Lord Baldock's attention became quite undifferentiated. Only the butler seemed to feel he had received a useful and unlooked-for factual lesson.

This aspect of things evidently struck Baldock after a time. 'I think you might get back downstairs now, Burke-Smith,' he said. 'And see if the duke needs a hand. We'll be along soon, tell him, would you?'

There was a small scuffle at the door whereby the red-haired butler managed with some difficulty to get out of the path of the red-faced man, who strode forward and seemed to say,

'Ah, Apollo jars. Arcane standard, Hannah More. Armageddon pier staff.'

Ronnie recognized at once that this was not what the man could really have said, not exactly. This was somebody talking to excite as much credence as he could in the native accents of Dixie. He excited more than that in Ronnie when he strode up and took hold of the lapels of Ronnie's blue hopsack hunter's-cut jacket, driving firmly away (at least for the time being) that ever-ready suspicion that a Southern accent was meant to be funny, and saying intelligibly enough and to spare,

'Who the hell are you? And what the hell are you doing here?'

Lord Baldock had apparently noticed this confrontation. At all events he immediately detached the red-faced man's hands from Ronnie's clothing. He spoke with a contralto authority that Ronnie heard with mixed feelings.

'George. Dear boy. Go to bed. We'll talk it over in the morning. Not now. Too tedious.'

'I got no quarrel with you, Chummy, but I came up here to have my say and have my say I will. This guy was hanging around Simona at the party those Jewish people gave, and I don't know who he is, but I guess—'

'Oh, I say, how frightfully rude of me. George, you haven't met Mr Appleyard. Mr Appleyard, this is Mr Parrot.'

'How do you do, Mr Appleyard.' Parrot inclined his head. 'As I was saying, Chummy, the guy was hanging around just waiting his chance. Simona tells me to lose myself and the next thing I know he's brought in here and you-all are feeding him whisky. I have certain rights, and I demand—'

'Get out, George,' said Baldock with his own brand of urgency. 'If you've any idea of what's good for you, don't say another word.'

'In my position,' roared Parrot, 'I have the right to insist that a man of whom I—'

'In your position?' Simon, still on the floor, was leaning back on her hands and looking at Parrot with very wide eyes. Her voice was much louder than Ronnie had heard it before. 'What position's that?'

'We have an understanding, Simona, as you very well—'

'I don't want to have it any more. It's always just been boring and horrible. We're going to Scotland. We're going to Nassau. We're going to Juan-les-Pins. Just the same as it's always been: boring and horrible. Put on a dress, you can't go out in those jeans. Where are your shoes, put on your shoes. Wash your face, do your hair. This is my aunt and this is my uncle and this is my cousin's daughter's husband's sister-in-law's son's wife's father's cousin. Different with me, it'll be different with me. We'll enjoy it together. Honey.'

'Simona, you just don't have any right to throw all this—'

'Sod your bloody right. Shut up. And go away. I told you to go away once already this evening. You know why I did that? Why I did it then? Because I'd just seen a man I fancied a damn sight more than I fancy you. And I got him. You didn't know that was why I did it, did you? Bet you didn't know that.'

'You just a goddam bitch, Simona, that's all you are.'

Ronnie admired the way George Parrot's anger went on escalating instead of switching to a phased withdrawal, which would have been the response of any but an ungovernably rich man to Simon's last revelation. He was virtually certain it was a pseudo-revelation, that he was far better at spotting people undetected than Simon was, but what was the difference for Parrot? Ronnie did his admiring and virtual certainty at a distance from the action, having walked away from it at about the time Scotland had been mentioned, a second after Baldock had set off purposefully towards the drinks table. With his back to everybody, Ronnie had his front to a green-and-gold wall thickly hung, as most other walls hereabouts were hung, with paintings. This lot, he saw while hearing and retaining every word of dialogue, included a sort of science-fiction carnivorous-shrub picture by Jackson Pollock and a Buffet showing some colourless stained glass against the side of a battleship. Yes, the big money was always two and a half steps behind the trend.

A relatively new but totally expected voice spoke. 'George, I can't have that. You'll have to go.'

'Hell, I'm sorry, Juliette, but you heard what she said. Real mean provocation if there ever was such a type of damn thing. Juliette, I'd have expected you to be defending me. I'd never have thought to—'

'No, George. Mona's still a child in many ways and you know perfectly well that she doesn't mean half she says and does. You're supposed to be an adult human being. Oh, I don't mind what you *say*, that's not the point. It's your attitude I deplore. I don't have much use for insensitivity and selfishness and lack of sympathy. And lack of imagination. It seems I was wrong when I thought you might just be the person with the adaptability of mind to make all the difference to our lives.'

In this rather remote key, discussion died down. There were muted protesting noises from Parrot, ones presumably meant to be soothing from Baldock. A door shut. Ronnie heard the approaching swish of skirts, and turned. Across the room the doleful figure of Simon sat with arms round knees.

'Mr Appleyard, I can't tell you how sorry I am that you should have had to suffer all this. I'm afraid you've had to find out rather a lot about us rather fast.'

'My dear Lady Baldock ... ' Ronnie drew it out. 'I assure you I've been listening avidly to every word'—a slight risk, but the smile came up with no more than the predictable delay—'and that my memory is a total mess.'

'How nice of you.' As before, the hand came on his arm and they promenaded, but not so far. 'I hate to say it, but I shall have to be getting back to those dull people of mine, without our having had a chance to exchange more than two words. Now I quite understand that you can never have a moment to call your own, but I would be so pleased if you could get away just for an hour or two on Friday and look in at a little luncheon-party I'm giving here. Very quiet, nothing formal, just the family and one or two old friends. Do you think you could possibly manage it?'

Ronnie pretended to consider. He had been going to lunch at the House that day with the Opposition expert on foreign affairs, but he would cheerfully have put him off if he had been the Head of Programmes at L.C.M. Television and Claudia Cardinale rolled into one. 'Yes. That would be delightful. Thank you.'

'Splendid. One fifteen. Now you'll see Mr Appleyard out, won't you, darling? and then I expect you'll be wanting to get to bed.'

As Ronnie came in sight of the White Lion, he continued to review certain enigmas: how much Lady Baldock knew about him and Simon and what she wanted from him, why Simon had been faintly surly when they said good night, what he was going to do about Lord Baldock (it was too long to wait until after the wedding). But his mind moved only sluggishly. It was eleven five, just right for a quick glass of champagne in the saloon, a stroll across the street back to the flat, and an exploration-in-depth of all that was fattest and best about fat Susan.

Two

MALAKOS, POUSTOS

'What time do we get to Malakos?'

'Ng? Get ... '

'Don't you speak English?'

Two-thirds asleep after a night flight and a six a.m. sailing, Ronnie Appleyard responded with less than his usual promptness. He was lying back in a sagging canvas chair on the after-deck of the steamer, being bumped into more often than every minute by one or another of three Germans in shorts and baseball caps. Now he looked up at the man standing over him, a bony middle-aged shag with a flat-faced wife who had jumped the queue coming on board.

After a moment, speaking very distinctly as if to a foreigner, Ronnie said, 'I am English.'

'Are you?' said the man in his upper-class honk. 'I asked you what time we got to Malakos.'

'Did you? Anyway, I don't know. I suggest you try the purser's office. One deck down.' Ronnie waited until the shag had started to move off, then added, 'Oh, by the way.'

'Yes?'

'Come back and tell me when you've found out, will you? I'd like to know too.'

'There's no need to be damn rude.'

'Isn't there?'

Ronnie shut his eyes, feeling slightly toned up. He had caught a glimpse of shag and wife going through Immigration at Athens Airport, indeed heard them honking above the tumult, and had already judged it quite probable that, like him, they were on their way to be guests of the Baldocks in their villa on Malakos. If so, the last half-minute had been well spent. He was short on the one attribute certain to win the immediate respect of the rich – i.e. being rich – and must therefore obtrude deterrents against being buggered about. There was little chance that, assuming he was right about their destination, these two possessed any other quality than being rich. That frown, and wrinkled lip, and sneer of cold command belonged to nobody in the least dependent on the goodwill of others. Statistics pointed the same way: in Ronnie's experience, the rich disliked any but a slight dilution of their gatherings by people with other claims to notice.

His first encounter with the cash barons went back nearly twenty years, to a big dirty house in Queen Anne's Gate, where a girl called Jerningham had invited him to have, among other things, *luncheon* with herself and her parents: a difficult occasion, as it proved, made endurable only by the thought of what he would later be doing to his particular Jerningham while all the others were at the theatre, and of what Mr Jerningham especially would have said and done if he had known of this. The head of the family had entered the dining-room late and left it early. At no stage had he noticed Ronnie's presence except, throughout the meal, to keep his left arm and hand curled round the half-bottle of claret he was drinking, in this way forestalling any attempt by Ronnie to snatch it up and carry it to his lips. At the time he had thought this merely a bit colourful of Jerningham, or even one way among many of going on when you were grown up. Now he saw it as a small result of just being able to do as you bloody well liked all the hours there were. A splendid state, worth any amount of effort to attain.

He had recalled this little episode several times in the nearly eight days since lunching with the Baldocks in Eaton Square: no quiet family party at all, it had turned out, but a twenty-cover thrash with a political cartoonist and a stage designer besides himself to leaven the lump of rich. There had been, it was true, an absence of arms crooked round wine bottles during the meal – expensive materials nastily cooked: nevertheless, one glass of white and one of red had been the limit at table, one fifteen had always meant one drink instead of two before sitting down, and (naturally) no cognac had been forthcoming with the coffee. Being even less inclined to booze in the middle of the day than later, Ronnie had not deplored these austerities, simply filled them in on his mental sketch-map of the area under exploration. This he had rolled hastily up and stowed away when Lady Baldock, of whom he had had a fourth share for about a minute and a half on arrival, approached him with casual emphasis as he was preparing to leave.

After a good deal of competent dirt-eating about being

out of touch and sounding quite ridiculous and would he please stop her before she got too boring, she had asked him if whoever it was could possibly spare him for a few days to cheer them all up on their fuddy-duddy little primitive Greek island starting some time like the end of next week, because seriously people like him could so easily overtire themselves without realizing it, and perhaps people like her could help a bit there, and it would mean so much to Mona. The last clause had on the whole seemed the least convincing. Miss Quick, wearing a dress and shoes, and with her hair dragged forward in an implausible fringelike construction, had put in an appearance recalling Mr Jerningham's in duration and lack of affability: Ronnie's share had been two surly waves of the hand and a single toss of the head. Neither of his statutory pair of telephone calls, one before and one after the lunch-party, had induced her to ring him back. (But he would get her into a ringing-back frame of mind before she knew where she was.) Anyway, Ronnie had said he just *might* be able to get away, had borne down gently on bearded, corduroy-jacketed Eric, had reckoned there was enough of himself on film to keep his memory green with the *Insight* viewers for a week, and here he was.

Where was here, exactly? Picking his way among a litter of used coffee-cups and empty glasses with bent drinking-straws in them, he made his way to the corroded rail. The light was very strong and there was a lot of reflection from the water, but as he leaned outwards he could distinguish ahead a dark patch, broken up by misty horizontal bars, that must be Malakos: the ship was due there at twelve thirty (as he had found out from a steward before settling down to his nap) and it was now twelve forty, so that arrival at one twenty or so would be about right for local conditions if nothing went wrong in the meantime. Ronnie had been to Greece only once before, as far back as 1958, but he could still easily remember the hour and a quarter he and a couple of dozen others had spent, in a boat admittedly much smaller than this one, watching the captain trying to start the engine while a stiff breeze blew them towards some rocks. When half the passengers, and the captain too from time to time, had fallen to prayer, Ronnie had become seriously alarmed. In the event, they had got away with plenty of open water left—a hundred yards of it, if not more—but somehow the experience had left its mark. Even the report of that trainee producer a couple of years before, to the effect that the local girls had all suddenly started screwing, had not been enough to lure Ronnie Appleyard back to the isles of Greece. It was to his credit that the larger, higher appeal of having lots of money and no work had been needed to bring that about.

Presently a stony brownish hunk of land, mostly uninviting hill but with a fat string of white and apricot-coloured buildings along the waterline, started getting close. That minority who had not, half an hour earlier, formed a laden queue to the gangway point hurried to join it now. Ronnie sat on, reasoning that shag and wife had got to be going where he was going and that neither would have dreamt of stirring from London without the assurance of being massively met off the boat. The ship began to turn and slow, while bells rang, orders were yelled and sailors in torn shirts pounded along the decks as if the vessel were approaching Scylla and Charybdis rather than the quayside. But in the end they docked smartly enough. When men with cylindrical moustaches and intent, responsible expressions crowded on board and set about carrying off anything and everything that might have been luggage, Ronnie moved. He had prudently kept by him his midget typewriter and managed, going down the gangway, to give one of the Germans a good belt on the bare calf with one corner. The baseball cap swung round; Ronnie's face expressed the awareness that some object had indeed obtruded itself into the destined path of his property, but not seriously enough to warrant his taking the matter further. On the quay, the shags were calling to each other.

'I don't trust the fat one carrying my little red case, Tubby. He's looking for a chance to sneak away with it.'

'He won't get far if he tries it, my dear.'

'Well, keep an eye on him, Tubby. Stay close to him.'

'What's happened to that fool Burke-Smith?'

'Flat on his back in some drink-shop most likely.'

Ronnie had already spotted the small red-haired butler from Eaton Square standing by what must be a taxi (the only one in sight) and doing his poor best to see over everybody's head. The shags, as people whom it had always been some bugger's job to seek out and look after, halted and concentrated on not having their luggage stolen. As one of those who have to go and seek out buggers capable of being bullied or bribed into looking after them, Ronnie found his suitcases, gave not very much money to a native standing near them and carried them over to the taxi.

'It's Mr Appleyard, isn't it, sir?'

'Afternoon, Burke-Smith.'

The butler was wearing different kinds of floral shirt and shorts and a floppy white hat. Sweat was running down his small face. With just a hint of incredulity, he said,

'These are yours, are they, sir?'

They were leather-bound olive-green canvas twin suit-cases from Asprey's. Ronnie had decided that pricey luggage was one of the cheapest ways of impressing domestics and their employers.

'Get them loaded up, would you?'

'Have you seen anything of Lord and Lady Upshot, sir?'

'No,' said Ronnie.

At that moment the crowds parted and a loud honk was heard. In no time the shags and their porters were milling round the taxi. The butler did a lot of your lordshipping and your ladyshipping. Ronnie handed his cases over to the driver.

'Did your lordship have a good crossing?'

'Now just a minute, just a minute, we're going to be in trouble if we're not careful.' His lordship, who had done a wonderful job of non-recognition on seeing Ronnie again, barred the taximan's path. 'If we take this gentleman's things we're not going to have room for half our own stuff. And we'll be crowded out. No, the simplest plan would be for him to take one of those carriage affairs from that little square at the end of the quay, don't you agree, Burke-Smith?'

'Yes, that's the simplest plan, your lordship.'

'Oh, I don't know,' said Ronnie, picking up one of his cases. 'These old crates are very deceptive.' He went to the side of the taxi and swung the case up past Lord Upshot's head and on to the roof-rack. 'They hold a lot more than you might think.' He picked up the other case. 'This rack will take a good bit more, and there's the boot.' He put the second case on the rack and took up a defensive position below it such that interference with his luggage would mean interference with him. 'And if the worst comes to the worst there's always our laps, isn't there?'

The worst came some of the way: Ronnie sat unencumbered in the front with the driver, Lady Upshot in the same state behind him, but Lord Upshot carried a hat-box on his knees and Burke-Smith supported a hefty black Revelation suitcase, clasping it to him like a fetichist in action. The journey took ten minutes, most of it on an upward incline and inside dust-clouds kicked up by one after another of the carriages Upshot had referred to, lofty two-wheelers with black leather hoods. Now and again there swam into view a man or boy sitting side-saddle on a donkey and apparently not at all disconcerted at being seen doing so. They passed a sign that mentioned dancing and cocktails and Ronnie's heart lifted slightly. Then the taxi stopped, two heavily tanned young locals started unloading the bags as if against time, and the final stage of the journey was revealed as a climb up a winding staircase of white stone that apparently extended several hundred feet above their heads. A figure on a distant crag showed like an ant.

Ronnie always kept himself in trim (not vanity, just a necessary part of the image) with work-outs and rowing-machines and stuff. Nevertheless, he was in some discomfort by the time he got to the top and found that the figure he had seen was Lady Baldock, standing not on a crag but at the end of a terrace and near a large boomerang-shaped swimming-pool. There was a really quite frightening quantity of marble about, more or less plain in the pavement and Corinthian pillars of the terrace, pink and honey-coloured round the swimming-pool. Lady Baldock still looked very, very slightly like an ant because of her slimness and the close-fitting black silk trouser-suit she was wearing. She took off her sun-glasses, held out her hand palm downwards and said,

'Ronnie. How lovely to see you. Did you have a good journey? How was the boat? I know it can be rather terrible. Did you run into the Upshots? I meant to tell you

you'd be travelling together but I had so much to see to at the last minute. Now at the moment there is some sort of luncheon-party going on, but I don't see why you should be bothered with that unless you want to. They're mainly Greek business people who were friends of my second husband. I know all I feel fit for after coming off that boat is a cold beer and a sandwich and a good long siesta. Why don't you go and find Mona and get her to look after you? If you take that second archway and keep on around to the right, you'll come to where she is. The child simply cannot wait to see you. Ah, Beaty and Tubby. How marvellous you're here. Isn't it a horrid climb? How was your trip?'

The last of this receded behind Ronnie as he moved obediently off. Earlier, he had turned in a good one-up-from-formal hand-kiss, then answered every phrase in full, as if taking some Stanislavski-type test, simply by movements of his head and features: simple headshakes and nods eschewed as beginner's stuff. It was beginning to look very much as if what Lady Baldock wanted from him was to keep her daughter off the streets, as it were (and as it was and all, bloody near), until a successor of George Parrot calibre could be secured. But little did any of them know that that time would never come. Appleyard would be in there first, and once there would prove beyond extirpation by any power on earth. There was just one detail that puzzled him slightly: what did his hostess think he thought he was doing here? She was far too smart not to have considered the point.

Ronnie forgot it for the moment. He entered a small open courtyard where there were lots of potted plants and a scrubbed-looking nymph endlessly pouring water out of an urn, then, following directions, went indoors again into a hallway strewn with large hairy rugs. For someone who could not wait to see him, Miss Quick was lying very low.

The only person in sight was an elderly man wearing a pale-green suit and lighting a fat, genuine-looking cigar. As Ronnie passed him he started to amble off towards the distant grumble of the luncheon-party, from which, no doubt, he had momentarily absented himself in order to rule out the danger of being forced to hand his cigars round the company. At the end of the hall there was a staircase with a stone youth, his genitals in unusually good repair, standing beside it. What a lot of stubble trouble the boys and their pals must have had, when everybody was having to shave with sea shells and olive oil, Ronnie thought to himself as he went to the stairs and called:

'Simon?'

'Is that you, Ronnie? Come on up.'

The voice sounded different, almost lively, almost welcoming. It called again when he stood peering through the gloom of a thickly curtained landing. He found her stretched out, looking very long, on a bed with pink sheets. She was wearing a sort of enlarged bikini, the top half extended to include the shoulders, the bottom half almost a pair of shorts, with a stretch of concave midriff between. The thing was lilac-coloured with spaced-out white stripes, and in it she might have been an overgrown and underdeveloped thirteen-year-old. One who would give rise to a great number of sexual felonies, though, Ronnie decided as she got quite quickly off the bed and came and kissed him: a good kiss, incidentally, not showing him how jolly randy she was and not just pally, either.

'How are you? Are you hot? Are you hungry?'

'I'm fine, also hot, also hungry. Also thirsty.'

'I'll get you a beer and I'll see what food there is. You won't mind if it's a bit sort of local, will you?'

'As long as it's not too local. I don't want any of that filthy goat cheese of theirs. Foetor or some such word.'

'Feta. I'll go and get it. You're meant to, you know, have it up here with me.'

'So I gather. Where's my room? Or is this it?'

'Through the bathroom.'

In the bathroom there was more marble. The bath was in the middle of the floor under a chandelier. The bedroom beyond was a replica of the one he had left, except that the bed had blue sheets. Ronnie sighed heavily at this, then walked across more hairy rugs to the wash-basin. In the sizable wall-cupboard he found a new razor of the cut-rate plastic-handled sort, a new tube of shaving-cream with a name unfamiliar to him, a new packet of local razor-blades, a new cake of soap of the sort recommended for its cleansing properties, a new packet of tissues with the initials of an air-line on the wrapper, a very small new bottle of after-shave lotion. At this lot, Ronnie grinned affectionately. He had never found anything about the rich half as sweet as their constant Stilton-paring: 50 centimes in the cloakroom saucer at the Tour d'Argent after a 2,000-franc dinner-party, the telephone in the guest bedroom available for incoming calls only. It was called being good not *with* money—people merely in the process of becoming rich were that—but *about* money.

Ronnie explored briefly outside. The two bedrooms and bathroom were at the end of a short passage that led off the landing. It was soon clear that nobody was staying, or was yet awhile expected to stay, in this part of the house. He went back to find, in the bedroom designated as his, Simon setting out a meal for him on a coloured-glass table by the window: the promised beer (Greek), some meat that had come off a skewer and looked as if it might still be smouldering but soon afterwards turned out to be less than lukewarm, bread, tomatoes and fruit. Her movements were hurried.

'I thought we'd be in here. I'm tired of being in there. Is this all right? It doesn't look much.'

'What are you going to have?'

'I don't want anything. I had a sort of cake.'

'One of the first things we're going to do is to get you eating properly.' He began on his food and drink. 'I see you and I are going to be living in a little apartment of our own here.'

'Right. Mummy always ... '

'Always?' he said, chewing hard, by necessity, not choice. 'I suppose you always have somebody along to share your little apartment. I don't mind a bit. Just curious.'

'You said you had girls.'

'I told you I didn't mind. What intrigues me is the idea of your mother setting this up. Always.'

'Mummy's very good about me and sex. And I think she likes to know. She can't stop me, you see. So I think she thinks the more she knows about the better. It must make her worry less or something.'

'That's it, I expect.'

'Ronnie, it is nice that you're here. I never thought you would be.'

'Oh, I knew I'd be. Why are you being so nice to me? After I took you home that night, and when I—'

'I know. Mummy does take people over. They're never quite the same after I've shown them to her. But then I thought you couldn't help that. How long can you stay?'

'I must be back in London on Monday week morning.'

'It's a lot of travelling for just seven, eight, nine days.'

Ronnie was tired. And he had been concentrating more than his gaze on Simon's midriff, nearly but not quite too hairy legs and forearms, and face. He almost brought out the wrong answer to the implied question, the one prepared for people like Chummy Baldock (should it occur to him to wonder, and where was he?), the one about being used to long inconvenient journeys on either side of a short stay—because he was so important—and having been advised that he really had to get clean away from the job for even the short time he could be spared for—because he was so important and so important. He took some trouble with a tomato skin and said, quite truthfully,

'I wouldn't have done it for anybody else.'

'Oh, you're starting to like me, aren't you?'

There was a brief rapping on the passage door and it was thrown open. One of the young locals entered with Ronnie's suitcases. As he was putting them down, Simon said something to him in Greek. From its tone, Ronnie decided it was offensive, and the young man's expression showed that he thought so, too. The door closed quietly.

'What a clever little linguist you are, Simon.'

'Why are you angry?'

'That laddie was only doing his job. What did you say to him?'

'Told him to knock in future and not come snooping around.'

'He knocked and came in straight away because he was expecting us to be expecting him. As we would have been if we'd thought about it. You mustn't be rude to servants.'

'Nothing to do with you.' For the moment, her voice was back to the drone it had been in London.

'It's a lot to do with me,' said Ronnie, again speaking the bare truth. The instance was nothing, the principle important. Rudeness to servants—other people's, those in hotels, in restaurants—could only be indiscriminately indulged in by those at or near the Lady Baldock level, which it would be unrealistic to aspire to as yet. Of all the girl's huge empire of offensiveness, this small province might be the place to start the process of subjugation. But that could wait for now. He started on some grapes.

'Don't see why it's anything at all to do with you.'

'Everything about you has to do with me. You know that, surely?'

'Oh.'

He ate more grapes. 'What's the programme?'

'Lot of boring things. Boat-trip tomorrow. We ... ' It was almost surprising when she checked herself and went on in her newer, less hypnotized tone, 'It's quite a sail we have to do, down to the next big island. There's going to be a luncheon-party there.'

'That doesn't sound too boring. But I meant today.'

'There's a dinner-party tonight.'

'I meant before that. Starting from now.'

'Well ... nothing. Mummy'll want you to have your dinner-jacket and things on and be in the drinks room at six thirty. That's all.'

'Splendid. Lots of time.'

He finished the grapes, eyed his suitcases, opened one and took out his Swedish black suede sponge-bag. From this in turn he took out his toothbrush and toothpaste, and with them cleaned his teeth. After that he went up to Simon.

'We're going to have a little rest now.'

'Ronnie ... oh ... '

'I said a *rest*, Simon.'

'You mean get into bed with all our clothes on in this heat?'

'Of course not: we'll have to—'

'Well, there you are, then. Oh, darling ... '

'Look, Christ, you're ... take your ... '

Striving to keep his balance, Ronnie stepped backwards, knocked into a suitcase and, much as before, only just avoided falling flat on his back with Simon on top of him. Then he grabbed her by the upper arms and shook her, not very hard.

'What's the matter?'

'Listen. I'm not having it like it was last time, you jogging about like an electric blender to stop me seeing how much you hate it. I—'

'What do you mean I hate it? I adore it, I'm crazy about it, I—'

'All right, you adore it, but I don't, not when it's like that. It's no good when the girl tries to run the show. The man has to do that, and that's how it's going to be this time.'

'Why are we talking about this time and last time? I thought you said we were just going to have a rest.'

'That's not how you've been going on. Anyway, you leave the whole thing to me. Don't do anything yourself. I'll do everything. You're only to do things when you honestly can't stop yourself. See? You're not to do anything on purpose.'

'What about undressing me? Are you going to do that?'

'No, you do that. It's easier.'

Her face set, she complied slowly. With his shirt half off, Ronnie saw her step out of her shorts; her feet were much cleaner than they had been the first time he met her. After that he saw almost nothing until they were lying on the blue sheet with the covers thrown back, and not much more then.

He could not remember what he had meant about having a rest. For some ridiculously long time he tried all he knew to arouse in her those involuntary manifestations of desire he had ordered her to confine herself to. Nothing happened. She went on being in his arms, quite passive, apparently quite comfortable, behaving as if she were watching over his shoulder an *Insight* programme about the case for and against the decimalization of Britain's weights and measures. So at last he stopped.

'Time for our rest, is it?' she asked.

'Time for anything you bloody well like.'

'Do you mean that?'

'How do you mean?'

'Can I do anything I like?'

'No. What sort of thing do you mean?'

She showed him, though this was not the first demonstration he had assisted at. He had found out what sort of thing she meant that time in his flat. As then, she trembled and was tense, she gasped rather than breathed, she moved about a lot. He recognized most of this, but thought to himself, very dimly, that the outcome might, would, must be different this time. And so, partly, it was. Instead of pulling him on top of her, she moved efficiently on top of him. And then, before he could begin to contemplate considering wanting things to be anything but what they were, long before loss of interest could suggest itself to any part of his frame, her body went into overdrive. With nobody at the wheel, the Porsche left the M1 in an accelerating ascending spiral. A kind of black box in Ronnie's brain registered what were probably unprecedented readings. At last the needles swung back.

You can't screw the rich, something in Ronnie muttered as Miss Quick got off him with quite as much alacrity as she had got on him. You have to let them screw you. Or else you leave out screwing altogether. No. Even at this moment of time, when anything of any sexual sort seemed as remote as landing on the moon or applying for French citizenship, he rejected that. Then depression took him in its unfamiliar embrace.

'Was that nice for you, Ronnie?'

'That was, yes.'

'What you wanted, wasn't it?'

'... Yes.'

'Good. Ronnie, if you don't mind I'm going back to my room now. This one gets terribly hot in the afternoon with the sun on it. Don't forget you're on parade at six thirty. Mummy'll be cross if you're late.'

Yachts like the Baldocks' yacht—the kind that sleeps twelve and has a saluting uniformed captain—can sail south-east from Malakos to the island of Poustos in about three hours. With half an hour added for a swim en route, any reasonably early start would get the party to their destination by one o'clock, in these parts and circles the statutory hour for pre-lunch drinking to begin, and that was just what had happened the previous year. But this year the man who was giving the lunch, an exporter of machine-made antiquities named Vassilikós, had said that he could not have his friends from Malakos getting up at an ungodly hour and breaking their necks to be with him so early. They were on holiday, let them relax, take their time, roll up about two o'clock (the statutory hour for at most one not oversized drink to be half drunk on the spot, half resumed at the lunch-table). An observer of these matters might have said that Vassilikós, whose capital in 1950 had been five thousand drachmas, was becoming less ostentatious, less *nouveau* in his attitude to being *riche*, better about money. What Lady Baldock had said was that she and her guests hated lolling around in bed half the morning and that their breakfasts were always cleared away by eight thirty. But Vassilikós had replied that she had forgotten to allow for getting everybody aboard and for stopping to have a swim, and although he knew this was not so, she had had to pretend it was and agree to arrive at two, because he was richer than she was.

To have been aware of all this would have alleviated the very faint puzzlement Ronnie Appleyard felt just before one o'clock that day, when he saw the small red-haired butler, now wearing white ducks, unlocking what would have had to be, and was, the hard-drinks cupboard behind the counter in the saloon. In one sense, this development was only to be expected. The rules said that, when one rich man was playing host to another rich man—or even, come to that, a poor man—and a traditional hour of refreshment arrived, then the first rich man must provide the refreshment, however ardently he might wish that he had manœuvred somebody else into having to do this. The last part was the faintly puzzling part. Ronnie felt it was uncharacteristic of Lady Baldock to leave even this small fraction of her cellar to the mercies of a bunch of guests who had put in several hours of mild sweating and among whom was numbered more than one tenacious boozer.

There were nine people sitting or largely recumbent under the awning aft of the saloon. Absent were Lady Baldock, her daughter, and an understandably unattached middle-aged woman called, it seemed, just Bish, so much and no more. After their swim, the three had gone to lie in the sun on the cabin-top. The butler served eight of the nine before approaching Ronnie and asking him what he wanted to drink. In doing this he stumbled in both leg and tongue. His own personal opening-time had preceded the official one by a generous margin.

'No, I find it upsets me,' said Ronnie, turning down the emphatic suggestion of a glass of ouzo. 'I wonder—'

'Brandy and soda, sir?'

'Not at this hour, I think.' It would be Greek brandy. 'Is there any champagne, by any chance?'

'No, sir.' The butler smiled a regretful, experienced

smile. 'It gets shaken up on the boat, you see, sir. A glass of cold beer?'

'Scotch and soda with plenty of ice,' said Ronnie confidently. The rules said that, whereas champagne need not be forthcoming at any given time, whisky, and good whisky at that, must always be. Immediately, muttering something that at any rate sounded polite, the butler went.

This encounter was nowhere near lost on the Upshots, nor on their immediate companions, an elderly and dough-faced American couple called Van Pup and a youngish fat lone American called Mansfield. In the past, Van Pup had had something to do with crab-meat—preparing it, marketing it, one or another process of that order. Whatever it had been precisely, Van Pup was rich because of it. Mansfield was just rich. All five now looked silently at one another, far from pleased to have seen a round of richmanship won so effortlessly by somebody so plainly non-rich. The three men were drinking Scotch and soda.

Ronnie surmised as much from where he sat on the opposite side of the deck with some people called Sir something and Lady Saxton and, a yard or two farther off, Chummy Baldock, who was drinking a glass of beer and, to all appearance, sneering at the sea. Ordinarily, Ronnie despised the sea himself: it was a part of scenery and therefore a waste of time, and today it was at its most boringly smooth. But no element that caused Baldock to show so many of his top teeth and look down his flexible nose could be all bad. If he were to fall into it, then he, Ronnie, would be on its side.

Setting off a fresh but minor stir of resentment across the way, Ronnie's drink arrived. At the last second it nearly failed to, for, on hearing Lady Baldock call his name from the cabin-top, the butler went momentarily rigid with his hand on the glass, as if calculating at computer speed whether or not it might be advisable to take it away incontinently with him and so eliminate the delay attendant upon setting it down on the table. Negative: spilling some of its contents, the butler nevertheless delivered the glass before bustling unsteadily off into the sunshine.

Lord Baldock had reacted belatedly and slowly, much as dinosaurs are said to have reacted when they reacted, to the sound of his wife's voice. He now reacted belatedly and slowly to the sight of Ronnie's drink and, after an interval, said slowly,

'Very pricey. Very pricey. Expensive.' Then he added quickly, 'I take it that is Scotch you're drinking.'

'Yes.'

'Very pricey, as I say. Probably the priciest drink in Greece. Fashionable too, of course.'

'Really?'

'Yes, really. As well as expensive.'

'Ng.'

'Damned expensive wherever you go in my view,' said Sir Saxton tremulously, not out of excessive emotion but because he said everything, or had said everything that Ronnie had heard him say, tremulously. He was not old: early fifties, perhaps. It might be how the drink took him. The drink would have had to take him somehow. With only sporadic assistance from Mansfield and a visiting Greek, he had meted out condign punishment to a bottle of Courvoisier the previous evening: made it look a bloody fool, in fact. (How pricey was Courvoisier in Greece?) At the moment the irreducible remains of a glass of ouzo stood before him. God bless his belly, and the rest of his alimentary tract, and his head. As he launched into a quavering but not hesitant tirade about how much everything cost, his wife almost seemed to listen. She was a good deal younger, and might have been pretty in a cadaverous way if she had moved her face more when speaking, and at all when not. On showing so far, the Saxtons were marginally the least actively and continuously offensive of all the Baldocks' guests, might turn out on further acquaintance to be little worse than family-size bores. Last night and at breakfast, Ronnie had been even more cordial to them than to the rest of the bastards. Nine days among the pretty well unrelieved rich might cause him to hanker for not quite inhuman companionship. He maintained something like eighty per cent sincerity while Saxton went palpitating on and Baldock stared contemptuously at the water.

'Makes you wonder how people survive. Of course, in many cases they simply don't. Can't. Driven out of existence. Gives you all the more respect for the people who do manage to keep going. Take the Scaifes, now. Eh? Eh?'

Lady Saxton showed that, to her, this was a sufficiently good example of people who managed to keep going; Ronnie thought it more prudent to look courteously blank.

'You know the Scaifes. Smudger and Clarissa Scaife? Well, they're marvellous. Aren't they, Chummy?'

'What's that?'

'Smudger and Clarissa. I was just saying how marvellous they are.'

'Oh yes. Yes.'

'Absolutely marvellous. They were in Nassau in the winter. I thought perhaps you might have seen them there.'

'No,' said Ronnie.

'Well, anyway, they just refuse to knuckle under. Kept up their house in Northamptonshire exactly as it used to be. Had to let some of the servants go, of course. Hung on to as many as they could. Gardens just as they were in his father's time. *And* none of the rooms shut up. Even redid the orangery completely a couple of years ago. The old order, you know. The old ... style. Thing of the past everywhere else, practically. You'd think you were back before the first war. Absolutely marvellous. I take off my hat to them, I tell you frankly.'

Ronnie could not think what he took off to the Scaifes for their continuing feat of rich people's intrepidity, but nobody noticed this, because just then Saxton happened to become aware of the empty glass in front of him, and knitted his brows at it.

'Where's that damned fellow?' he muttered, at the moment when the butler reappeared. 'Ah. Uhm,' he called, with rather more vibrato than usual, 'just, uhm,' picking up the glass and waving it above his head, 'would you, uhm?' The last uhm conveyed with total clarity that at that point Saxton would gladly have used the butler's name instead, had he only been able to remember it.

The butler took the glass in question, though not anybody else's, and made off into the saloon. Lady Baldock, Simon and the woman Bish filed into view, all three heavily sun-spectacled and Bish smeared with oil like a Channel swimmer. Van Pup got up and went and embraced Lady Baldock very heartily.

'Here's my little sweetheart,' he said.

When the embrace was over, its recipient looked round the seated company, or perhaps at its glasses. A dissatisfied expression that had begun to gather on her face dispersed at the sight of the glass of ouzo borne by the returning butler, who proceeded to ask her and the two with her what they would drink. Whether in a sudden burst of deference or (advisedly) not trusting himself to speak, he did the asking in dumb-show. Whichever it was—Ronnie wondered—what then had the man been summoned for a few minutes earlier? No doubt to be told to impose some mulct or amercement or curb on hospitality, some measure of self-taxation; other-taxation, rather, since they always got what they wanted—the belt they tightened was yours.

Simon was standing, perhaps deliberately, in such a position that the considerable bulk of Bish lay between her and Ronnie. Since getting out of his bed the previous afternoon she had been doing her withdrawn thing, slipping off to bed early, locking her door, not being seen at and around breakfast-time, so that she had seemed to be absenting herself from the expedition entirely until, without warning or explanation, she had suddenly appeared on the deck when the yacht was a mile out to sea, as if she had stowed aboard in the small hours, and then, finally, walking straight past him and going to sunbathe. It was enough to make even Ronnie Appleyard feel rather not wanted. Now he got to his feet and went over to her.

Wearing a two-piece of lime green with white stripes, of the same pattern as yesterday's one, she stood in a dejected slouch, arms quite loose at her sides. She did not look up when he came in range.

'Hallo, Simon.'

'Lo.'

Oh, bugger off, he thought. 'Are you having a drink?' he asked.

'It's all right, Burke-Smith's getting me one.'

'Come over and drink it with me.'

'Going to take it down to the cabin. Got to change.'

'But there's loads of time. It's miles yet. I'll show you if you'll just—'

'Got lots of things to do.'

Ronnie said interestedly, 'You know, Simon, you're not really making it very easy for me to like you.'

'Shut up.' Her mouth jerked involuntarily as she spoke.

Frowning in concentration, Lord Baldock had been carefully watching this exchange. He had not been able to hear any of it: nobody had, for that matter, because Mansfield had been talking and Mrs Van Pup laughing throughout, a combination only a public-address system could have penetrated. Baldock looked over the rail instantly when Ronnie started to turn away from Simon.

When he had been back in his chair for a minute or so, half-listening to Saxton's variations on parts of his paean to the Scaifes, Ronnie looked up to find Baldock staring at him much as if he had been the sea. After another few seconds he said to Ronnie in his neighing tones,

'How's young Simon today?'

'All right, I think.'

'Good. Not depressed? You didn't think perhaps she seemed a little bit depressed?'

'No, I didn't.'

'Good. Why don't you ask her to come and join us over here?'

'I did, but she said she had to go and change.'

'But that's quite absurd.' Baldock sounded fairly angry with Ronnie over this point. 'We've got another ten miles' sailing yet. At least that. At least that.'

'I know. I told her.'

'And she still wouldn't come?'

'No.'

'Why not?'

'I don't know.'

'You don't? You don't know? Don't you? Don't you know?'

'No. She didn't say.'

'*Oh*,' said Baldock on a long wailing note, as if this totally unexpected disclosure altered the case beyond recognition. '*Oh.*' Then a thought seemed to strike him. He looked down at the sea as before and nodded to himself a number of times, alternately screwing up and relaxing his face at short intervals. Finally he said, 'We haven't had a chance for a proper chat yet.'

'No.'

'We must have one. Soon.' With that, which held a certain equine menace, Lord Baldock heaved himself upright and did his scholar's shuffle across to the other group.

'Funny chap, old Chummy,' said Saxton.

'Yes.' Tragedy strikes yachting party, thought Ronnie to himself. Peer vanishes in flat calm.

'Yes. Very fine chap, of course. You don't think it was tactless of me, do you, to talk about the Scaifes like that?'

'Surely not. How could it have been?'

'Oh, well, you see, the old man, Chummy's father, very fine chap in all sorts of ways, just had no idea of how to run things. Didn't even do the thing, the, you know, the what the devil is it called?—the deed of covenant, that's it, deed of gift, didn't even do that in time. Signed the papers just after Ascot and was dead as a doornail by Cowes. Never been any good about money. Left poor Chummy without a bean. Poor devil had to sell up down to the last stick of furniture. So you do see it might have been tactless of me to talk about the Scaifes like that.'

'Yes.' Ronnie saw this and more. His researches on the Baldocks had concentrated on the lady, in all ways the senior partner, more than the lord, whom he had known to have made a fortunate marriage but not to have been plucked from the abyss of being left without a bean, i.e., probably, without more than two or three thousand a year to his name. 'But I'm sure you're worrying unnecessarily.'

'Mm. Hope you're right. Uh, these deed of gift affairs can be pretty tricky, you know. Not the end of your worries by a long chalk. Oh dear no. Take young Mansfield, now. Expect you heard about that unfortunate business with his mother. Put it all behind him now, it seems. Sensible of him. Still, what else could he do? Eh? Eh?'

Lady Saxton gave a single inch-deep nod. Appealed to in his turn, and motivated in part by actual curiosity, Ronnie was about to ask what the unfortunate business with Mansfield's mother had been, but just then Saxton again became aware of the again empty glass in front of him, this time without much evident puzzlement or chagrin.

'Where has that blasted fellow got to? Ah. Uhm,' and he went into a second demonstration of rich people's jussive, with identical results. Ronnie joined him, in the sense that he asked for and obtained another Scotch and soda. He also stepped up his cigarette-smoking. The thought of that proper chat with Lord Baldock weighed on him slightly, to a degree at which the unimpressive stimulus of such stimulants might be slightly helpful. The nobleman concerned could be on the point of chucking him out.

Nothing so drastic came into prospect for some time. Lady Baldock and Bish, after and with more laughter from Mrs Van Pup and others, withdrew below. Miss Quick showed her independence of spirit by standing with her back turned for five minutes or so after they had gone, sipping some drink derived from the cola nut while deferring the lots of things she had to do. Then she went. The ship sailed on, in due course reached a hunk of land indistinguishable from Malakos except by being a bit flatter and a bit greener, and tied up at a private anchorage beside a couple of rather grander versions of itself. No human habitation was in view, only a wooden shelter, in the shade of which were to be seen two small vehicles of unusual pattern. There was nobody about.

Ronnie disembarked with the Saxtons. The glare from rock and water and from the quay itself was tremendous, and streams of heat seemed to be constantly flowing from all three. The party straggled towards the shelter. The vehicles proved to be electricity-driven, balloon-tyred open trucks of the type used to transport certain sorts of people round their sorts of golf-course. Almost before Ronnie had taken this in, Lord Upshot was into a driver's seat and away, his wife, the Van Pups and Mansfield having managed to fling themselves aboard just in time. By the time Ronnie reached the second truck, Simon and Lady Baldock were in the back seat and hoisting Bish in beside them. Lord Baldock's arm, like that of a commissionaire imposing his will on a cinema queue, came down between the Saxtons and Ronnie, who quietly stood and watched – as, indeed, most people worth less than a million pounds would have found themselves doing – while Baldock explained the controls to Saxton. This took some time although the thing had only go-pedal, brake and steering-wheel; the last-named, in particular, seemed to strike Saxton as little short of revolutionary. But in the end, bucking and weaving, the equipage moved on to the road taken by its predecessor and was soon climbing steeply.

'So.' Baldock faced Ronnie, paused, and jerked his head with a violence that would have ricked most men's necks, presumably indicating removal to the back of the shelter. Here there was a wicker armchair, a bench carpentered to the wall and an empty beer bottle. Baldcok sat down in the armchair, picked up the beer bottle, sneered at it briefly and threw it at random over his shoulder. It burst somewhere among the rocks with a crack and a faint jangle of glass. (That's right, thought Ronnie. *You* won't ever go walking there barefoot.)

'About five minutes up to the house and half that back. Ought to be enough. Now, how shall I put it?'

Facing him from the bench, Ronnie was feeling—not nervous exactly, but a little keyed up, as if about to confront one of the more experienced Tory Q.C.-M.P.s on *Insight* to discuss some aspect of home policy: a topic requiring knowledge of the facts, in other words, not just of the trend. Facts, however, would hardly serve him here. Histrionics were the thing. He put some apprehension on to his face and at once, a seasoned actor at the rise of the curtain, felt himself relax.

'Of *course*,' whinnied Baldock, slapping his thigh, most of which was covered by part of his shorts. On these, different kinds of fish were portrayed, in contrast with his shirt, which was eventful rather than merely descriptive. 'Of *course*. Just ... I expect you'll have noticed that I haven't much time for you?'

Saying this, he fluttered his eyelids and flexed his nose in a self-deprecatory way, as if not having much time for somebody and making this plain to him were accomplishments on which one should not, perhaps, plume oneself too openly.

'Well, that is rather a, of course I have been conscious of, um, I, uh, there has been something of an atmosphere but really everything here is so new to me that I thought perhaps, uh, but if I've done anything, you know, uh, then I wish you'd ... '

There came a snapping, cracking, ripping sound, like a large animal making its way through dense bush. Lord Baldock had leant forward in the armchair. He giggled and said in rather efficient Cockney,

'Come off it, me old Ron. No need to play silly buggers, all right? I got your number, see?'

'Honestly, I've no idea what you—'

'Okay, okay. Stay with it, then. Stay with it as long as you're quite certain in your own mind that I've got your number. Much easier for all concerned. You're hanging about on the chisel, aren't you, Ron?'

'On the chisel? Oh, you mean I–'

'Yes. And it's no good, old lad. Not a chance, Romeo. Wherefore art thou Romeo? Here's somebody who knows bloody well wherefore, Ronnio, and don't you forget it. Nobody's going to marry that girl for her money if I have anything to do with it, and I have a lot to do with it.'

'Do you?' said Ronnie flatly.

'That's more like it, Ron. Yes, I do have a lot to do with it. You wouldn't understand that, of course. I'm afraid your ideas about money are rather limited, you see. Bit vulgar. Money and what goes with it, I mean. How would you know, after all?'

'I suppose you've ruled out the possibility that I might be in love with her?'

'You bet I have. What do you take me for? As I told you, I've got your number. Anyway, none of this is important. Question of what you're here for. Whatever you may think you're here for, let me tell you what you are here for. You're being given a free holiday, plus the chance of making some contacts, entirely for Simon's benefit. She took a frightfully hard knock over that George Parrot business ...'

'*She* took a hard knock?'

'You wouldn't know. You wouldn't understand the ins and outs. Your job. Your job is to give that girl a good time–in bed and anywhere else you like. Talk to her. Make her laugh. What used to be called taking her out of herself. That's your job. And you don't seem to be taking it very seriously. Which makes me a bit cross with you.'

'She's a very difficult girl,' said Ronnie, thinking to himself that if Baldock really believed that anybody could give her a good time in bed, not to mention elsewhere, then there was one important set of ins and outs that he, Baldock, had failed to understand.

'You've got that far, have you? If she weren't she wouldn't need therapy from any little Tom, Dick or Harry she might happen to fancy. Now look here, Appleyard. I want young Simon to be happy. If you can manage that for the next week or so I'll be very grateful to you. Your job. You'd better start doing it. Look at her so far. Bored, irritable and depressed. That must be your fault, musn't it? All right, then. Marked improvement in the next forty-eight hours. Otherwise Juliette is going to find she simply must have your room. Understood?'

'You make it very clear.'

'Good. No hard feelings, I hope. Not like me to wave the big stick, but I don't like having you round the place, you see. You may be good of your kind, but I don't like the kind. Nothing personal. Ah, here we are. Thought we could do it in the time if we put our minds to it.'

Driven by Simon, one of the electric trucks was approaching, white stone chips flying from under its tyres. The butler and the skipper of the yacht, a portly man who resembled a butler, and an English one at that, far more than the butler did, came up from the quay. As Ronnie followed Baldock towards the point where the truck would turn, he was looking shaken. This was partly because he was feeling shaken (at the blowing of such a substantial bridge in his line of advance), but also because it was always best to appear to take to heart any ballocking against which no defence was practicable. And, all unknowing, or perhaps not all that unknowing, Baldock had dealt him a strong opening card for the next hand.

In the truck, Simon looked from Baldock to shaken Ronnie and back. When they reached her, she took Ronnie's wrist and pulled him gently towards the seat beside her.

Vassilikós's luncheon-party—not one of his big ones, just seventy or eighty old friends—was held in the rectangle formed on three sides by the house itself, and on the fourth by a row of marble statues of the middle 1960s (A.D.) period: Spartan youths, hoplites with spear and shield, Xerxes' Immortals, Pericles addressing the Assembly, Aristotle and the young Alexander. Round the swimming-pool the balance of the sexes was redressed by enough splendid crumpet (Ronnie Appleyard thought) to last one a lifetime, or at least a very debilitating couple of years—some of Vassilikós's old friends could not have been his or anybody else's old friends for very long. Chilling gales were wafted into this space by four immense air-conditioners of the kind Ronnie had seen in airport halls, mounted on the three terraces and, on the open side, between a Greek and a Persian warrior. Overhead, to keep off the direct sun, there stretched a canvas sheet, with vents to let out the rising warm air. Its faded dark-green colour reminded Ronnie of marquees at country fêtes or cricket matches in his youth. Nothing else did.

Hand in hand with Simon, he went over to the drinks tables that stretched from end to end of one of the sides of the rectangle. Both in the fact and in the role of shaken Ronnie, he needed something, but a good half of his motive was professional curiosity. It was abundantly satisfied: rank on rank of gins awaiting their tonics and Pimmses their lemonades, whisky sours, champagne cocktails, curious purplish drinks full of fruit, all stood ready for circulation by waiters or for grabbing in person. While Simon was away in eager quest of a Scotch and soda—'Let me get you something: I'm sure you need it after that horrible Chummy'—Ronnie caught sight of Lord Upshot standing a little apart and surveying the deployment of drink. His face seemed to express surprise, resentment, envy, respect almost amounting to fear. So might the military attaché of some small backward state watch the manœuvres or street parades of its vastly more powerful benefactor, the display of quality, numbers and range, the line-up of powerful and immediately available front-line effectives, the background presence of innumerable reserves ...

But, at this stage, much of it had become no more than a show of strength. Even as Ronnie watched, an unopened bottle of White Horse went back from table to case, a servant about to slice up a lemon received some signal and at once abandoned the task. Lunch was starting. Led, presumably, by some trained member of the household or loyal guest, a small but growing queue had appeared on the far side of the pool, at one end of a bank of food that stretched down as far as Aristotle and Alexander. It seemed obvious to Ronnie that, in being scheduled to arrive at bar closing-time, the Baldock contingent had been singled out for a spot of rich people's mini-retrenchment, perhaps punitive in aim. He could not have known that Vassilikós's concern not to have got them up at an ungodly hour was a direct result of having been invited, the previous summer, to the wrong one of two closely similar parties Juliette Baldock had given for an American photographer and his boy-friend.

One of the pieces of cock-fodder by the pool, a blonde with a pigtail and an uncannily recessed navel, was looking alternately at the empty glass in her hand and at Ronnie, who nearly fell over as his body tried to sort out the contradictory programming of get-in-there instinct and dollars-before-dolls intellect. Not that his own future source of dollars could fairly be said not to be a doll, at any rate visually. She handed him his whisky now, her lips going thin in an intent way, then broadening out in a smile, a rather stiff one, as though she had toothache: no doubt she was out of practice at smiling. She fixed her eyes on him. They were inkier than usual and, despite the half-shadow she and he were standing in, very shiny. Near the left-hand one was a fair-sized crescent-shaped mole, or birthmark. He looked at the plain sleeveless linen dress she was wearing. His mind ground out the thought that a person need not be called thin simply because of being slimmer than the average slim person, then lurched almost to a standstill, like a lawn-mower going into a patch of long grass. For the second time in a quarter of a minute, while his higher centres cracked down on a surge of instinct similar in kind to the first, but undiluted and bigger, he came close to breaking a leg without moving an inch.

'Thank you,' he said.

'What did that ghastly Chummy say to you?'

'I ... ' He did a bit of shaken lip-biting. This one was going to wait for its moment. 'I'd rather not talk about it now. Do you mind?'

'Oh no, Ronnie, no, of course I don't mind. I understand, I really do. Any time ... Look, there's Mummy with Mr Vassilikós. I think they want us to go over.'

For all its radio-play style, this was undeniable. They went over. Vassilikós was hilariously handsome and dignified, like a clean-shaven Zeus: one who used plenty of after-shave, too. He smiled with a sincerity effortless enough to win Ronnie's professional respect; there was an artlessness component sited in the lower lip that might well repay imitation. Lady Baldock smiled too, and extended an arm.

'Here you are,' she said. 'Kyril, this is Mr Appleyard from London. Our good host, Ronnie.'

'Ronnie's very famous on television in London,' said Simon.

'Television in London, eh?' Vassilikós spoke with dazzled incredulity, as if informed that Ronnie had just spent a couple of days in space. 'That must be good fun.'

'Oh, you know, lots of hard work, a few laughs.'

'Oh yes. Tell me, do you know Bill Hamer?'

Ronnie heard this with something not far from panic. Had everyone gone mad? What could Hamer have been up to in the last thirty-six hours? Was there to be a Nobel Prize for television? Had Hamer married Jackie Kennedy, defected to East Berlin? The bastard. But Hamer himself would have admired the way Ronnie rose to the challenge.

'Oh, *Bill*,' he muttered, smiling and half-shutting his eyes, almost winking. 'A *very* old friend of mine. I know Bill of *old*.'

'Yes, Ronnie's a great fan, aren't you, Ronnie?' By her indulgent tone and patronizing hand on his shoulder, Lady Baldock undid a good deal of his solid hint that Hamer had advanced himself by blackmail or homosexual prostitution. Then her manner sharpened. 'But how have you come across him, Kyril?'

'I met him in London some time. Rather a good sap, I was thinking. Interesting Jap. I was discussing to go on his programme.'

'Kyril, you never told me.'

'My dear Zooliette,' said Vassilikós, going some of the way to clear up the sap-Jap phonetic puzzle, 'nothing has come of it. He was not getting enough millionaires to come on the programme with me. It was going to be everybody talking about Ritz people.'

Simon did a quick frown with her mouth as well as her brows. 'Ritz people?'

'I'm so sorry,' said Vassilikós, with a smile of such superhuman tolerance that Ronnie could hardly bear it. 'It's my bad accent. People with tremendous lot of money. Rit-sh people, you see. Yes, I was unhappy when the thing was cancelled. Hamer was getting ready to make a little film of my house—not this one, the one near Cannes: you haven't been there, I think—and then nothing has happened. I was disappointed. I liked this fellow Hamer. He has very nice ideas. Oh, people like me, we're all getting our hands dirty all the time with the money. Dollars, drachmas, pounds,'—Ronnie tried all he knew not to incline his head at this bit of graciousness, but failed—'all day long we're thinking of nothing else and having dirty hands. But fellows like Hamer are helping us to be better, they're making us remember that there are so many other things in the world, beautiful things which nobody can sell and buy, truth and love and friendship with everybody.' By moving the back of his fingers an inch and a half, Vassilikós negatived some offer or question put forward by a dark-haired girl whose figure could simply not have come about as the unassisted handiwork of nature, must have been partly the result of injections or something. With the other hand he silently took a glass of a kind of fruity nonsense off a silver tray (the smallest Ronnie had ever seen) put under his nose, or not far from his paunch, by a local person wearing white clothes. 'It's quite obvious, after all,' said Vassilikós, 'that the human beings have not come to this world by chance. We must be doing what God wishes us to be doing. That's what it is. So I can't stop you from your lunch any longer. Ask for a double order of the clams. They're very small but you'll like the good flavour. Bye-bye for now.'

With a majestic smile that changed indefinably as he shifted his gaze, Vassilikós made a short flanking movement towards another figure of myth – a minor hanger-on of Dionysus this time – in summer naval uniform, a commodore or perhaps a rear-admiral, dripping with gold braid, anyway. Lady Baldock's brown eyes, in a way suggesting that she too was looking forward to a proper chat with Ronnie, followed him as he trooped obediently off with her daughter. He sensed this. The bastards were closing in. Good. They must be feeling they had something to close in about. If that was what they felt they were showing a bloody sight more prescience than observation. He hoped to God that what they saw in their crystal ball was going to come to pass. And soon. All his instincts told him that he had no longer than until the evening to win Simon over. Another night apart would trigger off plan B, the telephone call to the *Insight* office and the mendacious cable from bearded Eric. Ronnie crossed the fingers of his free hand against this chance. His captive one was in Simon's.

'Plenty to say for himself,' he began experimentally.

'Never stops talking,' she said, reacting as hoped.

'And the terrifying thing is he means all that balls about love and truth and God and the rest of it.'

'And yet he's clever enough to have made all this money.'

'That's different. You can believe in flying saucers and still be a first-class microbiologist.'

'But money's to do with people.'

'Making it isn't. Still, I can quite see why a chap like Vassilikós goes on about love and truth.'

'Why?'

'I don't suppose there's much of either around in his world.'

'What about God?'

'Christ, I don't know,' said Ronnie, a little put out at having the effect of his last line—very strong and sympathetic, he had thought it—impaired by this eager query. 'These days he probably has quite a bit of time for that too. He's moving into coronary territory, fast.'

Although what they had just had was not really a conversation, rather a matter of Ronnie showing off and Simon agreeing to be shown off to, it had seemed more like one than any former exchange they had had, and he was quite sorry when joining the food queue put an end to it. A ten-minute shuffle began. Before and behind them were young foreign queers in silk shirts and tight little shorts and with heavy gold chains round their necks, old foreign queers wearing cheeky hats and tussore cardigans, foreign and American non-queers of most ages who were collecting two lunches and keeping an eye open for any untoward re-groupings by the swimming-pool. The lunches themselves were good material for the pluto-anthropologist. At the starting-line you picked up a black plastic tray with curious holes and hollows in it, suitable for the accommodation of, say, a twenty-seven-inch-screen-television dinner. This was much what you were then piecemeal served with: a very lightweight knife and fork wrapped in a paper napkin [embossed with *K.V.* in toiling pseudo-classical style) and fitting into an indentation along one side of the tray, a cardboard bowl containing a dozen toyshop-sized shellfish and bearing what was undoubtedly a sample tube of some sauce clipped to its circumference, a cardboard plate with meat and sliced peppers on plastic skewers, a salad contaminated by shreddings of gruesome authentic cheese, a peach doled out into a shallow depression specially prepared for it on the tray, a yellow plastic vessel two-thirds full of retsina, a finger-bowl that looked like but was not glass with an extremely thin slice of lemon floating in it, and 'Coffee later on the other side, sir.'

The clams were indeed good on flavour, but so gritty that a second dozen would not really have been acceptable, supposing the server concerned had granted Ronnie's entreaty instead of taking it as a strange, almost macabre jest. As it turned out, he could have had most of Simon's for the asking. She ate only three of her portion, complaining that they tasted strong and could give you jaundice. He decided against telling her to try not to be so crappily American, and went on humbly asking questions about guests, set-up, etc. By the time they were through the kebabs, which seemed to have more plastic in their composition than just their uniting skewers, and were on to, or were trying to get their teeth into, the peaches, Ronnie considered he had achieved his temporary object: convincing Simon of how unfeignedly relaxed he felt in her company.

They abandoned the peaches and Simon ran off to get the coffees. Ronnie drank the last inch of what, to him, had always tasted like cricket-bat juice – rubber grip and springs thrown in along with blade and handle. He decided against even trying to get more; clear head needed. Not that this stuff could be much of a head-fogger. How little did it cost? Very little. To devotees of micro-economy, operating in a country that produced its own wine (very much excluding France) must seem to carry a substantial advantage. You could serve the local product, however horrible in the mouth or provocative to the large gut, at any time, and not only incur no reproach, but win positive approbation for not putting on airs, having the good sense and the good taste to realize that what these sturdy folk had been drinking for centuries must appeal to any but a jaded palate, and suchlike. Jaded palates got their turn, for some discreditable and probably literary reason, in places where the folk, sturdy or not, spoke English. Not even the very best, the well-nigh perfect about money had yet, in Ronnie's experience, dared to keep the Taittinger for themselves and stock their parties with Taylor's New York Brut. Still, give old de Gaulle another two or three years ...

Simon came back with two paper cups of coffee that turned out to be instant. There was a satisfactory amount of glancing and hand-touching when she gave him his and took a cigarette from him. He dumped their trays and plates and the rest of the junk in a white-painted iron basket behind Pericles' statue, off the plinth of which, having nowhere to sit, they had eaten their lunch. The dumping was far from an anti-social act; notices in English and French exhorted him to do just as he had done. A Greek notice presumably said the same thing, though it could have been recommending him to stuff the things up his arse for all he knew or cared.

'When are we leaving here?' he asked.

'We sail at four.'

'Not till then? That's well over an hour.'

'Mummy has to have a sleep after lunch when she's in Greece, you see.'

'Has to?'

'When she's in Greece.'

'I see. What does everybody else do? Do we all have sleeps?'

'Oh no. There isn't anywhere to do it. Unless you want to lie down on the ground somewhere, of course.'

For a moment, Ronnie was honestly puzzled. 'But there

must be enough beds and couches and what-not in this place for everybody at this bloody party to have a sleep if he feels like one.'

'Oh, sure, at least that many, but only Mr Vassilikós's house guests can go into that part of the house. Except for Mummy.'

'What about peeing and that sort of thing?'

'There are johns round the corner you can get into from outside but you can't get into the house from.'

'Doesn't Vassilikós want to, uh, show people round his house sometimes?'

'He shows them round part of it, the part where the pictures and the statues and the vases and things are.'

'Supposing somebody just lay down on a couch in that part?'

'There aren't any couches in that part.'

Ronnie hesitated; Simon's contributions to the session were becoming more and more reluctant, but occupational curiosity must be allowed to round off its task. 'Supposing somebody like Lord Upshot demanded to be let into the part where the couches are?'

'The man would tell him he'd have to talk to Mr Vassilkós about it, and Mr Vassilikós would explain why it couldn't be done.'

'How? I mean why couldn't it be done?'

'It couldn't if he says it couldn't. It's his house, isn't it?'

'Of course.' He spoke warmly and gravely. 'Absolutely. I was just interested. Well ... what would you like to do until we take off?'

Immediately she turned her eyes and face full on his. 'Let's go for a walk.'

'In this heat? And where? Up the mountain or down the mountain?'

'Nearly all of it's through a wood where it's shady. And

except for one bit where you just have to go up and over and down again the rest of it's practically on the level. And it's not far.'

'What isn't? Some other rich ... chap's place?'

'A temple, actually.'

'Full of Germans.'

'It won't be full of anybody. You can pretty well only get to it from here.'

All these statements proved true, not least the one about it not being far. Nevertheless, it was too far for some. Several other couples, including an old queer and a young queer, set out about the same time to make apparently the same journey, but none finished it except themselves. Two by two the wayfarers trooped off the path, in one case to a poorly concealed spot about eight yards from it. This move took place no more than half a minute before Ronnie and Simon passed, long enough, however, for the establishment of a going concern. Ronnie felt envious and, spoke to distract himself, without much thought.

'Something to be said for old Vassilikós's no-admittance policy, I suppose. Your mother wouldn't fancy having to step over those two on the stairs. And the laundry bills would—'

'Ha ha, very funny.'

'Well ... You're hardly the—'

She stopped dead on the grassy, dusty path, standing with irregular patches of direct sunlight slanting across her midriff and thighs. One of them enclosed a small oblong birthmark on her upper arm. She looked very tall and very serious.

'*Shut* up, you *shit*,' she said hoarsely. '*Shut*-up-*shut*-up-*shut*-up.'

Immediately, looking her in the eyes, Ronnie said, 'I'm terribly sorry, Simon. I spoke without thinking. Please forgive me.' He had no very clear idea of what he was apologizing for, but knew that she had managed to read his feelings of envy. That was no way to kick off the afternoon.

'I know her. She's a high-class call-girl from Athens. You can have her if you want her.'

His mind, sparked by memory of the incident of the Reichenberger party, threw up a picture of Simon dragging the present incumbent clear by the ankles and personally preparing himself for action. 'I don't want her,' he said, moving half a pace nearer.

'She'd give you a good time. Everybody says she gives everybody a good time. I don't know why you don't.'

There was self-dislike as well as self-pity in her tone. Ronnie did not want her to feel either emotion. Speaking for once in his life with real sincerity, he said, 'I don't care what sort of time she gives people. I don't want her. I want you.'

'H'm.' It was a grunt, but a believing grunt. 'Mean that.'

'Of course I mean it. You know I do.'

'H'm. Can have me when we get back this evening.'

To be on the safe side, Ronnie kissed her instead of saying anything. Having Simon had turned out so far to be a bit of a pig in a poke. They walked on. There was just rather light-green foliage, white outcrops of rock, stringy clusters of poor man's dandelions and, in the middle distance, the tangerine flicker of a pair of trousers as somebody draped them over a bush. Soon a battered granite column showed through the trees.

The temple, being a temple, was nothing to write home about except to your auntie. Half a dozen pillars supported what looked very unlike a piece of the original roof. The remnants of an adjacent wall had some probably ancient blocks and some certainly more recent ones, of a period a little earlier, it might have been, than Vassilikós's Spartan youths. A good deal of original pavement had survived, with elementary designs in faded crimson and purple and an unhealthy-looking tree growing through one corner. Ronnie sat down on a stone stump somewhere near the middle.

'Whose is it?' he asked.

'All this land belongs to Mr Vassilikós.'

'No, I meant whose temple, god or goddess or nymph or something.'

'Oh, who cares about that? All over and done with, isn't it? What's it to us? Just a lot of bricks.'

She had spoken amiably enough for this to have been an opinion, granted for the moment that she could be said to hold such things, rather than an attempt to put him down. The new pissiness, he thought to himself. An older pissiness would have tried to make him feel inferior for not knowing about Homer and Venus and Plato and Euclid and people like that. Well, times changed. You could say that for them. He allowed a pause to form and half-saw her eyes flick over to him. Vestigially shaken Ronnie was ready to take the stand.

He was able to lead off with something so strong that, under an earlier convention, he would almost have been inclined to repay Lord Baldock, who had given him the chance, by killing him outright instead of torturing him to death. Whatever the reaction, he would be better off for having introduced this point than for its introduction to him in any possible form.

'Chummy accused me of being after your money,' he said matter-of-factly, rejecting the more obviously indicated blurt or mumble, and feeling for once in his life a bit of a shit.

'Did he. Are you,' she said in her dullest voice.

He looked away and noticed, to his slight surprise, that in that direction there was a view, with cultivation terraces, a village, a road, a harbour, boats, sea, islets, an island, more sea, and the horizon. Even the nearest parts of all this were quite a long way away, and all of it was spread out a lot on each side, so that the temple must be near the edge of some fairly chunky escarpment type of thing, up which any bus would need a jet or a rotor to make its way. Hence the uncanny absence of Germans.

'Do you know, I hadn't thought about it until he came out with it? But I've thought about it pretty hard ever since. Thought of precious little else, to be perfectly honest.' Mirthless laugh. 'Afraid I must have seemed a bit gloomy ... not much of a companion ... '

Sitting on the pavement, Simon moved up until she leant against him. A narrow dry hand took hold of his. 'The bugger,' she muttered.

'Funny. I quite thought he liked me ... Anyway, I tried to think about it sensibly. I cast my mind back to when we met at the Reichenbergers'. You remember? George Parrot went off in a huff and you asked me to get you a drink and I did and then I took you away from two other blokes and all that before you even told me your name. So even if—'

'You might have recognized me.'

'How? From what?' By this time he was off, his role taking charge of him in the way that—in the minds of interviewers on arts programmes—characters took charge of novelists, the obvious but risky hunch to be fearlessly backed. 'You've never had your picture in the papers.'

'That's true.' No monotone or mutter now.

'Why not, by the way? I'd have thought you'd—'

'Mummy thinks it would be bad for me.'

'I see. Well then, I couldn't have known who you were. I went for you because I thought you were bloody attractive. Which indeed you are.'

'Mm. But why shouldn't you be the sort of man who makes passes at girls all the time, and you take me to your flat for a one-night stand, and then you thought I wasn't any good, which I might not really have been much because I do tend to be a bit nervous the first time, but I wasn't as bad as you thought, and then you chucked me out for not being any good, but then you found I was rich, so then you thought why shouldn't you hang on and perhaps I'll get better from your point of view, and anyway if you turned on all your charm I might fall in love with you and want to marry you?'

This exact reconstruction of past events and diagnosis of current policy had gone on long enough for Ronnie to be able to polish the rough draft he had by him for such an eventuality. 'I can't answer that,' he said. 'There's no way I can prove to you that you aren't right in every detail. All I can do is just *say* to you that I don't give a *bugger* whether you've got a million pounds or ninepence, and I'd rather have you with ninepence than anybody else with a million pounds, and I've got an odd feeling that one of these days I'll have the chance of proving *that*.' This last lie struck him as unnecessary, and he resolved to live the part a little less whole-heartedly for a bit.

'*Say* it to me, then.' Her hand wriggled in his. 'Don't keep on trying to tell me what it isn't about me that you like. I want to hear what you do like.' The hand went like wood and the voice took the same turn. 'If there is anything much.'

'There's everything.' No need to live the part at all over the next stretch, thank Christ. 'I told you in the street that time and then again, and I was cross with you then, after we'd had that lousy bloody sex-session, I told you I thought you were beautiful, and I still think so, only more now because I know you better. And extraordinary as well as beautiful. But beautiful first.'

'Nasty body.'

'Nonsense. Lovely body. Slim and lovely.'

'Too thin. No tits.'

'No, just small. Dear little tits.'

Her face was lowered. 'Nasty girl.'

'Silly girl sometimes. Annoying girl. But very very nice girl.'

'Can't like me.'

'I like you a lot. You know that. I almost love you.'

'Mustn't love me.'

'Why not? What do you mean, mustn't?'

'*Mustn't*. Ones that love me always go away.'

Silence, apart from the racket of birds and insects. Pissy girl, remarked Ronnie to himself, then decided to withdraw the epithet on seeing two tears splash one after the other into the dust on the pavement. He waited, looking down at the close-cropped nape of the neck, from which a line of small inky moles ran and disappeared below her dress. She had not removed her hand, but seemed to have forgotten it.

'You see,' she said after a moment, gasping and swallowing from time to time, 'that's the worst thing of the lot. We get to a certain stage and then they ... just go away. There doesn't even have to be a quarrel. And that's why I don't want you to love me ... I couldn't bear you going away. I wouldn't mind anything else. You could ... just pretend to like me and really only want me because I'm rich, and I wouldn't mind as long as you didn't go away ... I'd let you have other girls ... '

Ronnie knelt down and put his arms round her. Her

hair smelt slightly of lemon peel, and very nice too. She was getting quite sound on such matters.

'Now listen,' he said. 'As long as you want me to stay I'll stay. I've got to go back to London at the end of next week, but that's—'

She nodded hurriedly, her damp cheek waggling up and down against his. 'I know, that's not going away. Go on.'

'But there's one condition.'

'Huh. What's that?' she asked in a tone of glum suspicion.

'We've got to get to perform properly in bed.'

'Huh.'

'In time, that is. And that can't happen unless two other things are fixed. One is that, not like yesterday or the time in my flat, I run things. You do as I say and you do what I want. Then I can do what you want. And that must happen, because I shall never enjoy it while you still don't enjoy it—no, shut up, Simon—and I won't go on not enjoying it. You understand?'

'Suppose so. What's the other thing that's got to be fixed?'

'You must tell me the truth. Oh, I don't mean all the time: nobody can do that. But when it matters. Now, will you tell me the truth?'

'All right. Ronnie ... '

'Yes?' he said without his glissando.

'Why couldn't you go on not enjoying it with me?'

'I thought I'd told you. You're too beautiful and I want you all the time and I couldn't stand not having you properly. That's why.'

'H'm. Looking forward to getting back.'

'So am I.'

'H'm.'

Ronnie had meant what he said about making love properly, but his air of confidence in his ability to bring this about had been assumed for the occasion. He was fond of women as well as wanting to go to bed with all the good-looking ones and, in the interests of his own pleasure, was considerate when he got them there. And he had got enough of them there in the past to have become efficiently considerate. Nevertheless, it was a condition of his amorous merits that he knew their limitations. He might simply be and remain ignorant of what it specifically was that would turn Simon's goodwill into desire. Or he might have underestimated the extent to which frustration would eat away patience—and a hell of a lot of patience was going to be needed, as he discovered almost at once.

Not quite at once. He had not expected anything very much from their first encounter under the treaty of Poustos, and he got a little less than that. On the boat-trip back to Malakos, Simon behaved like an inexperienced actress about to play the lead in a new production of *St Joan*: at first a lot of chatter, relatively unpissy stuff considering the subject was Greece and staying in Greece, then almost total silence, plus lip-biting and yawning. As soon as they reached the blue bedroom up at the house she stripped, clung to herself and stood waiting for him. She was so anxious to let him run things that when he kissed her she seemed scarcely to notice. On the bed she remained passive but could not disguise her tension, and trembled as soon as he touched her breast. He put both arms round her and they lay cheek to cheek.

'Sorry, Ronnie. I am trying, but all I can think about is how nervous I feel.'

'Don't worry about it. Nothing's going to happen.'

'I've started too late, you know, that's the trouble. Got

into bad habits. I made up a way of what I thought was pleasing people and now it's all I can do.'

'That can't have happened. You'll change now you really want to.'

'I do want to. This isn't much fun for you, though, is it?'

'I'm all right. I'm loving just lying here and holding you.'

'Oh, I'm loving that. At least in a way I am. I can't sort of completely, though, because I keep thinking if I let myself really love it, then you'll start ... wanting to do other things.'

'I promise not to. No other things whatever today.'

'You're a very sweet man, Ronnie. I'll just concentrate my mind on your promise.'

Bit by bit she did relax a little. Not much. At bedtime that night it was perhaps slightly better. Not much. The next day a pattern of behaviour began to emerge in Simon. Throughout the morning on the beach—or rather the patch of shingle, rock and coarse grass from which the party bathed—over drinks at the taverna across the road—ouzo, wine or metallic local beer—and until almost the end of lunch—six guests: four Greeks and two shags—Simon said things, some of them quite remarkably unpissy, and listened to what was said to her. Ronnie saw to it that as much of this as possible took place in Lord Baldock's presence. Then, as siesta time approached, she absented herself mentally. Ronnie got her away from Lord Baldock for most of this. There was the same alternation of mood during the evening.

'You mustn't get so wrought up,' he said to her that night.

'No use saying that. I can't help it, honestly.'

'You weren't like that before we went to bed the first couple of times.'

'I know, but that was when it didn't matter very much. I was just going ahead like always. Now it's like a test, and you know what that's like. You keep getting all afraid of failing.'

Ronnie recognized that being nervous of being nervous must be an unusually troublesome form of being nervous. You had to stop it before you could stop it. Other aspects of this situation, it occurred to him at lunch-time the following day, also had something circular about them. Just as Mansfield called for the bill (he had feasted the party frugally at a hotel near the harbour), Simon's shoulders went loose. Clearly and glumly, Ronnie saw that the only certain way of getting her to relax to the point at which he could satisfactorily screw her was to tell her, and get her to believe, that he had abandoned all intention of ever screwing her, satisfactorily or otherwise. Perhaps he should remodel his strategy, ask her to marry him in return for his promise never to screw her. She might jump at it. And, after all, a *mariage blanc* with that mule-faced bint five years back would have suited him down to the ground. Ah, but that was different. Because she had not wanted him not to screw her; quite the contrary. And he had not wanted to screw her, not any more. And he did want to screw Simon, more than ever. Yes, that was the difference.

Alternatively, then, since she seemed to dread not being screwed by him more than she had dreaded being screwed by him, it might be the best thing simply to plunge ahead, bash on regardless, rape her. This seemed a simple and splendid idea on the drive back and all the way to the bedroom; but one look at that elongated unvoluptuous body, and another into those anxious black-coffee eyes, and he knew that any kind of rape was out for good. He must do it in the way he had set out to do it, or never do it at all.

He lay down beside her and took her in his arms. Her body stiffened slightly.

'Have you always hated it?' he asked.

'Oh yes, every time. Hated the whole bloody thing.'

'Does it make any difference whether you like the man?'

'No. Not to it itself. That's always been the same, right from the first time. I was only fourteen then. A girl-friend of mine had just started and she told me exactly what you did. It sounded so marvellous that I went and did it straight away. And it was horrible. I thought maybe I was too young, so I held off for a couple of years, and then tried it again. And it was just like it was the first time, horrible in exactly the same way. And it's been like that ever since. Sorry, Ronnie, but it isn't *you*, you see.'

'I do see. But what I don't see is why you keep doing it. You told me you'd had forty-four men. Is it because you hope you'll find someone it won't be horrible with?'

'Forty-five, counting you. No, after the first two I stopped hoping. Until the other day, that is. Now I've started hoping again. No, I slept around because I wanted someone. Someone to be with me. You know, a man of my own. That was part of the time. The rest of the time it wasn't as grand as that. Just someone to be with me for a while.'

'Simon, have you never come? Had an orgasm?'

Her voice grew hoarser. 'Not with men.'

'Ah.'

'No, not girls either. I tried them. By the time we got into bed I didn't want to do anything to them, and what they did to me was just as horrible as a man. Different, but easily as horrible.'

'I see.'

'Are you disgusted with me?'

'No. I was just wondering if we could use that, if I could use it.'

'Trouble is, Ronnie,' she said in a laryngitic whisper, 'you have to sort of be over here to do it, where I am. Be me, really. I only know one way to do it and it takes ages. Doesn't always work, either. Sorry. Nothing seems to be any good, does it?'

'We're making a bit of progress. It's bound to be slow.'

'Hey, wait a minute, Ronnie, can't I do it to you? I mean, you know ... Or would that be difficult?'

'Nothing could be easier, love, I can assure you of that. But wouldn't you hate it?'

'Not hate it, just not mind it. And I'll like it being nice for you. If it would be.'

'It would be.'

After that, of course, she was more relaxed than ever before, until it started being relevant again. Then, and later, and as earlier, he found his touch confined to the totally neutral areas of her, and these were not many. The arm up to the elbow, the furry forearm, he possessed undisputed; the upper arm began to be sensitive territory, and the shoulder brought a tiny but perceptible stiffening from head to foot, because shoulder was near breast, and everybody knew what came after breast. The small of the back was all right, but as a hand moved from there to the angle of the waist it came closer to everything. Face was good, neck good, throat less good, base of throat bad. Ronnie came to dread their twice-daily sessions, but only a bit, not nearly as much as Simon did. Anyway, having no visible alternative, he went on with them. Towards the end of the week she began to improve slightly, both before and during, or so he fancied. She was best, obviously, when she got interested in what they were talking about, when, in other words, she could momentarily forget the hideous fact that she was lying naked with a naked man who was all too ready, demonstrably able and therefore by definition unreservedly willing to copulate with her. Handicapped by almost total ignorance of what made women frigid, he tried some amateur psycho-analysis, asking her for instance to recall her first man and just what it was that was horrible about him.

'It wasn't him that was horrible, it was it. What he did, or maybe how he did it. When he got going. I still thought it was going to be lovely up until I suppose he really got excited, until he realized that nothing could stop him starting to do it any minute. I hadn't told him I was a virgin and that didn't come into it: he didn't hurt me. He just ... the way he used his hand on me, in such a hurry all the time, as if he was putting out a fire, or dealing with a dangerous animal. And then when he got into me, so sort of urgent, I don't mean too fast, not that at all, I think he was probably quite good and wanted to give me a nice time. It was like he and I were in some sort of terrible emergency together, trying to escape from a flood or something, almost ... like riding a horse to get out of danger, and the harder he went at me the faster we'd go. And then at the end he had to go all out for a bit or something would have got us, and then we were past, we were safe, he'd got us through. Only I'd never wanted to come along in the first place.'

Ronnie said with carefully idle curiosity, 'Did your mother ever, you know, tell you about sex, explain to you?'

'We've never discussed it.'

'Oh,' he said, still very idly, 'I'd have thought it must keep coming up, you say she's very good about it, and things like the arrangements here, surely you and she ... '

'No, it's all taken as read. We don't discuss it.'

'Ng. What did your father say about it? Oh, of course,

he died when you were a child, didn't he? Your first stepfather, then.'

'Stavros. Well ... he never had much to do with me. He sort of left me to Mummy, really. We never talked about anything. So ... '

'Yes, so you've never had a man round the place much. Just boy-friends and lovers and people from outside.'

She moved slightly, apparently just for comfort, but one result was that her thighs were now farther away from his. 'I see. You mean I'd never had a chance to find out what men were like at all until I went to bed with one. And so it was all too much of a shock. There may be something in that. But can there be? Aren't you supposed to feel better right away when you know what's been making you feel bad? Isn't that what these psycho-whatnot fellows say?'

'I expect you've been to lots of them.'

'Oh no. Mummy doesn't believe in them.'

Whatever there might have been in the shock idea, Simon did not seem to feel better after being introduced to it, either right away or later. The whole thing was and continued much the same. On the afternoon of his last day, Ronnie found himself seized by the desperation that is the forerunner of despair. There seemed no thoughts in his mind when he started treating naked Simon as a naked woman, plying her with hands and mouth and body in motions no more voluntary than those of a man carried downstream by a torrent. At the last moment, as he settled himself above her, she made a movement or a sound, probably both, that activated some part of his brain. It was gone instantly without leaving the faintest recollection of itself, but he could recollect what it had reminded him of: somebody preparing to receive a physical punishment or catch a formidably heavy object. As unthinkingly as before, he stopped.

'Come on, Ronnie. What is it? I'm ready.'

'I couldn't. You'd hate it.'

'I don't mind hating it. I want you to have it.'

'I'd hate it too. Anyway, I couldn't now.'

He spoke the truth. By this time he was lying beside her and holding her in his arms. She started to cry violently.

'It makes no difference whatever we do. Nobody's ever been so nice to me and it doesn't make any difference. It'll never be right.'

He agreed with her, but said, 'One day it'll be right,' there being no other line by which to play out the next twenty hours or so.

'I'm so horrible and silly and childish and awful and selfish and babyish and scared of everything. And you're going.'

'Only to London. Not away for good.'

'If only I could come with you.'

At this point Ronnie could not prevent himself from feeling rather sorry for Simon. Feeling sorry for people was something he was far from used to, which was perhaps why he forgot himself sufficiently to say, 'Why don't you? It would be marvellous if you did.'

'I can't.'

'Why not? You haven't got to be here.'

She shrank away from him, and when she spoke her voice had gone dead. 'Not coming.'

'Why not? Remember you agreed to tell the truth.'

'Only about sex and things.'

Ronnie started to say that in his view they had not left that topic, but this time checked himself. 'No, Simon, everything. You must see that, surely.'

'All right, then. Mummy wouldn't like it.'

'I see. What would she do if you just said you were going?'

'Well, she wouldn't prevent me, of course. But she'd be terribly upset. She wants me here with her, to help her and things.'

'I haven't seen you doing much helping. And so she's terribly upset, but you just tell her kindly that you're going and go. What can she do?'

'Ronnie, you're completely off. You don't understand a damn thing. When Mummy gets upset it's just ... awful. She's so sensitive and she's had two husbands die and she's so brave.' There was a fresh onset of crying. 'You don't know what it's like when she really gets upset. It's not fair, she's had so much to put up with about me and everything. She gets so terribly worked up. I can't stand people getting worked up.'

'Of course not,' said Ronnie pacifically. 'Simon, quite off the track, but did your mother and what's his name, bloody shagbag, old Stavros, did they get on fairly okay?'

'Not too bad, I suppose.'

'No great dust-ups, rows, any of that?'

'Well yes, they did, actually. Stavros wanted his own way in absolutely everything. Including about me. The only time he took any interest in me was when he was trying to send me away to school or something. Mummy used to stand up to him on behalf of me and he'd be furious at being crossed, and then she'd get upset, and so it went on.'

'Were you sent away to school?'

'No. Mummy stopped him doing that. What about it?'

'Just off the track.' He held her in his arms a little longer and then said, as coldly as he could, 'Don't you think your trouble is simply that you're scared stiff of your mother?'

'Balls, ballocks, shit.' No more tears now. She wriggled out of his embrace and settled in a sort of uncommitted position, by him but not with him. 'You're so completely off you'll never know it. Mr Van Pup and Mr Vassilikós and everybody keeps saying we're just like sisters. *You ... wouldn't ... know*. All my girl-friends keep saying they wish they got on with their mothers like I do with Mummy. We can talk about anything. You just wouldn't know.'

She had observed the treaty of Poustos by answering his question truthfully, though not in words. He said for some time that he had no idea what had possessed him to go so far off the track, put in a lot of serious, wrung-from-him, lying stuff about his deprived childhood in the Midlands (his parents were flying to Naples the following week to celebrate their emerald wedding), and by the time they had showered and were dressing had coaxed her beyond grunts and monosyllables. She got into a black organza thing that Mummy had not economized on. In it, what with outlandish physique and colouring, haircut that might have been accomplished by half a dozen mighty but ill-aimed snips from a pair of garden shears, and no make-up, she looked like a female warrior from some remote North African tribe who has suffered forty-eight hours. inexpert Westernization. And beautiful, Ronnie thought.

Much more beautiful, without doubt, than youngish fat lone Mansfield, who was silently accepting a drink from the butler just as they came out on to the western terrace. Only the balustrade here was marble, but along it were urns made of some other and no doubt pricier stone with glassy bits in it. The view was steep wooded hillside and sea, above which a sunset had entered the tuning-up stage. Mansfield's clothes passed as evening clothes only by virtue of the odd allusion in rough shape or texture: a tie that, although diagonally striped and unnaturally thin, was tied in a kind of bow, a strip of cloth that, for all its warts and hanging bunches of thread and scalloped edges, occupied the position of a cummerbund. He was sweating a lot.

'Hi,' he said in his really tremendously loud voice, which he knew he had and would assert unequivocally he could do nothing about. Then he became quiet, almost as if politely allowing the other two the opportunity to order drinks. Not until they had done so, at any rate, did he go on to inquire of Ronnie, 'Off in the morning, huh?'

'The boat leaves about midday, I believe.'

'Hell, what do you want to go back for tomorrow anyway? London you go to, isn't it? So what's in London right now you have to catch? Just name me one thing.'

'Well, one thing is my job.'

'Oh: yeah. Yeah,' said Mansfield with a good deal of force, though he contrived at the same time to leave it open whether he did or did not appreciate the point that one does have to return to a job at certain times, that this is indeed part of the very nature of a job. He seemed to be thinking this over for a space, while his great head nodded up and down and his bulging eyes bulged on. At last, speaking roughly as well as loudly and so implying that he for one had had enough abstruse theorizing for a bit, he swung towards Ronnie and demanded, 'Well, what have you got to say about that view? Isn't it just great? All that ocean ... and the ... all the ... that ... '

Mansfield had made a gesture or two in an unpolished style and come to the end of what his party had to say about the view. The butler's return allowed the topic to lapse. With a certain show of efficiency he handed Simon a very weak Scotch and water. This move Mansfield watched approvingly on the whole, but broodingly too, reserving the right to withdraw approval without notice. Ronnie took a politic ouzo and watched Mansfield, about whom there was this evening something disagreeably extra, as if his voice had managed to grow louder. Perhaps a lot more money had come his way from one of his aunties.

'Well now,' he said, concentrating his attention on Simon, 'here's a sight to gladden the eye, I do declare. Good enough to eat. Mmm-*hukh!*' He lunged forward with his head and took a bite out of the air. Then, quite quickly, his manner became confidential, almost affectionate. He kept his eyes on Simon, laid a worryingly small hand on Ronnie's shoulder, and said in a thunderous mutter, 'You know what they say down South about the fried chicken when they want to tell you it's out of this world? You know what they say? They say it's *finger-lickin'* good! Isn't that just great? *Finger-lickin'* good! That's our little Simon! She's *finger-lickin'* good!'

By now Ronnie had moved between Mansfield and Simon, so that parts of him should hide parts of Mansfield from her. It seemed the least he could do. And he achieved more, for partly out of sight was out of partial mind to Mansfield, whose convex eye now swivelled on to the glass of ouzo Ronnie was holding.

'What's that stuff you're drinking there?'

'Ouzo. You must have come across it.'

'Come *across* it? Come across it, hell. You know what that is? Dregs. What's left when they've made their ... brandy or whatever they ... Dregs. Right! That's what they need around these parts. *They're* dregs. You hear? Greeks? They're Turks and Armenians and Bulgarians and Arabs and ... Greeks. What's so great about Greeks?'

Ronnie was genuinely sorry to see the Van Pups, closely followed by the Saxtons, filing on to the terrace, veering aside towards Simon, coming up to him and Mansfield. The man's sheer virtuosity had been beyond praise: the breadth of scope in a small compass, the violent transitions with a rightness that was only to be appreciated in retrospect, the inbuilt critical faculty ensuring that not a word was wasted, above all the *actual* effortlessness, far beyond anything attainable by any mere artist, whose uttermost toil and skill could only counterfeit that quality. And all this achieved for a mere fraction of a billion dollars.

When, very soon, the Upshots and the Baldocks and Bish arrived, Ronnie went over to Simon, who was looking at the sunset, now blazing away for all it was worth.

'Sorry about that unbelievable man. He was sober, too. That's the frightening thing.'

'Oh, that was just him trying to be sociable.'

'Christ and all his angels stand between me and him trying to be unsociable, this day and evermore. Why's he here?'

'He's just a friend. His father was a great friend of Mummy's years ago. I think he wanted to marry her, but she'd always been going to marry Daddy.'

'How did she feel about him, Mansfield senior?'

'Don't know.'

Here was a good case, though a bad situation, for invoking the treaty of Poustos, but either way there was no chance: Saxton came over to them, walking in a straight line but with the gait of one balancing an unusually springy plank on one shoulder. In the opposite hand he held an empty glass.

'Evening, my dear, looking very splendid, and, uhm,'—this bit was to Ronnie—'good evening. Seen that damned fellow anywhere, either of you? Of course, you know, he's boozing in his pantry half the time. Just goes off at his own sweet will. No—got him. Uhm, would you, uhm ... '

But the butler paid him no attention, and this for the sufficient reason that Mansfield was talking at the time; as well might a goat have tried to bleat down a roaring lion.

Saxton went on trying, stepping up both pitch and volume, and it was a splendid *uuhhmmhh* that soared through the comparative quiet when Mansfield abruptly fell silent.

'Loud-mouthed customer, that,' said Saxton when the butler had come and gone. 'Young fellow my lad, I mean. Typical. Well, in a way. He was in the army for a time, you know. American army, that is. Father was a general. Needn't have been, but he was. So young, uh, young, uhm, young *Mansfield*, yes, young Mansfield was going to be a soldier too. Went to that damned place, what the devil is it called? West something? Never mind. Expect you know where I mean. Anyway, wasn't long after he was commissioned that things took a wrong turning. Pity. Expect you heard about that unfortunate business in West Germany. Years ago now, of course. Managed to put the whole thing behind him. Rather admire him for that. Blasted sight more than I could have put behind me, I tell you frankly. Eh? Eh?'

In the temporary absence of Lady Saxton, Ronnie stepped into the agreeing spot with all his interviewer's smoothness. His (by now) burning interest in Mansfield's history, in those two unfortunate businesses that the bastard deserved so much credit for putting behind him—a good preliminary location, thought Ronnie, for a lot of things to be associated with the bastard—had to remain unsatisfied for the time being. The Upshots closed in. Bish and, belatedly, Lady Saxton closed in. The Baldocks closed in. Ronnie wished that they had not done that, or at any rate that Lord Baldock had not. Screwing up his eyes in advance, the peer turned his habitually half-bowed head first towards Simon, who at this stage was looking very down in the mouth, then towards Ronnie. There had been no proper chats since the one in the shelter by the anchorage, and it was no secret that Ronnie was off the next day, but for a moment, meeting that screwed-up gaze, he wondered whether he might not find himself required all of a sudden to spend the night on the beach. The moment passed; the gaze switched to one Upshot or another; Lady Baldock smiled at Ronnie and said that they would be sorry to lose him.

She said this again a few minutes later as they sat at dinner and tried to eat *dolmades*: grated chalk and blotting-paper wrapped up in wrapping-paper. Ronnie had been placed on her left, an honour less signal than it might have seemed, there being, for some undisclosed but no doubt cash-oriented reason, no guests tonight. Ronnie responded. In a little while, set on by a question or two about what *Insight* was going to be up to, he was doing his stuff, or one of his stuffs, about today's youth. The final effect of it was to lower very slightly your opinion of all the groups and institutions concerned – delinquent youth, non-delinquent youth, parents, schools, the law, probation officers, youth leaders, youth clubs, the political parties, the mass media and all that – and raise slightly more than very slightly your opinion of Ronnie Appleyard, for knowing, for going on taking the trouble to find out, above all for *caring*. Lady Baldock, in a high-necked scarlet thing with Hellenic or even priestessy associations, took it all pretty well, but without seeming to see that the point of it was what you ended up thinking about Ronnie. Lord Upshot, sitting opposite, missed it too, and instead listened with total concentration to Ronnie's eye-witness account of that strange territory from which, one day, marauders with designs on his household, his fortune, his life must surely emerge.

They got through the baked fish, shark-reject equipped with a preponderance of bone over flesh that must have made it an ichthyologist's byword, and garnished with lemon rind and tomato skins. With it came strips of fried egg-plant tasting of strong Indian tea, local so-called spinach which Ronnie could have sworn he had seen doing its level best to grow out of the garden wall, and half a dozen chipped potatoes each. (Lady Baldock did not eat potatoes.) This was washed down, a needful process, by a retsina whose parent cricket-bat had been oiled with unusual thoroughness and persistence. Finally, there was a sort of pastry, interspersed with quite a few nuts and a certain amount of honey, that somebody had taken the trouble to squash energetically. Somebody else, somebody with a malign, twisted view of things, had made the Turkish coffee, and bloody good it was. Ronnie refused the brandy, which had more stars than an American general. This perception put him in mind of Mansfield, silent for the moment at the far corner of the table. There was room for thought in that quarter, and not only about the bastard's two unfortunate businesses.

First warning her husband not to be too long, Lady Baldock led the women from the room. The men rearranged themselves round their host. When they had done this, he looked at Ronnie for a time and said,

'Getting the boat tomorrow, aren't you?'

'Yes.'

That was as much as there was of that. Nobody said anything of even anthropological interest to Ronnie until some time after the party had re-formed in the long, narrow, sort of gallery-type room lying adjacent to the terrace where they had been drinking earlier. One thing that made it easy to think of a gallery in connection with this room was the pictures along its inner wall. All of them, in their not widely differing ways, offered versions of local sights in such terms as to make those sights appear ridiculous, unpleasant or trivial: a row of columns like chopped-off bits of bowel, dancing peasants with blue faces and dropsical hands and feet, a village scene only just identifiable behind a drizzle of scarlet and grey-yellow. Ronnie had no trouble in deducing that they were the work of promising indigenous artists.

At the far end of all this, and across a stretch of the usual hairy rugs, were two padded wicker sofas at right angles. Here sat Simon, Bish, Lady Saxton and, raising her hand to Ronnie even as he caught sight of her, Lady Baldock. By the time he had picked his way thither, he found that Bish and Lady Saxton had removed themselves elsewhere. He also found that Mansfield and Sir—Cecil it had turned out to be—Saxton had come with him. He ended up somewhere in the middle, with Lady Baldock next to him on one side and Simon half-facing him on the other, Saxton and then, at the end, Mansfield being placed farther off. Nobody except Saxton seemed to think that Saxton ought to be anywhere near where he was.

What was going to happen soon started to happen. Lady Baldock circulated a smile and said, 'Ronnie was giving us a most fascinating account of youth problems and what's being done about them. It's a subject we should really all be thinking about most seriously. I had absolutely no idea that things have reached the stage they have. Do you realize that thirty-two per cent, that's very nearly a third, of young people under twenty-five are going to get into some sort of trouble with the authorities? Did you know that, Student?'

This last word had turned out to be Mansfield's Christian name, or to do duty for one. Ronnie had given it some reflection. As a nickname it could hardly have been appropriate at any stage of Mansfield's career, unless on the *lucus a non lucendo* principle that had got bony Upshot called Tubby. But this was British, and Mansfield was not. The same applied to another possibility, whereby you had made a roughly reproducible mess of saying your name as a child and 'somehow it had stuck'—hence many a rich/upper-class Oggie and Ayya and Brumber and Ploof and Jawp of Ronnie's acquaintance. Most likely it was simply the bastard's name. There was nothing under the sun that an American could not be called.

Student Mansfield, anyway, bawled consideringly, 'This is England we're talking about?'

'Yes, but you'd find the same situation in all the developed countries. The United States would certainly be worse.'

The moment his question was answered Mansfield lost interest. Saxton maintained an expression of calculating disquiet, as if such a staggeringly low figure as that quoted must point to a conspiracy of tolerance among the authorities. Simon smiled and blinked at Ronnie.

'But tell me,' went on Lady Baldock, making it clear that she was about to do some telling rather than being told, 'what is it about all these children that makes them rebel and revolt and just not want to behave? It's a refusal to take on the responsibilities of being an adult, isn't it? A refusal to grow up? I know all about that, you see, because that's what's wrong with my problem child here. Isn't that right, darling? You just hate the idea of growing up?'

With a nod that might have been no more than a nervous tremor, Simon dropped her head and began to fidget with a strand of the wicker seating.

'Permanent adolescence, isn't that what they call it? Emotional immaturity? She's always been backward, I'm afraid. Oh, not mentally backward. Don't you agree, Ronnie?'

'About delinquents or about Simon?'

'Well, both.'

'As regards delinquents, I think most of the social psychologists and straight psychologists I've talked to would be roughly with you there, Juliette, yes. Of course, the relaxation of parental discipline –'

'What about Mona?'

'Well ... I suppose there is something in it.' He saw the faint movement of some small muscle or nerve in the girl's cheek.

'*Something* in it? It's her whole sickness. And what she needs – you've just said it: discipline. Somebody who will run her whole life and see that she does exactly as she's told. The trouble with Chummy ... '

That trouble remained undisclosed, at least for the moment. Saxton got up rather quickly and neatly from where he had been sitting and walked away down the room. After a very small pause Lady Baldock turned to Mansfield.

'Don't you agree, Student? About Mona needing to be disciplined?'

'Sure, Juliette. Oh, uh ... sure.'

'I'm afraid I don't,' said Ronnie. Whatever he might be going to tell himself later about lightning appraisals of the situation, at the moment he spoke entirely on impulse.

The change in Lady Baldock was immediate. She sat up straight, her demeanour lost its former fluidity, and the tilt of her chin brought home to Ronnie the full sense of the phrase that features looking down one's nose, supposing him to have understood it only sketchily before. Nor was her voice unaltered. 'What do you mean? Do you think I don't understand my own child?'

'Of course not,' said Ronnie, turning the mildness full up and keeping it there. 'Nobody who knew the two of you even slightly could possibly think anything so absurd.

But I differ from you about the best way of coping with Simon's situation. I think what she—'

'Well, what does she need, then? According to *you*.'

'I would say she needs continuing kindness and sympathy and affection and—'

'You mean we all, Chummy and I and Student and all our good friends here, we all treat Mona brutally the whole time, locking her up with bread and water and beating her?'

It had been easy enough to foresee that one, but Ronnie only got as far as, 'Certainly not: that was why I said *continuing* sym—' before being ridden over.

'And it just shows how little you *know*. Kindness, indeed. Affection. She's had nothing else for twenty-six years and look where it's got her. And everybody else who's ever had anything to do with her. Student. Help me out here, please. Isn't it true that Mona has always had every last thing she ever wanted? Everything she ever asked for?'

'Completely, Juliette, completely,' said Mansfield in tones an evangelist might well have envied. 'Mona always had every goddam thing she wanted.'

'I'm absolutely sure of that,' said Ronnie, 'and I know it's very rare. But wouldn't you perhaps agree that one of the things we're dealing with is somebody who doesn't know what she wants? Knowing what you want is a very—'

'What do you *mean*?' Juliette Baldock was beginning to use oral italics in a way Ronnie had thought confined to the royal persons he had met or to those of Vassilikós's capital-group. 'You can't *deal* with people who don't know what they want. I don't understand what you *mean*, anyway.'

Ronnie was aware that Lord Baldock had moved into earshot somewhere in Mansfield's quarter and was going on standing, or swaying to and fro, thereabouts, but he knew he had to concentrate all his attention on the immediate issue. What this was by now was less clear to him.

'Part of what I mean, no, part of what I want to say, is that I'm not happy about the way we're all sitting here chatting about Simon as if she were a piece of furniture or something. Can't we go into all this another time?'

'So you think it's bad,' said Lady Baldock, dabbing her forehead with a handkerchief, 'that I don't choose to discuss my daughter behind her back?'

This was actually a not unfair approximation of what Ronnie did think, but all he said, fully as mildly as before, was, 'No no. I simply feel that it's a, well, a bit of an ordeal for her, listening to herself being—'

'Let's hear what the child herself has to say. Mona. Mona, look at me.'

Except to tease at the wickerwork, Simon had hardly moved during the discussion of her shortcomings. Now she glanced up, suddenly but after an interval, as if her mother's words had taken seconds to reach her. 'Yes? Yes, Mummy?'

'Do you object to our talking about you?'

'No, Mummy.' She looked down again.

'*There.*'

Lady Baldock's air of triumph, like the demonstration she seemed to think she had conducted, could surely not have been expected to come off, thought Ronnie, even on the stage (except possibly a gaslit one). But come off they did: the bloody little upstart, abuser of hospitality, goddam Britisher—you could take your pick of those and others—had been decisively demolished. Unconditional withdrawal was his only recourse now. He started to speak with really mucilaginous mildness, and at the same moment the top half of Lord Baldock's body snapped forward, to all appearance because somebody had shot him in the back with an arrow, but actually because he wanted to hear what Ronnie was saying.

'Well, in that case I've evidently made a—'

'In that case I suggest you apologize. I refuse to tolerate being told how to conduct myself towards my own child. For all I know, that sort of behaviour may be perfectly acceptable wherever you come from, but it won't do in any household of mine. I bring you here and feed you and take you about in return for your services as Mona's ... companion is, I suppose, the politest word, and you repay me by telling me my duty in public. And I won't have it.'

The italics had gone, but the tone had fully matched the words. Ronnie reflected that somebody who could be so angry and so coherent at the same time had a great future in any fact-finding, objective TV team, then very quickly addressed himself to his task.

'I really am most terribly—' he said.

'It seems I must have made an error of judgment. I should have realized that somebody of your background just wouldn't fit in here. I've seen your type before, Mr Appleyard. Many, many times. You thought you had me fooled with all your seriousness and all your innocence and the way you—'

'Hell, Juliette, the guy only—'

'Be quiet, Student. I should have been guided by what Chummy said. He told me I'd just be—'

'Oh come, darling, you know perfectly well that whenever I try to—'

'Shut up, Chummy. No, Mr Appleyard, you'll need a little less television technique and a little more common decency the next time you come pushing and shoving your way into civilized society.'

Ronnie was still doing his best to reflect, trying to feel

judicial about the limitations of the rule which says that the man who keeps his temper in an argument will always appear to defeat an enraged opponent. That only applied where there were rules about the sayable and the unsayable, and it was plain that any such Geneva conventions had long been repudiated. While he was grimly getting ready to be humble as never in his life before, Lady Baldock's attention passed from him as suddenly as a searchlight beam sweeps from one object of interest to another. She said to her daughter,

'I ask myself why he bothered. Have you any idea? Why he took such a chance on your behalf? Oh, we know what he's after, so why did he go against me? For someone like you.'

'Please don't get upset, Mummy,' said Simon in a drugged voice.

'I'm not upset. You know I'm not. I just want to know why you didn't tell him. I had to drag it out of you that he was wrong. You went on sitting there like a zombie. I wonder if you care about anybody. You have no feelings. And I know where you get that from.'

At this, Baldock and Simon made simultaneous and identical gestures of the hand, jerking it upwards from the wrist so unself-consciously that an outsider might have supposed them brother and sister, joint inheritors of a parental mannerism. It was a warding-off movement in miniature, very much called for by the nature of the momentary silence that had fallen. Ronnie recognized it as the kind that comes just before the perpetration (or, far more rarely, a decision against the perpetration) of the old, old piece of outrageousness, the tattered hobby-horse known in every lineament to family and close friends, the attack on the Jews or homosexuals or the Queen or the vicar or your brother's upper-classness or your sister's lower-classness or your drinking or your cooking. Good luck to the lady, Ronnie said to himself: even she could hardly blame him for Simon's ancestry.

'Not from me,' said Lady Baldock, getting a good deal of inexorability in, and again Baldock and Simon reacted together, though this time less definably. 'It's funny, it's very curious'—tone and manner now had become contemplative, detached, cinematically philosophical—'how we live our whole lives among people. Even when we're alone—and how often are we really alone?—even then we're still doing things for people and because of people, things that are going to affect a whole lot of different people. And yet ... some of us just don't ever seem to notice people, don't care about them, not only that but would sooner they weren't there, with all their feelings and demands and regrets and dreams.' Here there was a pause for effect which achieved its effect. 'I used to know a man like that.'

There is a sincerity about the rich shared by few other groups, an indifference to the claims of occasion or company or relevance or—in every sense of the term—style, an unforced and total willingness to say exactly what is in the mind at any moment that should commend itself alike to psychologists and to aestheticians interested in the relation between form and content. Part of this occurred to Ronnie straight away and part of it later. As things were then, what he mostly noticed was the set, or lack of set, of Simon's shoulders in the black organza dress.

'Well, that's something I can't throw any light on,' he said at once and with an effect of vivacity. 'But I'm quite sure that Simon is a totally different sort of person. Not in the least like your description.'

Mrs Van Pup's laugh—the first noticeable sound from down the room for as long as could be remembered—

made its noise. Mansfield leant forward with an unfocused intentness. Lord Baldock peered at them all as through a pall of smoke. Simon stayed as she was. Lady Baldock responded even more directly than Ronnie could have foretold.

Standing up, and looking impressive as well as unpleasant in her high-necked scarlet thing, she said, 'Are you telling me you know my daughter better than I do myself?'

'Not in general, no, of course not. But on this one point perhaps I do. She cares about people and she has feelings. There's no doubt of that whatever.'

'Mr Appleyard, you're leaving tomorrow, so we need say very little more to each other. That's fine with me. And don't let's spend the rest of the evening together, shall we? I don't want to see you either, Mona.'

Ten minutes later, Simon was lying naked, but turned away, on the pink bed. She had said nothing at all in the interim. It was just before ten o'clock, and on this late-summer evening the air was pleasantly cool. Ronnie was not doing much thinking: there would be more than enough time for that on the boat tomorrow and then on the aeroplane. He glanced incuriously out of the window and saw moon, rock, vegetation, sea, all given a rather pretentious *pointilliste* quality by the wire mesh of the screen. Oh well, there it was. He finished undressing, cleaned his teeth, and got into bed. Simon turned into his arms.

'Sorry I upset your mother.'

'She wasn't upset, just cross. Don't talk.'

Trembling, but not tense. And not trembling in the old way. She kissed him briefly and sighed. He heard her swallow. Then she pulled his right arm from behind her shoulder, took hold of his hand and held it against her left breast. As she did this she trembled more than before, but still not in the old way, and she was still not tense. Even if he had wanted to, Ronnie could not have so much as hesitated. It was very fast and extraordinary until the end part, which was very slow and extraordinary. Then Ronnie found he was sweating like a very fat man in a Turkish bath and breathing like almost any sort of man who has just been chased for a mile or so uphill by a bull in the pink of condition. In the three-quarters of an hour or so that it took his body to return to normal, he wondered at these phenomena. He remembered now that he had gone a long way out of his way to keep it short and as non-vehement as he could manage, for Simon's sake, the equivalent, say, of a couple of hundred yards' gentle trot along the flat on an English spring morning. Then why ... ? Perhaps he was getting old. No, if anything he had felt as if he were getting young. Like the old days, the days of Miss Jerningham and her coevals.

'How was it?' he asked when he was able to. He was about to go on to invoke the treaty of Poustos, but stopped himself at the last moment.

'Oh, Ronnie, it was lovely. For it to be nice for you, I mean.'

'But what was it like for you?'

'It was absolutely the first time it's ever not been horrible.'

'But it wasn't nice at all?'

'Not really, no. But I don't mind that a bit and you're not to either. It was so absolutely non-horrible that it was very very nearly tremendously nice. And just think, Ronnie. It being completely non-horrible must mean it could start to get nice one day, isn't that right?'

'Of course, it's bound to. It'll be better and better every time from now on. You'll see.'

'Oh, Ronnie, I ... I want to ask you something while I remember. Why did you say to Mummy I didn't know what I wanted?'

'Yes, that's been bothering me too. I don't really know why I said it, except that it seemed so much the thing to say at that point. That's the trouble with corny things, isn't it? Because you mean you do know what you want?'

'You bet I do. I always have. A nice man all to myself. What could be simpler than that? To want, I mean. Getting one's another matter.'

'Well, you've been going about it in such a bloody silly way, haven't you?'

'I know, I must have known all the time, but it was the only way I could think of. I was so afraid of people noticing I thought the whole thing was horrible that I kept making this big point of how keen on it I was. Like if you were marketing a car that was really tremendously unsafe you'd go on and on about how frightfully safe it was. Well, you might.'

'Yes, you might. I'm going to have a cigarette.'

'Go ahead. And it worked, you know, in a way, that was the funny thing.'

'Eh? What worked?'

'Well, I mean nobody did notice. That I thought it was horrible, I mean. Until you came along. Ronnie, don't you think it's a pity in a way that there has to be sex? You know, between two people?'

'No. Anyway, how do you mean?'

'It would be so much easier all around if you could just get your sex done on your own and then have a lovely time talking to people and being affectionate with them? Like eating? That's not a thing you have to do *to* someone.'

Ronnie put his cigarette down. 'Listen. Darling.'

'Oh, darling. Yes?'

'That's all balls. Isn't it?'

'Yes, I suppose it is.'

'Because you've got a man all to yourself. Me. A nice one, I hope.'

'Oh yes, a marvellous one. It's not going to be easy, though.'

'No, I know.'

'There's Mummy, you see.'

'I know.'

Three

FORT CHARLES

Ronnie Appleyard stood next to his pair of Asprey suitcases outside the Arrivals doorway of Fort Charles International Skyport and looked round for the small red-haired butler. No sign of him at the moment. It was five o'clock in the evening, a bit early for the man to have started drinking, or even for the damned fellow to have been delayed by a request of Sir Cecil Saxton's to, uhm, just, uhm, would he, uhm. Not that Sir Cecil, or any of the other old lags from the Malakos party, were much to be expected on this one not six weeks later, unless indeed they accompanied Lady Baldock about on her travels almost without rest to ensure the maintenance at all times of a band of rich people within call. There was no sign hereabouts of Simon, either. That was at the same time entirely to be expected and faintly ominous.

Near by, ten or a dozen white persons were settling themselves in something that called itself a limousine, an elongated car that cleverly avoided any suggestion of the possibly degrading omnibus principle. Cabs painted like children's models filled up and drove away. Quite a few pairs of oldsters, arrived here (like himself, in a sense) for Thanksgiving, hobbled towards the parking lot accompanied by their luckless descendants. They were pursued by monstrously burdened Negro porters, three of whom, as they passed Ronnie, turned in unison and looked at him. They seemed, while in no doubt about his not being black, unsure of what other colour he might be. Green, perhaps. The transatlantic hop had featured nothing more emetic than the reaction of the stewardess on learning that he was, as she had guessed, Ronnie Appleyard: she had asked him whether he knew Bill Hamer. But, crossing the Smokies a little while back, there had been a nasty bump or two, bad enough to justify the captain in frightening most of the passengers still further by an announcement that everything was perfectly normal.

Ronnie was almost getting inured to being asked if he knew Bill Hamer, almost stopping minding the way the bastard had, for an indefinite period, become part of his life. Not quite, though. He had to repress a groan of weariness at seeing Hamer himself, accompanied by a porter, emerge confidently from the swing door and look about, catch sight of Ronnie, give a smile of transparent friendliness and come marching over. Nodding, waving, smiling back, Ronnie chewed over the carrion memory of having made the stewardess's day by announcing that he was meeting Hamer at Kennedy and flying south with him, and of having then unmade it again when it was established that timings would not permit of her catching even a glimpse of him.

'Okay?' asked Ronnie.

'Just. They were trying to send it on to Nashville.'

'Where's that?'

'What, Nashville? Christ, I don't know. Florida or Missouri or one of those places.'

'Nashville, that's in Tennessee, sir,' said the porter.

'No doubt it is, my good fellow,' said Hamer, under-tipping him with fairly rich man's panache, 'no doubt it is. And now what about this transport?'

'I get you a cab, sir?'

'No, no, that's all. At least I hope it is. Ronnie, you did *say* ... '

'He'll be here.'

In five minutes he was, accompanied by a Negro chauffeur wearing lilac-grey gloves. The butler himself had on a tartan jacket of curious timidity, such that its lines and checks disappeared into a dark-blue fuzz to an observer not almost on the point of assaulting or embracing him. He spoiled Ronnie's intended demonstration of what old friends they were by effusively greeting Hamer and telling him how much he enjoyed his show when he got the chance of seeing it. Ronnie considered the omens were not good. Not far from here, he had heard somehow, the South had suffered one of their bloodiest defeats of the entire Civil War, and he felt himself booked to follow in their footsteps.

Ronnie and Hamer occupied the back seat of the black Jaguar 420 G, as once in a humble Humber Hawk on the evening of the Reichenbergers' party. That had been a bare three months ago, and the interval did not seem to Ronnie much different, but what that party did seem to him was a hell of a long way *away*. He had calculated that since meeting Miss Quick he had travelled (or would have, by the time he got back to London) well over ten thousand miles in pursuit of her, the equivalent of spending the whole period of their relationship, twenty-four hours a day, on the move at a very brisk walk. Now and again it felt rather like that. It was now, or again, now. Quitting *Insight* for two sessions at short notice had meant, not only bearing down rather brutally on corduroy-jacketed, bearded Eric, but a lot of genuine work for both head and leg. The recurring question of just what he would find at the end of his journey had been taxing in a different way.

He wondered how long he would have to wait before he got the chance of finding this out. On leaving the airport the car had climbed on to a splendid road that was now bearing it and innumerable other vehicles at full speed towards the Gulf of Mexico. At the moment there seemed little likelihood of any logical stopping-point before arrival there. No kind of building was to be seen, only grassland, advertisement hoardings, a few trees and, here and there in the distance, vast white-metal bulbous structures upheld by stilts and of vaguely interplanetary aspect.

'Vast bloody country,' said Hamer. 'Look, how soon can I get away from this place?'

'I don't know. I'm off on Sunday morning.'

'I really ought to be back in New York first thing on Saturday to set up this Margot and Rudy thing.'

'I thought you did that yesterday.'

'Only some of it. You're not dealing with the B.B.C. or Rediffusion or swinging old L.C.M. here, you know. Great American television, still trying to catch up with where we were ten years ago, wondering what to do about the reaction-shot principle and the rest of it. Ever done much with them, Ron?'

'Not a lot, no.'

'Lucky man. Anyway, it was just as well I was able to fit

in a spot of telly like this, or it wouldn't have been on for me to make the trip down here.'

'Yes, so you said. When will you use it?'

'Depends a bit on how it goes. What do you think?'

'What about?'

'Well, I can't really say I know them, not so as to have much idea of how they'd react to my kind of approach. I was wondering whether perhaps you ... '

'I've never met either of them.'

'Ah. How much more of this bloody transcontinental trip, do you think?'

'We'll be coming into the town in just a minute, sir,' said the butler, turning so far round in his seat that he seemed to have put his knees up on it, like a child. 'Then it's just a couple of miles on the other side of the centre. I'd like to ask you, Mr Hamer, if you'll forgive the intrusion, what are the main technical problems confronting one responsible for presiding over a television programme such as yours.'

Hamer narrowed his eyes keenly. 'Do you mean in preparing the show or after it's on the air?'

Ronnie stopped listening. For the last few seconds he had been looking forward to hearing Hamer deliver one of his mellifluous but definite recommendations of instant withdrawal from the conversation. Then he realized that the bastard would be taking the obvious chance of buttering up the man who was going to have so much power over his drinking destiny for the next seventy-two hours or so. After that, he asked himself why Hamer should have gone out of his way to put him, Ronnie, 2–0 down in their exchange just now. Not to impress the butler with the required view of the Hamer/Appleyard status picture; that was already in full existence. The chauffeur? Whatever Hamer's declared views about *apartheid* and all that, it was at best doubtful whether someone of that colour appeared to him as a card-carrying member of the human race. Habit? Or a desire to throw into relief the heights from which he was condescending by having kept his promise to come here.

Certainly anyone who came here was thereby stepping down from some sort of height. Quite suddenly a town had appeared, or rather they were moving along a six-lane road bordered by motor courts, gas stations, hamburger joints, funeral homes, health clubs, cocktail lounges, pancake parlours and other such places that everyone in England knew you were not supposed to have. Multi-coloured neon hectored and wheedled in such profusion as to weigh heavily against the notion that the oral word is driving out the visual. There was enough reading matter in a hundred yards of this stuff to keep you going for hours. It all looked so bad that Ronnie could have sworn he had seen it before as part of some unbiased documentary report on American civilization. Then, after they had passed a synagogue built in ranch-house style, the whole business disappeared again, and there was nothing but apartment blocks in grounds the size of small parks.

Hamer decided he had done enough for the moment towards seeing that his glass would be kept filled. He did not know how hard out-of-hours drinks were to come by at Lady Baldock's, how thorough and reliable the medical attestation of a heart attack would have to be in order to produce a small brandy at such times. Settling one or two points with the little shit beside him was in his mind now. He left unanswered a question from the butler about the future of television as an educative force, and muttered to Ronnie,

'Look—I suppose we could be getting there any minute now—what has this woman asked me along for?'

'I told you all I know about it. She wants you to set up your rich-bastards programme all over again and put it on with this Greek turd in it so that he'll know it was she who fixed it.'

'I still don't see why I have to come to this bloody backside of beyond for a five-minute chat we could perfectly well have had in the bar of the Ritz at home, or at her Eaton Square joint.'

'It's immaterial to her what it costs other people to do what she wants. And it won't cost you a bean, anyway, not in cash. Don't tell me you won't put the whole of your trip on expenses.'

'Wouldn't dream of trying to tell you that, Ron. But you're in the game.'

Ronnie laughed. 'You don't know people like her, Bill,' he said, driving the ambiguity home with vocal inflection and improving the score to 2–1. 'Ways of not spending your own money is her life-study.'

'Mm. And the whole kerfuffle is just to impress Vassy-what-not?'

'Get one up on him. Get herself invited to the three-star parties. You know.'

'Mm. I suspect there's more to it than that. Anyway, with her money and her houses in Europe and the rest of it, why does she spend any of her time in this frightful spiritual disaster area? From what I've seen of it, even so far, it's like a wet week-end in Watford. It can't just be that she comes from round about. As you probably know, I come from South Shields, and you couldn't have seen my arse for dust getting out of there as soon as I could buy a railway ticket.'

'Agreed. The thing is, she's horribly rich by your or my standards but she's not really uncontrollably rich, like Vassilikós, say. I gather – I rather *gather*,' said Ronnie, rubbing in his gathering abilities, 'that she's unloaded sums of money that would make your hair stand on end on the stock market. She's an intelligent woman but, well, headstrong.'

'What of it?'

'So this would be the sort of place where's she's queen. If she hasn't got the most money, which she may well have anyway, she's still got the most glamour. Europe. English lord for a husband. All that, you see, Bill.' 2-all.

'Could be, I suppose.'

Hamer seemed to fall into a muse. The dusk was gathering, relieved by private lamp-posts, coaching lanterns and other fanciful sources of light that stood or hung here and there about the houses they were now passing. These increased steadily in size and in distance from the roadway, until a governor's-mansion type of thing swung into view almost on the horizon. This was it all right. The car turned in and took them up through a wood of oaks and horse chestnuts, which had evidently had a great many leaves on them at one time. Hamer's bulk leaned over towards Ronnie.

'One last question, old lad,' he said in his mutter. 'What's in this for you?'

'What's in what?'

'You understand I have recently refused an invitation to visit your good friend Lady Baldock in the United States of America.' Hamer spoke in a prissy, quoting accent, as unlike Ronnie's as his own, but still offensive. 'Can you not persuade me to change my mind? Perhaps we could get together over a drink, and take the opportunity of also discussing the possibility of my appearing on the world-famous *Insight* programme. Now don't get me wrong, Ronnie,' he continued in his ordinary mutter. 'We all know of course you were going to ask me anyway. Just the timing is all I mean.' He now had the grace to lower his voice still further. 'The daughter, I take it?'

'Yes.'

'Serious?'

'Yes.'

'Marriage?'

'If I can.'

'Christ, you'll have your work cut out there, I should imagine, though you never know, do you? Wash she hike in head?'

'Bloody wild-cat,' said Ronnie out of loyalty.

'I know, some of these upper-class bints'll bounce you to the bloody ceiling. Well, all that and'—he gestured towards the lofty shape of the house, round the front of which the car was now picking its way among legions of others—'all this too, eh? Well, bloody good luck to you. Watch out for Mum.'

'Like a hawk.'

Ronnie and Hamer were set down in front of a portico two storeys high, incorporating pillars Grecian in inspiration (God, thought Ronnie, not again. Not here), and approached by a broad flight of steps. The two men climbed these and soon found themselves in an extensive hall under the dome of a cupola embellished with much stained glass. On the walls were pictured groups of early Americans signing things and still earlier Americans shooting arrows at things. But all over the immaculate mushroom-coloured carpet, and in what could be seen of a sort of Empire-style room opening off on the left, stood groups of present-day Americans drinking things. Present-day Americans of a different sort, wearing white jackets, moved round among them enabling them to go on doing this. Within five seconds Lady Baldock had appeared, the blackbird hair coiled even higher than usual and more rings than ever on her extended right hand. This Hamer kissed, Ronnie having to make do with seizing the outflung left hand by way of token of his inferior status.

'Bill, how marvellous. To think you've come all this way. Welcome to Broad Lawns. Hallo, Ronnie. You must be utterly exhausted. How were Margot and Rudi? Aren't they simply two of the most impressive people in the world? Now after all that if all you want to do is stretch out for an hour or two you've only to say. But there are so many people here who are just dying to meet you that it would be such a shame. But we must find you a *drink*; what's happening?'

Before he could be left to himself, Ronnie said jocularly, 'Where's my old friend Miss Quick?'

'Mona?' The momentary but perceptible wonderment was beautifully done, as to the gas-meter man asking to see the Rembrandts. 'Oh, she's somewhere around, I think. Try the drawing-room over there. Now, Bill, you must promise not to mind too much if I ask you to turn on the charm for some of my old friends. God knows they're not the most exciting people you ever saw but I did grow up with some of them. And then you and I can just go and ... '

As Juliette Baldock drew Hamer away, Ronnie mentally supplied what they could just go and do. He took a whisky and water, which he wanted, and was handed a paper napkin, which he did not want, from a passing tray. He drank half of the whisky. One of the incidental enlightenments of the Simon Quick campaign was to do with why some chaps who drank a lot drank a lot. He lit a cigarette. Then he moved off, his feet given substantial wings by the sight of Lord Baldock a few yards away apparently sniffing the air. One at a bloody time, please. In the drawing-room, where there were a great many silly pink chairs and needlework pictures of persons being very idle, Ronnie caught sight of the Bish woman talking to others of her sex, age and attributes. He changed course before pushing on with his search. At the end of the room, open glass doors with Adam-green frames gave on to a conservatory full of the usual stuff, fuller indeed than was common, so full of geraniums and bougainvillaea and plumbago and such that there was not a lot of room for people. But two people had made their way in here. One was Simon, wearing trousers, a trouser suit in fact of biscuit corduroy, and with her back to him, so that Ronnie was reminded of his first sight of her. The other, not raging as red-faced George Parrot had been, but leering and grimacing, was Student Mansfield.

Of course, you fool, said Ronnie instantaneously to himself, of *course*, you *fool*. So that was why she had stayed on so long in Greece, written only twice and in that information-packed, uniformative style, been as hopeless as ever in bed when she came back to London for the inside of a week, gone off with the Baldocks to the place in Ireland where Chummy did his shooting, not written at all from there, pleaded the time of the month when he had flown over unasked and tried to get her to bed in that dreadful hotel in Bray, never been available during the four days between her second return to London and her departure for this place. He had nearly known, he had really known, but he had thought that so much of her had stayed genuine, her self-reproach in bed, her desire not to go to Ireland, her grief at the Bray fiasco. [He still thought this, in so far as he could think at all.) All right, Mummy had been keeping them apart and leaning on her meanwhile. But, he had imagined, he only needed one fair chance and Mummy's blockade would be broken. And, he had imagined, that fair chance had come popping up in the shape of Mummy's telephone call from Ireland. Very neatly phrased.

' ... But do you think you really can get Mr Hamer to come?'

'I'll do my best, Juliette, but as you know he's a very busy man.'

'Of course, he must be with such a tremendous responsibility, but I do hope you'll absolutely strain every nerve ... '

'Naturally I'll—'

' ... because if Mr Hamer can't make it I shall have to fall back on a completely different alternative plan for my Thanksgiving party which I'm afraid won't include room for you. I do hope you understand, Ronnie.'

Oh yes. Now he understood practically everything, even a very minor mysteriousness he had not even considered since Malakos: what Lady Baldock thought he had thought he was doing there. Answer: pressing on with a (hopelessly foredoomed) plan to marry her daughter, while in fact keeping her happy, or not too unhappy, until Mansfield had been vetted, sounded, talked into taking on a twenty-six-year-old notorious neurotic who went round London with no shoes on. The only outstanding question was why he, Ronnie, was here now: Hamer once hooked, as he had been—and had been reported to be—within forty-eight hours, and surely he, Ronnie, became dispensable. Time would no doubt answer that one too.

Ronnie had been standing for about half a minute thinking all this with part of his mind, while the rest of it was considering whether to run up and hit Mansfield a lot would convey to him something of what he felt about him. Maybe it would, but Simon was there, and in some curious way he felt he did not want to have anything to do with her, to move any closer to her, while Mansfield was anywhere around. Getting her alone would be a pretty problem.

At this point, Ronnie became aware that somebody was watching him from the flank. It was red-faced George Parrot. To see him in the flesh so soon after being oddly reminded of him made Ronnie want to scream. Memory of their last encounter just had time to intimate a punch-up before Parrot came up and shook hands, mentioning Ronnie's name. Ronnie returned the mention. Then he noticed that Parrot was looking at him with an expression of slightly contemptuous sympathy.

'I think this is real funny,' he said, drawing it out a long way in his native tones. 'Re-you-all funny.'

Instinctively, Ronnie turned a bit British. 'How so?'

'Ah, Ronnie curl,' Parrot seemed to say, but soon cleared things up. 'The irony of fate, if you like to put it that way. You're just exactly where I was the time we met before. Realizing that you have just set eyes on the guy who is destined to be your successor. Gives you kind of a funny feeling, don't it?'

'It does. Look, can I talk to you for a minute?'

'I'd say that's what you were doing already, Mr Appleyard.'

'You know what I mean. Somewhere private.'

Two minutes later they were sitting behind locked doors in what was presumably a guest dressing-room somewhere near one of the top corners of the house. On a low table between them was a silver tray, and on the tray were eight or nine glasses of whisky. 'We may not need every one of these,' Parrot had explained as he drove the servant carrying this load upstairs before them, 'but you never know.' Now he said,

'All right. I was never engaged to Simona. I guess nobody ever was. That would get into the papers, and more to the point the break-off would too. We had this understanding. Did you ever get that far?'

'No.'

'No, you wouldn't. You were never a serious candidate. You were just a boy-friend. You ain't rich. I presume it's Simona's money you after, Mr Appleyard?'

'To begin with it was, but then I started getting fond of her.'

'Yeah, well before you get too fond of her I got news for you. Simona don't own a dime. Maybe she did way back, from her father, but Juliette has it all now. Like in trust. That must be real bad news for you. I'm sorry.' Parrot did not look sorry, just momentarily more contemptuous. He drained a glass of whisky, making a good deal of noise, and set it down with a rattle of ice and a clunk.

Ronnie considered it was the numbing effects of shock that, for now, had taken the edge off this disclosure. He said dully, 'She'd have to come round. Juliette would, I mean. She'd never cut Simon off.'

'On account of being so solicitous for her daughter's welfare? That's the damn lousiest piece of character-analysis I ever heard.'

'I don't mean that,' said Ronnie, who was recovering even faster than he was drinking. 'I mean Juliette couldn't face letting her not be rich. That would put her outside Juliette's world and orbit and everything. She'd lose all control over her. That would never do.'

'Mm, you got a point there, Mr Appleyard, there's no question about that. You know, I don't believe I care for Juliette very much. It was she who broke up me and Simona; I guess it's always that way. That little girl and I were getting along not too bad.'

'That's not the line you were taking that evening.'

'Sure, but I didn't know then that Simona was acting under orders. Under pressure, at least.' Parrot started on another drink. 'Well, I can't see you achieving your ambitions in a coon's age, but here's luck. Not because I give a damn for you, but because I like anything that may cause my old friend Student Mansfield even minor and temporary inconvenience.'

'You know him well, do you?'

'We almost grew up together, God damn it. He's from around here, the panhandle part of the state. Spent some years in the East curing his accent, the cotton-picking bastard.'

'Listen,' said Ronnie excitedly, 'what were his two unfortunate businesses?'

'Pardon me?'

'Sorry: somebody called Cecil Saxton told me there was—'

'Old Sir Cess? Say, ain't he the most marvellous old guy? Talking that way, like someone out of P. G. Wodehouse, and him the son of a railroad engineer in is it Leeds? He cured his accent too, and good. I tried to get him to talk the way he used to talk one time, and do you know he'd forgotten? He couldn't do it any more. Wonderful old guy. But I interrupted you.'

'You're welcome. Anyway, Saxton told me that Mansfield was mixed up in a couple of rows, or scandals. Saxton called them unfortunate businesses. One was about Mansfield's mother and something to do with a deed of gift. The other one was when he was in the army in West Germany.'

'Oh, Jesus Christ.' Parrot managed to laugh quite heartily without giving any sign of liking Ronnie better. 'Student and his mother had never gotten along too well. I didn't much care for the old lady myself, as a matter of fact. Came from Boston and let you know it. Well, she thought maybe she could soften Student up some if she made all her property over to him and let him kind of sit on top of it as well as spending money faster than you could count. Not that she wasn't thinking pretty damn hard about death duties too. So, comes the day when the papers are all signed, and while they all putting their fountain-pens back into their pockets Student says, "Does that mean this house and all is mine now, Ma?" and she says, "Damn right it is, Son," and he says, "Right, Ma: *out*." That was the unfortunate business about his mother.'

'Christ,' agreed Ronnie. 'And did she go?'

'It took a long time, but she finally obliged him by going back to Boston. And then a little while back she obliged him even more thoroughly by dying, just three months after the time-limit. The other affair was a long time ago, around 1955 I would think. Lieutenant Student Mansfield – by the way, you know why he was given that damn fool name?'

'I've been wondering.'

'As a perpetual memorandum to him that in our progress through life we never cease to learn. You could say he paid mind to that idea. Well: Lieutenant Mansfield gets stationed in this German town, I don't remember its name. His old man was still alive at that time and was setting his allowance at an unrealistically low figure. So old Student sets about supplementing his income. By the date we talking about, there ain't too much money in selling Uncle Sam's gasoline and cigarettes and what-have-you to the Krauts. So Student teams up with his platoon sergeant, and they take to waiting on a lonesome stretch of road until one of the locals comes by in his car. It has to be a good-looking car. So they stop him in the name of the U.S. Army and they say, "Get out, mine hair, and get walking. But give us your wallet and your watch for us to remember you by." They pointing their guns at mine hair quite steady-like, so he complies with their request. Then they drive the car to a friend of Student's, and he gives them a whole lot of marks for it. They divide them two for Student and one for the sergeant, because it was Student's idea. Well, in the end, naturally the U.S. Army gets to noticing what's been going on, and it makes them real mad. So mad they stop Student being an officer any more and they put him in the stockade to kind of underline their displeasure. The sergeant comes off bad too. Finally they ship Student back home, and you might think his prospects ain't too good, but in the meantime his old man has passed over, some say on account of Student's activities and the reaction of officialdom, but anyhow Student's financial problems are notably alleviated. That was the unfortunate business in West Germany.'

'Good ... *God.*' It was never easy to get Ronnie (who occasionally felt that some of his own behaviour might not appeal to everyone) into a state of moral disapproval, but he was very nearly in one now. What had conveyed him there was not nearly so much Mansfield's reported actions as the way he had—how did it go?—put the whole thing behind him. Widespread and unstinted collaboration must have been needed for that. Ronnie drank copiously and said, 'But how the hell has he got away with it? So that Juliette can consider him as a husband for Simon? I suppose she does know about him?'

'Oh, of course she does. Simona does. Everybody does. He's rich, you see. That means he belongs to a very confined circle and a very tight circle. Kind of a mutual defence system. And the numbers are so small that if one goes it's like an empty chair at the table. So you can get away with damn near anything, long as you stay rich. You eligible in the marriage market on account of almost nobody else is, whatever you've done and even if you can't perform.'

'Even if ... '

'Hell, there may be nothing in it at all, but in the days when the world was young that was the word on Student everywhere you went. Some tale about double dates where the other guy had to do Student's duty as well as his own. And when you come to think of it, Mr. Appleyard, we dealing with a situation in which incapacity is a recommendation. What better husband for a girl who don't like it than a guy who can't do it?'

Ronnie said, 'I understood you weren't sleeping with her.'

'Whatever she told you, that state of affairs had not yet come into being when we parted. We'd fixed to go away together with sex strictly out, so she could relax and we could get to know each other. But, as you very well aware, that never happened. Oh, let's forget it. I think you stink a little bit, Appie boy, but if you can do anything to annoy Student you sure of my full support. Now come on and get loaded.'

'Looks as if I might as well. What I can't see is why I'm here. Any ideas?'

Parrot finished his current drink in a ruminative manner. 'I must say nothing springs to mind. Are you in a position to do Juliette any kind of a favour?'

'I'm not. Only the chap I came with.'

'Yeah, she was in quite a tizzy waiting for you-all to arrive. Or I guess I should say for him to arrive. Mm-hm ... Did you frustrate her about something recently? Go against her wishes, that type of thing?'

'I did have a bit of a disagreement with her when I was—'

'In public?'

'Yes, it was about the way she and—'

'It wouldn't matter a goddam in hell what it was

about. You here to pay for that little error of judgment, Appie old man. If you meant it when you said you were getting fond of Simona, Juliette would know all about that. So you've been brought here to see precisely what you did see when I first spoke to you. Repeated and intensified. The happy couple, with you not one of it.'

'Yes, that has got the right sort of ring, I admit. I wonder if he'll last any longer than you did.'

'I'll kill the bastard if he does.'

'Of course, Juliette may push him because she liked his father. Wasn't there some story about that?'

'Yeah, according to my old man Juliette and the general were going great at one stage. Blighted Southern romance. You may be right. Drink up.'

'Why not? What are you here for, by the way? Same as me?'

'No, I've expiated my crimes. Not that they were ever as grave as yours. I got to hand it to you, some of it anyway, for disagreeing with my Lady Baldock. Anyway, I'm here because why shouldn't I be now? Because I've gone back to being an old friend of the family and there never were many of those. Because I'm rich. Like I told you, Appie old fellow, it's a small circle. Real small.'

'And how do you like Fort Charles?'

'Well, I've only been here for less than four hours, so I can't really—'

'I think you'll be impressed. We have some very gracious buildings in our city. Our court-house is based on a reconstruction of the temple of the goddess Diana at Ephesus, Greece.'

'Isn't that interesting?' said Ronnie hoarsely. Was he never, not for so long as an evening, to get away from the glory that had been Greece? 'So is the main entrance of the television studio I work at in London.' Good enough: some such tumbledown stone shack, or a photograph of it, must have so served. And who was there to care if it had not?

Another member of the group standing near the supper table, a lean man in black whom any appropriate head-gear would have turned into a judge or doctor out of a Western, heard this with more than surprise. 'London?' he queried on a falling note, as if Ronnie had claimed to earn his living in Saigon, or even Hanoi. 'You-all got trouble there. Real bad trouble.'

'Trouble?' Ronnie visualized the abolition of expense accounts, the appointment of George Brown as Chancellor of the Exchequer. 'What's happened?'

'What's happened? You-all have got all these coloured people coming in all the time from the Caribbean and Africa and India and Pakistan ... '

'Not so much now as—'

' ... and you-all are not doing one damn thing about it. Now I speak as somebody who loves and admires England, and I think all of us here would say the same.'

'Yes, indeed. Surely. Where we all came from. Damn right.'

'What I want is for England to preserve her traditions and her historical institutions and her culture. And here you-all go, letting them mix with you-all and work and live alongside you-all and having their children in the same schools and putting them side by side with you-all in your hospital beds. It's crazy, any way you look at it. In fifty years' time, less than that, they'll have dragged all of you-all down to their own level. We've lived with them all our lives and we know them. Why won't you-all be guided by us?'

Ronnie made some evasive and indeed quite wild reply. Now was not the moment for a stand on liberal principle, or on anything else. His feelings about coloured people, as about old people, hardly went further than a mild dislike, plus in this case an occasional twinge of discomfort on being momentarily outnumbered by a group of them in pub or street. Since nobody present, near or far, was going to report him to the *New Statesman* for backing down on race, he let the conversation take its course, rather savouring, in fact, the relief of not having to come back at this boring old fascist with pseudo-facts about how much the U.S. Negro's living and educational standards left to be desired, to say nothing of pseudo-concern.

Across the room, Hamer (who on reflection would have been delighted to advertise any new shortcoming of Ronnie's he might become aware of) was being very charming and punchworthy, chiefly to Vassilikós, at his most Jovian in a bottle-green velvet suit. Lady Baldock was watching them both, but chiefly Hamer, with conscientiously mimed approving amusement. Simon, her back to Ronnie, seemed to be passively listening. And Mansfield continued to diffuse an air of part-ownership over her, occasionally bawling some question or comment, rather in the way of a sports commentator over loudspeakers, so that Ronnie could have followed the general progress of the conversation had he cared to.

He did not care to, was merely waiting, waiting for the group to dissolve so that he could get hold of Simon for two minutes. He had been waiting for over an hour. On coming downstairs after the session with Parrot and a brief wash and brush-up, he had found the five of them just on the point of converging. Since then they had moved about quite a bit, eaten as well as drunk, chatted to others, but all along stayed together as if for a bet. Ronnie knew gloomily that it was Simon who was doing the staying: on his account, too, or why had she not come up to say hallo to him, not even been caught looking in his direction? At least the five had stayed where they were for the last quarter of an hour or so, enabling him to snatch a hasty supper from the table at his side—the claws of some shell-fish with petrol-and-gherkin sauce, cold turkey like slices of dead chaps' chaps, morsels of ham in miniature bread-rolls, and little sour tomatoes, cubes of pale cheese, cock-tail onions, these last on sticks impaling what might have been a ham vaster than all the morsels put together; but what it really was must remain for ever in doubt. No ten persons would have had the patience to eat their way through the innumerable tit-bits stuck into its rind, and even if they had there was nothing to carve it with. Ronnie wondered how many times the supposed ham had done its duty, recognizing with interest and respect a fresh stratagem of rich people's housekeeping.

The shag in black—he even had the cheek to have a black ribbon attached to his glasses, thus stressing the legal rather than the medical aspect of his appearance—the shag in black had been going on about the irremediable inferiority of the coloured man. 'Have you ever met any-body who really likes the Negro?' he was asking.

Ronnie knew at least two men in London whose liking for the Negro was so all-embracing as to have attracted the attention of the police in days gone by, but he saw the irrelevance of this. 'I can't say I have.'

'Or who wants his children to mix with Negroes?'

'I can't name anyone, certainly.'

'Of course you can't. And the same goes for all of you-all. Everybody in his senses knows that the black man is an inferior form of life.'

This went down very well with all those in earshot, Ronnie noticed, with the exception of the black man who was handing round drinks at the time, though this man did no more than lower his head abruptly. Just for the moment, Ronnie felt an irrational desire to tell him that this was not necessarily his, Ronnie's, own view of the matter. But then a movement across the room caught his eye: Juliette Baldock seemed on the point of making off with Hamer but without Vassilikós. That would be tricky.

At this point, a girl said, 'Mr Appleyard, I'm called Betty-Belle Chase.'

'Are you?' Ronnie had no attention to spare.

'I understand you flew here all the way from England with your friend Mr Hamer?'

Ah: Vassilikós too was stirring. 'Well ... yes, I did.'

'I really do adore that British charm that Mr Hamer has.'

No: the Greek turd had done a ta-ta-for-now grimace at Juliette. 'Hell. I mean good.'

'Watch that Britisher, Juliette,' thundered Mansfield facetiously. 'None of them are up to any good.'

'Did either of you-all come to the South before?'

Right: Lady B and Hamer were off arm-in-arm. Now it was all up to Parrot, if the red-faced sod had not fallen flat on his back half an hour ago. No sign of him. No, yes, here he was, striding across from the library, seizing Vassilikós and Mansfield by the upper arm, forcing them into the beginnings of motion, saying something to Simon that kept her where she was.

Speaking without any conscious thought and very fast, Ronnie said, 'He-all may have been for all I know but I-all never have and neither of us-all have ever been to this bloody place and now you-all-all must excuse me.'

He reached Simon in five strides just as Parrot (blessings on his little red cheeks) was steering the other two men out of sight.

'Hallo, Ronnie, how nice to see you. I kept meaning to

come over but I got sort of stuck with Mummy and the rest of them. What do you think of these ghastly people? They really are the –'

'None of that, Simon,' he said as gently as he was able.

Her face, the features more severe than he remembered, the skin sandier, the eyes inkier, fell at once and completely. 'I suppose George told you.'

'Somebody would have had to before long, wouldn't they? Even you in certain circumstances. Or perhaps –' He checked himself, not too early. One of the disconcerting features of this affair was the way it kept giving scope for that failing of his whereby his personal feelings could override his advantage. He said, not perhaps gently but at any rate fairly quietly, 'Sorry. Simon, I must talk to you. Not necessarily tonight, but some time. You say when and where.'

She immediately went hangdog on him. 'No good. Nothing to say to each other. No point.'

But Ronnie Appleyard had been ready for that one. Putting his faith in the fragmentary code of amatory ethics he had known her to act on once or twice (notably when the supposedly imminent arrival of another girl had got her out of his bed that first evening), he said abruptly, 'You must. I love you, Simon.' Saying it made him feel a bit of a shit, another recurring hazard of the present operation, but perceptibly less of one than he had expected. Good show.

'Oh, Ronnie, don't. That's a dreadful thing to say.' Her lower lip spread out like that of a child about to cry. For a moment it seemed clear that this was what she was about to do. Then, much to his surprise and relief, she screwed her mouth back to something like its original shape, swallowed noisily and unhunched herself. 'All right: eight o'clock tomorrow morning in the office.'

'Eight o'clock? Christ!'

'Mummy comes down at eight thirty.'

'Eight o'clock, then. Where's the office?'

'The servants'll show you.'

One of them did in the end, though he took a good deal of finding and just as much instruction in what it was that Ronnie wanted. He got to the office, a small but lofty panelled room near the front door, at exactly eight a.m., shaved, showered and feeling bloody awful. Getting up in time had been nothing like the problem that, the previous evening, it had looked like being. Quite the contrary – the difficulty had been to go on lying in bed until a sufficiently non-early hour while reviewing various disagreeable possibilities: that Mansfield was in Simon's bed or the other way on, that he had tried to do his stuff last night, that he was trying to do his stuff now, that he had succeeded in doing his stuff last night or was succeeding in doing it now or both, that she was finding it not horrible, great fun, gorgeous, more more more ... Et sodding cetera.

He had awoken for good at five thirty. The bed was too short and the top sheet also too short, so that its edge kept flopping against his face, and the pillows, though generous in number and fetchingly varied in hue, were all baby's-cot size. His room clearly lay on the very borders of servant country, was perhaps even a tiny guest-territory enclave within it. There were lots of hurryings up and down stairs, metallic crashings and occasional deeper thumpings he could assign no source to, frequent gigglings from persons whose sex was sometimes uncertain but whose skin-colour was always unmistakable. He had nothing to read except *Drugs: the New Dissent*, which he considered he had tried quite hard enough with on the transatlantic aeroplane, *LBJ – Tool of Fascism*, which he just could not face at this hour, and part of a year-old copy of *The Fort Charles Citizen-Mail* he found lining a drawer in the (no doubt) colonial-style dressing-table. This last he decided to do some serious work on. To quote a rag of such a sort as the source of even a mild anti-American story would give an effect of terrifying omniscience almost anywhere. No good, though. Apart from a piece of impartial stodge headed *Nation at Polls* there was no news except of the doings of Fort Charles's financial, mercantile and criminal communities, all three of which seemed on this evidence drearily respectable. The rest was chatter, sport, cookery, more chatter. And he did not feel like it, anyway.

Now, mooning about the empty office, he felt like nothing on earth. Why? He was not seriously underslept: last night's company had been driven out by ten thirty, the household dispersed soon after. Hereabouts they started early and finished early, as he had already had time to be assured more than once. Even by his own modest standards he had not had a great deal to drink, having slowed down almost to a standstill after the Parrot get-together. But then American drinks were stronger than British ones (though the American drinks in question had not tasted very strong). And then, of course, he had spent a lot of time in aeroplanes yesterday and had not had time to unwind. No wonder the act of sitting down anywhere seemed strange, fearful, not to be contemplated for hours and hours.

He returned to the hall, which was empty and silent, and looked through the extensive glass panes of the front door. There was bright sunshine among the trees and shrubs. A breath of air might be good. He opened the door, went through and shut it behind him, reasoning that, if he stayed more or less where he was, Simon would see him on her way into the office, unless she proposed entering it by way of a trapdoor or something.

The sun was warm, the air faintly cool and faintly

scented with some kitchen spice he could not name. A thick dew still lay beneath the trees, some of which were bare, others ostentatiously autumnal. Despite this, the whole thing looked very green, and with the milky-blue sky thrown in made him think of England. He had no feeling of being in the south at all, even though the place was on the latitude of somewhere like Tunis. A lone cicada, whirring like a muffled telephone bell, did what it could to correct this impression. In a mild stupor, Ronnie watched the steady movement of the lines of vehicles on the highway. They were a long way off. He wondered how far the property extended to the rear. Would he, become rich, famous and not quite so lecherous with the passing years, stand here one day as master of the whole show, fill the house with racialist shags, send son of small red-haired butler to the airport to meet people who had travelled four thousand miles to visit Sir Ronald and Lady Appleyard? This prospect struck him as on the whole unlikely, considering ...

He came to and looked at his watch. Eight nine. Christ. He pushed his way back into the house with no clear idea in mind and saw, through the office doorway, Simon sitting at a roll-top desk with her back to him and looking through some papers. He hurried across to her.

'Didn't you see me out there?'

'Hallo, Ronnie.' She smiled at him, whether anxiously or just blankly he could not tell. 'Yes, of course I saw you.'

'Well, why didn't you tell me you'd turned up?'

'I've only just turned up. And I thought you'd come in when you were ready. And you have.'

He could think of nothing to say, except that this managed to be more characteristic of her than anything he had known her do, or not do, and he could not say that. So he stared at her. She was wearing a high-necked white pullover, lime-green trousers and a different-green ribbon in her hair that seemed not to be holding it up or together or anything much. She looked thin, splendid, not very healthy, and, as always, so strange that she might have been tinted by some quite different colour-process from that used on everything round her.

'Oh. Here.' She took a glass from a small copper tray at her side and gave it to him. 'Fresh orange juice.'

'Thank you.' He had to admit that this was characteristic of her too. 'What about you?'

'I've had mine.' Her voice was beginning to lose what animation it had had when she first spoke to him. 'I hope you slept well.'

'Not too badly. How did you sleep? I mean on your own or with Mansfield?'

The ribbon in her hair wobbled as she turned her head away.

'Simon, you remember how in that temple on that island I promised not to go away and you promised to always tell me the truth? When it mattered? Well, here I am. And the truth bloody well matters now.'

She said something too muffled to be intelligible.

'Take your hand away from your mouth, I can't hear you.'

'Meant no lies. Not I'd got to say everything.'

'No, it meant saying everything as well.'

'Won't like it,' she said, meaning him.

'Bugger that. Now. Simon, are you sleeping with Mansfield?'

'Mm.'

'That's better. But I gather he can't get it in. Is that true?'

'He's very bad at it.'

'But can he manage it at all?'

'Not much.'

'Not *much*?'

'Only twice. He's terrible at it.'

The outside of Ronnie's glass of juice was slippery with condensed moisture. At this point it slid out of his hand and fell to the floor, remaining unbroken but flinging its contents over quite a wide area of Turkish rug. He had seen the whole thing coming very clearly since the previous evening, but that was no help. Simon's revelations had acutely distressed and shocked him. At a remove from this, he felt a painful bewilderment at being so distressed and shocked. He tried to think and feel that what he had heard was nothing in itself.

'I told you you wouldn't like it,' Simon had said. Now she added, 'It was as horrible as ever,' got up and crossed the room.

'Oh, that's all right, then, if it was as horrible as ever. What are you doing?'

'Telephoning ... Henry, would you send someone up to the office with a wet rag and a bucket? Somebody's split something. Right away.'

'Why did you put on that accent?'

'They understand it better. It's how I talked before I went to school in Europe.'

'Sorry I made a mess, but can't it be left for a bit? We haven't got long.'

'No, it'll stain. It won't take a minute.'

'Are you going to marry that flaring shit?'

'He's not so bad. He can be quite funny. He hasn't asked me.'

'Yet. But he will. Or more likely you'll find the whole thing's suddenly fixed itself up overnight, complete with date, place, best man, the lot. You see, this time I think she means business.'

'What are you talking about?' A slight edge came into her tone.

'Mummy. She hasn't meant business before, certainly. For instance with old George Parrot, who's neither stupid, nor illiterate, nor insensitive. Obviously he'd be no good at all. Now Student, there's a really strong candidate for you. You only have to hear him talk to see that.'

'He can't help his voice. And I don't understand all this meaning business and candidate thing.'

'If he can change his accent he can turn down his bloody volume control. Anyway. This whole situation is very simple, but unusual too. It's the simple things that are unusual. Sit down there and listen carefully.'

Simon had sat down on a flamboyant chair of ebony or ebony-substitute when, with unexpected and yet wouldn't-you-know promptness, a middle-aged Negro maidservant knocked and entered. She was carrying the equipment asked for.

'Over there, Betsy.'

'Yes, Miss Simona.'

Ronnie violently lit a cigarette. He was standing by the desk. Now he looked down at the papers Simon had been handling when he came into the room, and saw that they were bills, with envelopes, a cheque-book, and a couple of cheques filled in but for the signature.

'You said I didn't help Mummy but I do.'

A detail caught Ronnie's eye. He picked up one of the made-out cheques and the bill it referred to.

'Titanic Foods,' he read aloud.

'That's the supermarket.'

'Eighteen hundred and eighty-six dollars and nineteen cents. Quite a lot of food, considering you only got here last week.'

'It's from last *April*,' she said impatiently.

'So it is. Some time ago. And ... the bill's made out for only eighteen hundred dollars. Not enough.'

'We always round them off that way.'

'How tidy. But won't Titanic Foods stick the eighty-odd dollars back on next time?'

'Not if they want to keep Mummy's custom.'

'I see. But that's ... ' He had said too much already. 'Well, it's no business of mine.'

'Huh.'

There was silence, apart from the noise of the maid's activities. These were taking a long time, not because she was thorough but because she was slow. A memory of Ronnie's national-service days suggested to him an explanation of this slowness. You took as long as you could to do every task, because when you had finished the one you were on you were going to be given another one that might be nastier. Something to be said for that view in this case.

He looked at his watch. Eight seventeen. Double Christ. This could go in indefinitely. Perhaps he had better ... But then, against the odds, Simon said that would do now and the maid said something back and went. He tried to get the two of them back into the right key.

'Here we go again, then. You must attend to every word. You won't like it, to quote you just now, but you must listen to it all. Will you?'

She exhaled sharply and nodded.

'In one way, your mother would like you never to get married at all, so that she could keep you by her side and go on bullying you, and also because she knows you want to be married. So men appear, and sleep with you, and that's fine because she knows you don't enjoy it, but even so you get attached to some of them, because you're a loving and affectionate person in spite of everything that's been done to you, and you're beautiful as well, so quite a few of them fall in love with you. That's dangerous, because one of them might get you to run away with him. So they disappear pretty promptly. They don't just go away, as you said that time, they get the push.

'But this can't go on indefinitely. For one thing, an unmarried daughter over twenty-five is getting to be a worse and worse advertisement for her. And you're an expense. And a constant risk. And perhaps she feels like varying the treatment—instead of preventing you from getting married, make you get married to an absolute bugger instead—that is to say, not only a very unpleasant man but a clown who talks like a loud-hailer and a crook as well, and a known crook. He's not much good in bed, which is a bit of a drawback from her point of view, but on the other hand that's another thing everybody knows about him, so it's an added humiliation for you, so the balance is in his favour even there. Then—'

'She wants me to marry him because he's the son of the man she was in love with when she was a girl before she married Daddy,' droned Simon.

'Yes, that's the absolute clincher. Her official reason. All her friends would understand that. Yes, dear, I know he seems a funny sort of choice but you must have heard the story about Juliette and the boy's father. She may even use that to herself some of the time.'

Simon looked up. Her eyes were half-shut and her lower lip stretched out. 'Mummy loves me,' she said, and gave a violent gasp.

'Stop it. Try to behave like a woman. In a few minutes you can cry as much as you like, but for now your job is to listen. To every word. Right?'

She nodded. 'Moment.'

He looked round the room, but before he could do more

than begin to wonder if the panelling on walls and ceiling was real, a strange loud noise, or medley of noises, started up quite abruptly, apparently within those walls. It fizzed, clanked, whirred in gradually decreasing tempo, clicked very loudly, wailed in gradually ascending pitch, hummed, all with such variety married to a kind of periodicity that he was tempted, though not strongly or for more than a couple of seconds, to think that somebody had switched on a tape of a piece of concrete music, rather conservative in tendency.

'What the hell is that row?' he asked.

'Heating.'

As if triggered by this exchange, new effects were added: a powerful boot going into and through a bass drum, the lowering of the lid of a giant's saucepan, the snap of the catch of a giantess's handbag. Then a prolonged diminuendo.

'Ready.'

'Well done, Simon. What she really feels about you, whatever the hell really is, I don't know. But the only way for you, you yourself, to treat her is as if she hates you. I don't know how that comes about either, but there's plenty to choose from, by Christ. You're Mr Quick's daughter, not General Mansfield's. Your first stepfather—what was his bloody name?—Stavros, that's it, he took notice of you instead of only taking notice of her. Same with Chummy. He—'

'Chummy's horrible. *He* hates me.'

'He's horrible all right, God knows, but he doesn't hate you. In his way, and it's not any kind of way I care for, he is concerned for you. It's me he hates. We won't go into why. Going on with the list now. She wanted a homosexual son who doted on his darling mum, not a heterosexual daughter. There's a couple of things about you that go with that, but don't let's get too ballockingly Freudian about this. Best tip: you're not only better-looking than she is, you're the same physical type, I mean size and general shape, only your colouring is so much better and extraordinary. So that people might compare the two of you, you see. Which they couldn't if you were a big busty creature with hips and a great arse, say, which you're not. But as it is they can check, and if they do they can't help seeing you're better. Because that was your father's colouring, I bet. Eh? I'm right, I bet.'

'Think so. Not better than Mummy.'

'Yes you are, though I'm sure you've been told the opposite since before you can remember. Anyway, you've got to do something about her before it's too late. Oh, Christ.'

Saucepan lid and handbag catch had begun a sort of slow movement in dialogue, with fizzing, clicking and wailing accompaniment. Ronnie waited for it to subside. When it did not, he went over to Simon and stooped down by her chair. He did not touch her.

'You must leave her. When I go back to London on Sunday, you come with me. I'll look after you.'

'Couldn't.'

'Yes you could. You mean she'd get upset on a grand scale. Of course she bloody well would. It's her ultimate deterrent. Don't give her a chance to use it. Sneak out without a word to anybody. Don't pack a suitcase, come in what you stand up in. Just bring your passport. Meet me at the airport at ten fifteen on Sunday morning.'

'Can't.'

'You must. Simon, if you don't come with me on Sunday you're finished. This is your last chance of ever leading a normal life like other women and enjoying sex and being happy. You know that's true, don't you?'

She nodded, then shook her head. 'Not brave enough.'

'You'll have to be. And you won't need to be very brave. A better idea is to make out you're coming to see me off. You can bet no other bugger will, except perhaps old Burke-Smith, and I can't see him grappling with you at the departure gate. You've got to do it.'

She made no response.

'You can't take it in that she hates you, though I'm damn sure it's crossed your mind plenty of times in the past. So think about it. And listen to this. Why's she got me here? It looked at first as if she wanted to get her own back on me for crossing her about you by sort of showing me you and Student together. But now I think it's you she's aiming at. She'll find a way of doing something with me to get at you. She knows you like me, you see, and you liking a man is unforgivable.'

'Don't just like you.' Simon got up and started for the door. She looked quite composed and very miserable.

'Where are you going?' He took her lightly by the arm, which felt like a doll's arm. 'To have breakfast with her?'

'No. Going to bed.'

'Why? Are you all right? You're not ill, are you?'

'No. Just want to go to bed.'

Ronnie tried to come up with some final thought for the day, but he realized that she was not listening now, and a cadenza for bursting bass drum had begun in the wall. So he let her go, lit another cigarette, and followed.

Hands in pockets, Lord Baldock stood peering with apparent incredulity through the panes of the front door. He turned and looked at Ronnie and nodded several times.

'I must say, Appleyard,' he said, somewhere near the top of the tenor clef, 'you do seem to pursue your objectives in a curious fashion. All Simon needs to be driven to despair is a few minutes' chat with you.'

'You don't understand,' said Ronnie, 'but we won't argue about it.'

'Indeed we won't. Sunday you leave, isn't it? Mm. Three whole days.'

Those three whole days were a myriad times more cheerless a prospect to Ronnie than they could have been to either Baldock. Apart from keeping out of as many people's way as possible, not in itself an activity to fill the mind for hours on end, what was he to do all the time? Had nothing much been at stake, he would have been on the wire to Western Union in two shakes of a lamb's tail, passing the word to corduroy-jacketed Eric for a stiff dose of plan B. But it seemed clear to Ronnie that three days was an absolute minimum for Simon to deal with and act on what he had said to her (if she was ever going to be able to), that more time than that might well be needed, that he might even find himself running up a plan C involving feigned illness and God knew what.

There was breakfast in a sun-room adjoining the conservatory: a cereal full of nuts and tough-looking pieces of dried fruit, eggs and bacon, English muffins, but he could face nothing more than coffee. Lady Baldock was there, so heavily attended by Hamer as to have no attention to spare for anybody else, which showed that even the most repulsive of God's creatures had their uses in the scheme of things. Vassilikós, Mansfield and so on were absent; Parrot, though due to turn up again in the evening for Thanksgiving dinner, had driven home the previous night. Ronnie would almost have welcomed the sight of a Saxton, a Van Pup, even an Upshot, but he knew there was no chance of that. Introduced into the set-up here, such as they would either have diluted Lady B's title or—without conferring the prestige of a Vassilikós—overtopped her riches.

Ronnie got through some of the morning with the unwelcome aid of *Drugs: the New Dissent* and *LBJ—Tool of Fascism*. The former suggested to him that the penalties for going out of your way to inflict on chaps an unshocked and deeply understanding human document about bloody little fools who took drugs should be in line with the penalties for peddling the stuff, the latter that whatever L.B.J. might or might not be a tool of he hated him slightly less than most of the people the author liked. All this took place in his bedroom, whence determined attempts were made to evict him in order that the place could be tidied and the bed made; alternatively, let him allow this to be done in his presence. He resisted either proposal stoutly until Hoskins, the big white-haired butler who looked as if he could not but have played clarinet for Louis Armstrong in the 'twenties, came up to add his dignified reproaches.

'All right then, I'll be off. I just had some reading to finish.'

'Very well, sir. I'm sure if you want to work in the library you won't be disturbed there, sir.'

'That's an idea. Where's, uh, Lady Baldock, do you know?'

'Her ladyship and the other English gentleman have driven over to see Henry Hall, sir.'

'Really? What on earth is he doing in these parts?'

'Henry Hall is the ancestral home of the Henry family, sir, of which the patriot Patrick Henry was a distant connection. General Calhoun Henry was at one time the commander of a Confederate army in the war between the states. The home is now a family and military museum, sir.'

'That sounds ... Tell me, what happens next? When does everyone sort of assemble again?'

'There are to be drinks in the buttery bar at noon, sir. The buttery bar is at the north-east corner of the building, to the right of the green room, sir. At twelve thirty a buffet luncheon will be served, sir.'

'Thank you. Right, you can tell the maid to come in now.'

'Very well, sir, thank you kindly.'

Eleven o'clock. Not worth the trouble and expense of following the vestige of an earlier plan, taking a taxi into what he supposed you had to call the town—and presumably finding everything there shut today. And he must stay on the spot, somehow combine keeping behind cover in general while staying in full view of Simon as much as possible. She must be kept up to the mark. Besides this, there were Hamer's activities to be watched, firstly as always out of common prudence, secondly in the hope of anecdotal material for the *Insight* hospitality-room. But this last notion quite failed to appeal. Hamer himself would fairly soon be drinking away in that hospitality-room for a long time before and after an actual appearance on the show, in all probability wearing that sodding gamboge antelope-hide jacket thrown negligently across his shoulders, almost certainly getting on horribly well with that new, well-hung girl in the research team, and beyond question having done nothing whatever for Ronnie in return, except act as the indifferent instrument of getting him here. *Here* ...

These and other images, some of them a good deal less welcome, revolved in Ronnie's brain as he first found, then incuriously explored, what must be the library. There were not a great many books in here, and what there were had long lost their newness. Ronnie verified a guess that this must largely be the late Mr Quick's collection. Apart from some works on great houses, furniture, silverware and such forgettables, it consisted of stuff on the Civil War. Ronnie had already heard so much about this (when he was not hearing about the shortcomings of the Negro) that he wondered occasionally, as now, whether the Americans had not somehow managed to slip in a second civil war when the rest of the world had not been looking, in 1914–17, perhaps, or 1939–42. Anyway, if they had, the South had clearly been beaten again. Jolly good for them. There was no sign of Stavros having been a great reader, and none either of Chummy Baldock's incumbency.

All in all, this seemed a good spot to lie low in. True, it contained pictures, frightful magazine-cover oils of Lady Baldock (twice over), Simon (at about twenty and, by what amounted to striking talent, made to look quite colourless), somebody who must have been Stavros (an unsuccessful poet in glistening tweeds), Lord Baldock (with his familiar air of having that moment received his death-wound). Nothing of any possible Mr Quick. Ronnie decided he was safe in here, with these five likenesses to deter any culture-lover who might consider coming along in search of a good read. He was just torpidly trying to choose between *The Thin Gray Line* and *Treasures of Old Richmond*, when the door was flung open and Hamer and Lady Baldock came in.

They moved in a scampering kind of way, with a certain amount of giggling and Hamer making playful unlocated grabs. It was a couple of seconds before either of them noticed Ronnie. Though strongly flap-resistant on television and as regards his own escapades, he was the most disconcerted of the three now. Without drawing breath, Lady Baldock went on to the offensive.

'I hardly expected to find anybody here at *this* time of

the day,' she said, as if reading in the mornings (or looking at portraits of her in the mornings) was the resort only of touts, homosexuals and other low persons.

'I just came in here to get a book,' quipped Ronnie.

'Well, I wonder if you could just take one and move along. I'm sorry to appear rude, but Mr Hamer and I have some-urgent-business-matters-to-discuss.' The closing pentameter was disdainfully thrown off.

Ronnie selected *Confessions of a Copperhead* with almost no delay and started walking, but struck some sort of blow for his side by saying to Hamer as he passed him, 'How was Henry Hall?'

'Breath-taking.'

With an ill grace, the day took itself off into the past. Ronnie was able to give part of it an extra shove. On his way to the buttery bar at three minutes to twelve, he reconnoitred the luncheon-room and found, lined up on a sideboard, a couple of dozen glasses of red wine already poured out. Five of these and part of a sixth he drank off with absolutely no fuss at all, unaware of the small red-haired butler watching him through the crack of the nearly shut door. Ronnie was an inexperienced drink-thief; Hamer could have told him that the very time to avoid was immediately before curtain-up, when staff were sure to be moving about and checking supplies. Anyway, with two pre-lunch whiskies and a sixth-plus, licit glass of wine inside him, he was able to get his head down, at the extraordinary hour of one fifteen p.m., and keep it there until four twenty or so. Five o'clock saw him dinner-jacketed and downstairs, as ordered, and feeling bloody awful again, or still.

The evening started like his last one on Malakos, with the main difference that then he and Simon had joined Mansfield, whereas now he joined the two of them. She was in a white Thai-silk thing printed with gold. It was well cut for her shape, and Ronnie asked himself why Mummy allowed, perhaps even forced, her to appear in becoming clothes, since to get a rival or enemy into something that did not suit her must already have been a favourite stratagem of Neanderthal woman. Vicarious vanity, he answered himself, or a social form of it, such that in this department at least the problem child should be presented as a star in the Baldock diadem. What of it, anyway?

Mansfield's evening clothes, vespertinal as before only here and there, were probably as well cut for his shape as they could be, so that he did not look totally gross, only about eighty-five per cent of that. His jacket lay open to reveal a cummerbund bearing a device Ronnie had seen a lot of in the last twenty-four hours: white stars in a St Andrew's cross on a red ground.

'Hi,' he roared; then, gesturing with a ladylike thumb towards his midriff, added, 'Know what this is?'

Yes, Ronnie thought of replying, and ever after reproached himself for not replying: a bloody great pot-belly, eloquent of years of unearned hard liquor, and situated in close proximity to the softest dick in Dixie. But the arrival of a coloured servant with a tray threw him off, and, taking a drink at random, he said no more than, 'I *think* so. Isn't it the, uh, rebel flag?'

There was no immedate response; Mansfield was frowning and peering at the tray, touching it with his meagre fingers. 'Is this bourbon?'

'Yes sir, Mr Mansfield, bourbon and water.'

'I can see the water. Last time you gave me Scotch.'

'I'm very sorry, sir. This here is bourbon, sir.'

'Ghmm,' said Mansfield like a half-placated lion, and tasted the indicated drink. 'Mm. All right. Now. *Rebel* flag? Are you some goddamn Yankee in disguise or what? This is the flag of the Confederacy, sir, the flag of freedom. That's what it was then, and ... ' he seemed to cast about for a phrase—'and that's ... what it is now. It hasn't changed. We have a way of life in the South that is ... our own. Hold yourself beholden ... have yourself ... be beholden to no man, and have no man beholden to you. That's the ... '

Ronnie's attention wandered at a fast trot. He glanced at Simon, who stood with her hands clasped in front of her and her head bowed in a religious sort of way. He was still trying to get in a remember-what-I-said look at her; so far she had not once met his eye. Over her left shoulder he could see the servant standing next to a large wall-mirror in a baroque silver frame, his tray of drinks on a marble table at his side. Next to him was Hoskins, the Negro butler, in a formal pose like Simon, but military rather than ecclesiastical. And now, over Simon's right shoulder, Lord and Lady Baldock came into view round the curve of the staircase. At once Hoskins turned towards an archway and snapped his fingers. Out of sight, the popping of a champagne cork answered him within seconds. By the time the Baldocks were advancing on Ronnie and his two companions, who were situated exactly beneath the dome in the centre of the hall, a second servant, with a tray that bore only a champagne glass white with frost and an ice-bucket containing an open half-bottle of champagne, was also approaching, Hoskins and the first servant at his side. The front-door bell rang; a third servant moved briskly up the hall.

'Hallo,' cried Lady Baldock, evidently in a genial mood, for the warmth of her smile went down by no more than a bare couple of therms when she moved it along to Ronnie. A moment later, however, it departed altogether. 'What's happened to my champagne? Why is there always this delay? I want it now.'

'Right here, your ladyship.' Hoskins lightly pushed the relevant servant forward and nodded to the other, who extended his tray to Lord Baldock.

'I was just saying, Juliette,' yelled Mansfield, 'that in these parts the traditional American way of life is still practised in the way it was ... practised when our nation first became a nation. In the past. Around here a gentleman is still a gentleman. We ... '

He went on for several minutes, austerely sparing of fact and often of simple denotation, vociferating his way almost without pause through the arrival of Parrot and two friends of his and the introduction of these, nodding suspiciously with no pause at all when Hamer and Vassilikós and three more house guests joined the group. None of the dozen or so persons gathered round Mansfield made any attempt to interrupt him or move away. Collectively, they paid him the mildly curious attention of a street crowd watching a man who has proclaimed that he will shortly take off his shirt without removing his jacket. The servants hurried to and fro.

'*And*,' shouted Mansfield finally, using this particle for the twentieth time as an indication that he had more to say, however long it might take him to decide what it was, '*and* ... we've solved the Negro problem. By realizing there is no problem, except keeping 'em down. That's what I said, keeping 'em down. They're inferior, they always will be inferior, and we in the South have the honest-to-God common sense to realize it. There's your so-called Negro problem solved. Simple.'

None of the servants present gave any sign of having heard, though even those as far away as the kitchens, the dining-room, the cellars must have done so. Hoskins, at his post by the wall-mirror, was motionless in the at-ease position. Ronnie barely noticed. His brain was in turmoil. He was experiencing an emotion, a desire, a thought—whatever it was, it was altogether new to him, remote, unpredictable by any intuition or technique, as if it had suddenly dawned upon him that what he had always most wanted to do was to induce a naked girl—or possibly a girl naked but for a transparent mackintosh—to stand before him while he pelted her with cream buns. All at once he knew what this sensation was. It was pure, authentic, violent sentiment of a liberal or progressive tendency.

'The only way to keep the Negro in his place is by *fear*. The only argument he understands is the *lash*.'

'Balls,' said Ronnie loudly.

'Pardon me?'

'Oh, come on. You heard. *Balls*. What you're saying is *balls*. Rubbish, nonsense, tosh, junk. And also extremely offensive, barbaric, inhumane, foolish, ignorant, outmoded and in the circumstances unforgivably rude.'

After an instant of silence, Lady Baldock said, 'I'll handle this, Student,' and moved across the circle until she was standing very close to Ronnie. Her lower lip drooped down from her teeth in a surprising way.

'I take it you're drunk.'

'Not in the least,' he said. 'I wish I were.'

An amateur would have held the next bit back for a knock-out blow; Lady B. used it to put the opposition irremediably one down from the start. 'Surely, since you stole all that wine before luncheon, you must have—'

'I may have helped myself to a—'

'Burke-Smith watched you drink six glasses, which is a whole bottle ... '

'That little red-haired—'

'... and he's searching your room now for the whisky.'

'The *whisky*?'

'There are three quarts missing from the buttery.'

'I bet I know where they've—'

'We need not discuss the matter any further. It's not my way to raise an inordinate stir over a few bottles of liquor. In any event, it's my view that you're to be pitied.'

For once in his life, Ronnie was at a loss, for words and everything else. At the disavowal of inordinate stir, Vassilikós flinched slightly, as if someone had gently dashed a few drops of water across his face. Hamer, very grave, was evidently in full agreement about the pitiable aspects of Ronnie. In different ways, puzzlement seemed to hold Mansfield and Lord Baldock firmly in its grip. Simon had not raised her head.

'However,' continued Lady Baldock, articulating over her bottom lip as before, 'what I won't tolerate is your behaviour to Student a moment ago. Fortunately I'm in the position of not having to give my reasons. Leave my house.'

'What ... you mean now?'

'Hoskins! As soon as is reasonable. You may have time to change and pack your suitcases. A taxi will be at the door in fifteen minutes. Hoskins, arrange it.'

'Right away, your ladyship.'

'There's an aeroplane to New York City at eight twenty; you'll be in plenty of time for that. Alternatively there are hotels in the town. Now go.'

'Zooliette, the poor sap was only ... '

'This is none of my business, of course, but I can't help thinking ... '

'Hell, Juliette, on Thanksgiving ... '

'Darling, a mere difference of opinion ... '

That lip of Lady Baldock's, still in the lowered position,

lengthened and grew rigid. 'Within these four walls I have things the way I want them.' She turned to Ronnie to order him from the room, but was distracted by the sudden appearance of the small red-haired butler, arrived rather behind cue after his search of Ronnie's bedroom.

'Well?'

'Nothing, your ladyship.' The man concealed most of his regret. He had intended to produce an incriminating bottle, as much out of simple dislike of Ronnie as to strengthen the cover for his own pilfering, but had not been able, at such short notice, to lay his hands on one of the right brand. He had been too drunk at the time of finishing them to remember now what he had done with the three original empties.

'Huh.' Lady Baldock again prepared to serve instant notice on Ronnie, who stood his ground in a torpor of bafflement, and was again forestalled: Simon burst out crying in a particularly noisy way, wailing very loudly when she drew in her breath.

'Oh, God, I can't stand that racket. Someone ... Chummy, take her up to her room, will you? Now ... '

But by this time Ronnie was half ready for her. 'I mustn't let you keep me. Well, it's been fun.' He searched the limited available regions of his brain for an exit line, without success. 'So long, all, then. See you in London, Bill.'

'So long, old boy.'

As when about to leave Malakos, Ronnie decided to postpone thought as far as possible until there would be nothing else to do but think. He changed into his grey man-made-fibre travelling suit and had started to pack when there was a knock on his bedroom door. George Parrot came in, a drink in each hand and a curious bulge under his dinner-jacket that turned out to be a bottle of Scotch.

'Stash this in your baggage. You've paid the penalty so you might as well commit the crime. I'd have brought the whole three but I couldn't carry 'em.'

'Thanks. Wasn't it a risk for you?'

'No. A whole raft of guests just arrived and she's doing her stuff with them. Well, Appie my boy, you certainly did it. A little on the short side, but by the living Christ it was sweet. Kind of an expensive gesture for you,' – Parrot settled himself on the bed – 'being consigned to the outer darkness like this. Still, you got through to old Student all right. You weren't watching him after her ladyship decided to take part in the discussion, which is understandable. The guy was like a landed fish. Nobody's told him balls in fifteen years. Well ... this washes you up, I guess. You'd need tanks and artillery to blast your way through to Simona now.'

'I guess that, too.' Ronnie snapped the catches on one of his suitcases and turned to the other. 'I should have kept my big mouth shut.'

'Hell, it wouldn't have made any difference. Juliette would have found a way. Very inventive woman. It doesn't matter what she does, you understand. There's nobody around to say she's wrong, except God, and his voice don't carry worth a damn. You going right up to New York tonight?'

'Yes.'

'Wise decision. Best thing is buy yourself a piece of hind-end to help you through the long, long night. More fun than any sleeping-pill.'

'Piece of what? Oh, you mean ass and all that. I'll see how I feel.'

'Do that.' Parrot swung his legs. He had plenty of room

for this, not because he was short in the shank, but because the bed itself (for what Ronnie had earlier suspected to be some horrible colonial reason) stood unnaturally high off the floor. Drinking, Parrot looked over the glass at him with sardonic commiseration. 'I don't know why, but it's surprising to me that you such a nigger-lover. I wouldn't think you'd have found it worth your while.'

'It hasn't been, has it? Anyway, that had nothing to do with me saying what I said. I just wanted to put bloody Student down somehow.' At this stage, such was Ronnie's honest view of what his motive had been.

'And you got such good results I feel I should take up the practice myself one of these days. If you could just have seen the way his eyes went ... '

Ronnie shut his second case. Like its fellow, it was barely half-full. A little personal shopping expedition at Kennedy Airport had been planned for the return trip. Well, he would have plenty of time for that now. He handed Parrot the torn-off back-jacket-flap of *LBJ—Tool of Fascism*, on which, with some difficulty because of the insane glossiness of the paper, he had written, 'Sorry about everything. Don't forget what I said to you in the office. Look after yourself. Love, R.'

'Would you give this to Simon? I don't imagine she'll be on hand for any big farewells.'

'I'll see Simona gets it right away,' said Parrot, putting the slip of paper into a pocket and draining his glass. 'Well, I imagine you about ready to get on to the next stage of your whirlwind turn-around.'

'Yes.' Ronnie began to pick up his luggage.

'Drop that. I'll get one of your coloured brethren to fetch them down.'

'Won't Juliette have given them orders not to do that kind of thing?'

'I have a way with your coloured brethren. Not a way you'd care for, Appie, my old pinko, but a way. Let's get going.'

Three minutes later, after passing through a deserted, quarantined hall, Ronnie stood at the front door with the small red-haired butler. Without having said goodbye, Parrot had suddenly been not there.

'Your luggage is in the taxi, sir.'

'Thank you, Burke-Smith. I'm not going to tip you, because I've only been here twenty-four hours, and it would be quite frightening to compute what I'll have done for your future refreshment. That Mr Appleyard, my lady, that's where the case of Napoleon brandy went.'

'What a mind you have, sir. If I may say so with all respect, you understand this sort of thing. Of course, you overstate matters, I'm sorry to say. Her ladyship and I understand each other. But you have the main drift. It's a clear night, sir. A little chilly, but excellent visibility. First-class flying weather. Goodbye, sir.'

The taxi-driver was a young Negro in a check suit, capless and badgeless. 'How are you?' he asked, and in no mechanical fashion either.

'Not too bad,' said Ronnie, rather surprised. 'How are you?'

'Listen, you want me take you some place?'

'The airport.'

'Fort Charles International Skyport?'

'That's the one.'

'All right.'

They began moving slowly between the parked cars under glaring illumination from lights on the outside of the house and on poles spaced a few yards apart, then halted for a minute or more while a new arrival made its cautious way out of the wooded part of the drive and passed them. Once they were among the trees the night closed in firmly and thickly. Ronnie lit a cigarette. He remembered with self-reproach that his book of addresses and telephone numbers was sitting on the table back in his flat. How absurd of him to have been so sure he would not need it on this trip. Alternatively, how could he have been so remiss as never to have memorized the names of any of his pieces of hind-end in New York? He worked on this briefly, trying to recall what came after Marilyn and before Bigelow, then gave up. A more serious trouble was that he could not remember fat Susan's telephone number, which had recently been changed as well as having had its letters taken away from it. Working on this one, at some length, deferred the thornier problem of whether it would be possible (and morally defensible) to get her out of her flat and round to his flat, there to await a second call from him with his telephone-number book before her. He would not reach the airport before seven, which must be midnight or even one a.m. in London. By that time, the surly Pole who lived above might refuse to admit her, and oh God, thought Ronnie, he was not absolutely sure he had left the second key in its place on the lintel above the interior door of the flat. Oh God ...

Apart from the shape of the driver and the glow from his dashboard, there was not much to be seen but headlights, tail-lights and, above the horizon, a shifting aurora of nebulous colour from the town. Not a moment's worth of distraction anywhere. He struggled conscientiously on for a bit with Marilyn something and something Bigelow, then with no apparent transition found himself thinking entirely about Simon, not thinking in any remotely constructive way, just having her in his head. Then feelings rather than thoughts came dimly up into his mental field of view: never really had a chance, could have done so much better, that bitch, that bastard, and, above all, oh *God* ...

Abruptly and unexpectedly he had distraction in plenty, so much of it indeed that for a moment or two he could not make out its source. That phase passed as quickly when he noticed that the car that had been overtaking them, doing perhaps sixty-five to their sixty, was cutting in ahead much too soon to allow them to continue at their former pace, and that the taxi-driver appreciated this and was braking hard and shouting unintelligibly, and that the car in front was continuing to move over to the right and forcing the taxi to do the same, and that they were leaving the roadway at what was still quite a smart pace with a lot of noise from the wheels, and that the taxi was now very near the car, and that there was a tremendous jolting, and that they had stopped.

'Shit, man,' said the taxi-driver with transparent sincerity. 'What does that mother think he's doing? Damn near got the whole lot of us killed.' He rolled down his window, leaned out and spoke up. 'Come on back here, man. Son of a bitch, Jesus, mister, you lost your marbles or what?'

In his present mood, Ronnie was prepared to let the incident go, take it as just another part of life's pageant, Southern life's anyway, so that he half accepted it as an enacted rebuke for speeding, perhaps, with a couple of shot-gun blasts and a tear-gas grenade or two about to be added for emphasis. Then he saw Simon Quick, wearing her white-and-gold silk dress, theatrically illumined in the taxi's headlights and walking towards them. It was a second or so before he discarded the notion that she was somebody who had just happened to be passing by. Then he realized that she must have been driving the car that had stopped them. At the same time he dully saw a lot of bushes and grass and generic greenery and stuff farther off. She approached briskly and peered in the open window.

'Ronnie, is that you?'

'Yes.'

'Oh, super.' To the driver, who had not made a sound since catching sight of her, she said in her Southern accent, 'I'd like you to bring this gentleman's baggage over to my car. He'll be riding with me.'

With great deliberation Ronnie got out. He held on to the side of the cab and stared at Simon.

'I hope I didn't scare you,' she said.

'Oh no, it happens to me every day. What was the idea?'

'I know, but it was the only way of stopping you. I tried hooting and flashing my lights and everything at a taxi farther back and he just drove on, so I had to do this to him. He was very nice about it. His passengers weren't, though. Jolly lucky I only needed to do two to find the right one.'

They reached the car she had been driving. It was large and of some American make.

'Is this yours?' asked Ronnie, who was still running on semi-automatic.

'No, it belongs to George, George Parrot.—Would you put them in the back seat, please?'

'Does he know you've got it?'

'Oh yes. We sort of worked it out together, about me chasing after you. He said to go straight to the airport but I thought that would take too long. Any minute they're going to find out I've gone.—Thank you very much.'

'Thank *you*, ma'am. Good night.'

'How much did you give him?'

'Twenty dollars. Don't stand there.'

'Sorry. Christ, anybody would think you weren't rich.

So you're coming with me after all. We'll have to go to the airport. We could go to another one, couldn't we? She can't cover the whole of the South.'

'No good, I'm afraid.' She backed the car away from the considerable tree that stood a couple of feet in front of its bumper, and drove it back on to the road. 'I couldn't get my passport. She keeps it locked up with hers and Chummy's. I had to slip out with just a purse.'

'Then where are you coming with me to? Are you coming with me? Where are we going?'

'Place called Old Boulder State Park, just across the line in Tennessee. She won't even have heard of it.'

'Look, if you think I'm going to have myself driven a couple of hundred miles to spend the night in a bloody tent ... '

'There are little log cabins and there's everything there and it's only about eighty miles. It's a gorgeous place.'

'I see. Hey, calm down, for God's sake,' said Ronnie animatedly, as Simon pulled out to pass a car that was itself going at a speed he considered quite break-neck enough. 'She can't have got any roadblocks set up yet.'

'Want to get away from here.'

Her voice had carried the first hint of drone since their reunion. Accordingly, he switched to another tack in which he had an honest interest. 'What about eating? Anything planned?'

'I have the whole thing worked out,' she said, back to full energy. 'First we go and shop ... '

'Won't everything be shut today?'

'Nathan's is always open. We can get everything there. Then we grab a bite at the Home of the Whopper ... '

'What in Christ's name is that?'

'Hamburger joint. It's the best sort of food around here.

There isn't a decent restaurant nearer than Memphis. Well, then we drive up to Old Boulder and we spend the night. Then tomorrow we'll go down to Andiamo, that's the town, about five miles away on the other side of the lake, and we'll do a real shop: clothes and things. I've only got what I stand up in.'

'Well, you won't be needing anything to lie down in.' Belatedly, Ronnie had come out of his mild shock. For the last half-minute he had been listening intently to Simon while wishing very hard that he could touch her. He knew her reactions quite well enough, however, to be in no doubt that so much as to touch the back of her hand with a finger-tip would have an untoward effect, like sending them across the dividing strip and into the oncoming traffic at eighty miles an hour. But just then Simon brought them to an abrupt and reluctant halt at the first traffic-lights at the edge of the town, so he grabbed as much of her as he could and kissed away like fury. She met him fully halfway. It was their best kiss yet, and he felt more triumphant than he could bother to try to remember feeling in his life before.

'Beautiful Simon.'

'Darling Ronnie.'

'You cried when she sent me away.'

At the corner of his eye the light went amber; she was back behind the wheel and had got them on the move before it had gone green.

'Actually it wasn't that,' she said. 'Oh, I was sorry all right. I felt awful. But what made me cry was seeing that she'd sent you away so as to hurt me. She kept looking at me. She does hate me.'

'Anyway, you've finished with her now.'

'Let's talk about it tomorrow.'

Ronnie had thought that of course Nathan's would not be open. To have thought this implied a view of Simon he instantly condemned as superficial, unworthy of one who knew her as well as he did, when she drove the car up in front of a gigantic building using up about as much light as the city of Warsaw, wide open, and called Nathan's. They went in. Nathan himself, or his local plenipotentiary, was in attendance at the check-out. Nobody but one or the other would have been talking as loudly as he was—fully three-quarters of Mansfield's working volume—or smoking a cigar with such ferocious smacking noises. He suspended both activities like a knife when he caught sight of Ronnie and Simon. With a gesture recalling innumerable films he drew his cigar slowly from his mouth and turned on a narrow stare. Ronnie was struck by the fancy that Lady B. had already managed to have had circulated photographs and full descriptions of the wanted couple. Nonsense, but nonsense that made more sense than a lot of sense did, a well-merited tribute to her not altogether explicable powers over the morale of those she came into contact with. It would not be going too far to say that she tended to get you down.

Simon, moving fast, was already loading a kind of robot's perambulator with goods: a dozen cackle fresh eggs, two transparent packets of finest hickory-smoked Canadian bacon, a cardboard carton containing a homogenized mixture of pure farm cream and tuberculin-tested Jersey milk, and comparably lauded quantities of Wisconsin cheddar cheese, English muffins, butter, wheat cookies, instant coffee, grapefruits, oranges, lemons, Oxford marmalade, tabasco, pepper, oysters in a round box, oyster stew in a tin.

'What's all this oyster thing?'

'Snack before we go to bed. We won't be settled in our

cabin till after eleven o'clock. They aren't as good as the British ones, but I can make us a real thick stew that won't taste like it was canned at all. If you want beer it's over there. Get me a six-pack of cokes. Regular, not calorie-reduced.'

By the time Ronnie rejoined her bearing the requested cokes, some of the beer that made Milwaukee famous, some club soda to put in the Scotch that Parrot had stolen for him, and some ginger beer to remind him of home, she had added to her store some coffee ice-cream, some melba raspberry sauce, a fruit-squeezer, a kitchen knife, a toothbrush, a packet of dental stimulators, a hair-brush in a box of what looked like rock crystal, and a green sweater in a plastic wrapper with lots of instructions about how to wash it and hang it up.

While a white girl jabbed at adding-machine buttons and a coloured boy filled a cardboard box with their purchases, Nathan first inspected these, then Ronnie and Simon afresh. Without removing his cigar he said, indistinctly on that account,

'Folks planning on a trip?'

Ronnie nodded.

'Aim to do some fishing? Where you headed?'

'No. Florida,' said Ronnie, and immediately heard Nathan, on an inaudible sound-track, declaring that sure he was sure, lieutenant, folks said they was headed down to Florida. 'Miami Beach, as a matter of fact.'

'You be needing plenty dollars down there. You understand? Dollars? You know about dollars? You British, ain't you?'

'Yes. Thank God.'

'Hey? Can't see no tea here. If you British, where's your tea? You forgotten it? We carry tea, you know. You like me to get you some?'

'No thank you,' said Ronnie quickly, before the man could ask him if he knew Bill Hamer. He picked up his change. 'We're off.'

'Long ways to Miami Beach.'

'That's what I like about it. Cheers.'

'Come see us again.'

'In a pig's arse I'll come see him again,' said Ronnie outside. 'Why didn't I tell him? Shall I drive? No, I haven't got a licence for here. You drive.'

'Are you all right? You sound funny.'

'Bit tired for some reason. I didn't want to drive anyway. We've got a tremendous amount of thinking and talking to do.'

'Needn't do it now. We've plenty of time.'

'Yes. Anyway, I love all this.'

He put an ill-advised hand on her knee for a moment and the car bounded out among the traffic as if powered by turbo-jets. Horns blew when this was noticed.

'Sorry. I love it too.'

'That's all right. Good. Eighty miles, you said.'

'More like a hundred really. Didn't want to make it sound a long way. Sorry.'

'That's all right. I might go to sleep later. Are you British or American? Passport, I mean.'

'I have dual nationality. But let's talk about it tomorrow.'

'That should make it easier to get you another passport. Or will it make it harder? Tomorrow's Friday. They'll be shut on Saturday. I've got to go on Sunday. We should have flown to New York.'

'Tomorrow.'

'What's Eric going to say? What's that bloody place, for Christ's sake?'

'Bel-Adieu Home of Rest.'

'Must be an airfield or a baseball ground or something. All those sodding arc-lights ... '

'It's a cemetery.'

'Nonsense,' said Ronnie firmly. 'No tombstones.'

'They're all flush.'

'Flush?'

'Flush with the earth. So that the motor-mowers don't have to go round them.'

'Good God, how British can you get?' said Ronnie, and fell asleep. He dreamed about the landlord of the White Lion at home, then about the Minister he had made not seem to give a shit for old people. The jolting of the car woke him.

'What?'

'You've had a lovely sleep. We're nearly there. This is the mountain road out of Andiamo.'

'Aren't old boulders all?' Ronnie fumbled for a cigarette. 'I mean old boulders all? Jesus, I mean all boulders old? What made them name a bloody park after this one, I wonder?'

'They found scratches on it.'

'Scratches? Big deal. They must lead pretty sheltered lives, American boulders. Sure there weren't some chips out of it too?'

'You must learn to listen, Ronnie. I don't want you getting like Chummy. No, all right. They're cavemen scratches. Kind of old-fashioned writing.'

'I see. Yes, I suppose it would be a bit outmoded these days.' Ronnie stared ahead, where everything was either very bright or very dark and there was no sign of anything. Because he was thirsty and still sleepy and in medium-grade need of a pee, he hoped that they would arrive somewhere eventually, but in other respects he was content. He asked himself, not very urgently, how much

Simon knew: about things like facts, for example. Her rough implication that U.S. cavemen might well have not been around in force at the time of the first Gold Rush, say, had not greatly surprised him. It was a rich-girl sort of phenomenon. He remembered his donkey-faced love of the old days holding, and holding on to, the view that the painter Van Gogh was at the time in question [1962) working in Paris on a Ford Foundation grant. Simon might easily turn out to be as far off on some comparable point, but she would yield in the face of evidence. That was how they differed. That and facially and so on.

Two low brick walls, flanking a non-existent gateway, came into the headlights. Ronnie was simultaneously welcomed to Old Boulder State Park and warned that it was illegal for him to possess beer in it. He said dreamily,

'What happened about the Home of the Whopper?'

'It's only a half-mile from Bel-Adieu and you were sleeping so soundly I didn't have the heart to wake you.'

'Oh, you shouldn't. I mean you should. What about you?'

'Oh, I was all right. I went in and got a hot-dog.'

'That's not much of a meal.'

'It was one of the foot-long ones and I had a cup of ketchup with it and an order of cole slaw.'

'I suppose that's a meal if you look at it in the right way,' said Ronnie, peering at a light that showed through trees.

'I thought you could make up with the oyster stew.'

'Sure. What happens now?'

'We go along to the office just along here and we check in.'

'With our marriage certificate and no-black-ancestors certificate and disbelief-in-evolution certificate.'

'Oh, they don't care. They're glad of anyone they can

get this time of the year. They have to stay open until the first snows by State law.'

'Who comes here in the last week of November, apart from refugees from Fort Charles and neighbourhood?'

'Fishermen and hunters and people.'

'Which were you on your last visit?'

'I was with a man, and he was much richer than you, but he wasn't nearly as nice, or as nice-looking, or as nice to me, and when we went to bed it was just as horrible as it had ever been if not more so, and you don't mind about him at all. Do you?'

'Yes I do. I mind a bit. Not minding at all would be wrong.'

'All right, just a bit, then.'

Most of the things in the office seemed to be for sale or hire: guns and parts of guns, rods and parts of rods, boxes of ammunition, belts and bandoliers in a style that set the mind running unwillingly on pioneer and frontier themes, hooks, lines, all sorts of stuff for getting dead animals and birds and fish from one place to another, and a magazine stand on which all the periodicals were of an outdoor persuasion except *Time* and *TV Guide*. While a man in a red-and-green tartan shirt and quite possibly deerskin trousers looked through his register in search of the relevant page, Ronnie's eye fell blearily on a manuscript notice mentioning night crawlers (50c doz) and spring lizards ($1.25 doz). This bothered him a little in some way he could not closely define. Then he reflected that whatever night crawlers might be they could not be so very formidable if they were less than half the price of these spring lizard characters, and cheered up again.

The man asked if they wanted a lakeside outlook and they said they did. Ronnie signed the book on behalf of Mr & Mrs G. F. Handel of Washington, D.C., was given a key attached to a small plank with carefully fretworked zigzag edges, listened to some halting directions, and turned to go.

'You from England?'

'Yes, and the car's loaded with tea, and we still play cricket, and yes, it's probably raining at this very moment, and the Queen was full of fun when I saw her last, and we're changing over to your side of the road soon. Good night.'

Burke-Smith's weather report had been entirely accurate, and yet had not gone nearly far enough. There was a slight chill in the air, but of a very good and original sort. No amount of extra expenditure could have improved the clarity of the sky and the stars and the tops of the trees. Some creature was making an infinitely harmless and non-assertive noise.

'Are you sure you're all right?'

'I love you,' said Ronnie, and braced himself in time, but even so teetered momentarily when Simon closed with him. The two of them swayed, once to and once fro, beside the car. He kissed her, thinking how she really never said anything when there was more than one person with her.

'Are you sure? Oh, I love you and I always will. I never told anybody that before. Just loving, I mean, not just the always part. Not that it matters. But I've got so much I want to tell you. But are you sure you love me?'

'Yes, and you'll have to do your telling in Cabin 8 before I forget where it is.'

Cabin 8 could be driven up to, but there was nothing to be seen anywhere near it except large quantities of vegetation and a neat stack of firewood; no lake. Ronnie hardly noticed this omission. He followed Simon indoors and looked round. Apart from a fireplace of rough stone and a brick chimney, the place was evidently constructed of pine planks. These too, however, were not points calculated to make a deep impression on Ronnie at the moment. He just about took in bunks, refrigerator, television set, cooker, bed, air-conditioner, sink, shower and lavatory, electric blankets, wash-basin, fire-extinguisher, and the fact that it was far from warm. After forty or so trips to the outdoors and back he had brought in all the groceries and luggage and a tremendous amount of wood. While Simon put things away, he poured her a coke and mixed himself a Scotch and soda. He was contemplating the empty fireplace, turning over the uniformly stout logs he had dumped there, and wondering whether there would be much to choose between *Drugs: the New Dissent* and *LBJ—Tool of Fascism* as combustibles, when he heard a motor vehicle approaching. Immediately he thought of Lady Baldock, but was too ashamed to mention this thought to Simon, who went on in the kitchen as before. The sound of the motor grew, became very loud, was throttled back just outside the cabin. Ronnie took up a defensive position next to the fire-extinguisher. After a short pause, some heavy and unimaginable missile crashed or burst against the front door. Physically and verbally, Ronnie's reaction was lavish. In one way or another he made a near-by chair fall over.

'Only the kindling,' called Simon.

'Who?' (Some Germanic wood-spirit by the sound of it.)

'The kindling. Stuff to get the fire going.'

'Oh.'

He got the fire going, and in ten minutes the cabin was comfortably warm. By that time, too, Simon had put her stew to stew on the stove, come out of the kitchen and snuggled herself up in his arms on the lower bunk.

'I meant to tell you I loved you ages ago,' she said. 'As

soon as I started to. Which was when we started going to bed together in that funny way in Greece. I know it was hell for you, all that, and I didn't like it either, but as a way of making me fall in love with you there couldn't have been anything to touch it. But I couldn't say anything, because you hadn't, and the man has to say it first. When did you fall in love with me?'

'As soon as I saw you. No, that's not quite right. After I'd talked to you for about half a minute. But I didn't realize I had until we were in Greece.'

'When in Greece?'

'When I realized that you were going to do everything you could to keep your promise to tell me the truth.'

'Oh.'

'What's wrong with that?'

'Thought you thought I was beautiful.'

'You know I think that, darling, you bloody fool. Listen to what I say. I fell in love with you because you're beautiful, but I didn't know I had at the time, I just thought I thought you were just beautiful, you see. Well ... Anyway, I realized later, but it all started with me thinking you were beautiful.'

'Sorry, okay, but it is important for a girl. And she's got to think the same thing about the man in a way. At least I know I have to. I mean I think you're attractive. I started thinking so in Greece. And at the same time I realized I'd never thought it before about anybody, all the time I was going on to myself about how super men were. What I really thought was that men didn't look very nice with their clothes on, you wouldn't feel like touching them unless you had to, but oh boy, that was nothing to how horrible they looked when they'd taken their clothes off. And felt. But you look nice. Even'—she put a friendly, demonstrating hand to his crotch—'all that, which I realize now I'd always thought was absolutely ghastly, with you it's not too bad. Not the Venus de Milo, but not too bad. I do love you, Ronnie. I'm jolly glad you said you loved me.'

'Good, but I might have picked a better time to tell you than just outside that office place, like now, or when we're in bed together.'

'Oh, I thought it was a lovely time. Much better than when you said it before, the night before last, but I know that was just so as to get me alone. I've never loved anybody before. You have, though, lots, I expect, haven't you?'

'Well, yes, in a way. I've certainly had lots of girls, and some of them lasted quite a long time, and I suppose I'd have said I'd been in love probably half a dozen times, I mean I'd have said that before you turned up. But now I don't really know what to say. I can't say I didn't really love any of them, because I think that's about the meanest thing you can do to a person, say you didn't love them when you did, even to someone else. But I went over them all in my mind the other day, and I couldn't honestly feel I'd loved any of them as much as I love you. So ... '

'What I can't understand is why you never married any of them. They can't all have not loved you or been married to husbands who wouldn't divorce them.'

Ronnie hesitated. Halfway through his previous speech he had become aware, to his vague and uncomprehending but not mild alarm, that nothing he had said to Simon in the last five minutes, or indeed the whole evening, had made him feel a shit. He sensed that this piece of self-discovery ought in some way to help him to answer Simon's implied question. And similarly, or perhaps not similarly, he ought to have a choice about what line to take, but could only think of one, short of changing the subject to orchids or Czechoslovakia, and he had hesitated too long for anything like that. Oh Christ, here we go. 'They weren't rich enough,' he said.

'Oh.'

'But I'm not going to marry you just because you are rich enough. That's how I started off, I admit. Or nearly started off. I didn't know it at the time, but I'd fallen in love with you before I knew you were rich. But in a way everything you said to me in that bloody temple thing that time, about me trying to get you to fall in love with me so that you'd want to marry me and I could have all your money, was true. I mean I thought it was true at the time, I could have sworn it was true. I decided you were beautiful. Then I was after you for your money. Then I ... started worrying about you. Then I fell in love with you. Or I realized that I had. Now I'm not a bloody fool, and I'll help you to spend a million quid very cheerfully indeed, but it doesn't matter. I'll take you in what you stand up in. Or lie down in. Do you believe me?'

'Dearest Ronnie, don't sound so anxious. Of course I believe you. Because I knew all of it all along. About the money. Well, I realize I did. But it's so marvellous that you've told me. It's like you saying you love me twice over.'

She gave him a kiss that made him wonder for a full second whether the bunk they were lying on might not have started to turn out to be one of the sort that drops you into a vat of boiling oil in the basement, then disengaged herself and got up.

'I must see to the stew. I tell you what you say to yourself about your other girls and me. You loved them and you love me, but you love me best. How's that?'

'Fine. Thank you.'

The stew was delicious, and Ronnie ate a lot of it, so

much that he just made it to the bed and got his clothes off before falling into a deep sleep, a state in which he continued for over nine hours. When he awoke he got quietly out of bed and put on his silver-blue Sulka dressing-gown, another of his standard butler-impressers (not that it had caused Burke-Smith any uncontrollable emotion). Strong sunlight was coming through the window. As soon as he had crossed to it he saw the lake, stretched out no more than a hundred feet below him, and in no niggling quantity either. Even where it fell into the shadow of the hills over at the far side, there was a lot of blue in the water. Several boats moved or stayed relatively still, one of them tied up at a small wooded island from which a line of smoke rose almost straight into the air. The collective sight filled him with so much energy that he almost had serious trouble preventing himself from climbing down the rocky slope and hurling himself into the lake, as if he were some clot in a boys' adventure story. Instead of that, he got the fire going, having intelligently put aside some of last night's kindling-wood for the purpose, and set about breakfast. This was the only meal he normally ate in at home, and he had got himself good at it, though it was something of a breach of tradition that he should be preparing it in person when there was a bird on hand for the job.

At the end of twenty minutes he had squeezed two tumblers of orange juice, prepared two halves of grapefruit, toasted four muffins, made a lot of coffee, poached four cackle-fresh eggs and fried eight strips of finest hickory-smoked Canadian bacon. All this, plus butter and marmalade, he arranged on a plastic tray got up to resemble, at some distance, a buffalo-hide shield, and carried it round the corner into the bedroom. Simon awoke, said 'How super' and sat up. She had finished her orange juice before, reaching out to put the glass down, she advertised her nakedness to Ronnie. He looked at her, and she looked back at him with an expression he had never seen on her face before. (Neither had anybody else, actually.)

It was a pity in a way, but there it was. By the time they thought of food again, the grapefruit was probably rather better than it had been, but all the other stuff was stone cold.

'I will next time,' said Simon. 'I very very nearly did. It was nice right from the beginning and it was lovely at the end. I know I will next time. If you don't mind doing the eggs and bacon again, I'll do the coffee and muffins and some more orange juice.'

After they had eaten, what was left of the morning soon went. While Simon drove into Andiamo to buy clothes and more food, Ronnie went over to the park office and did some vigorous telephoning, agreed to by the warden with Southern discourtesy. It was not very laborious to secure tickets for an evening flight from the nearest airport to New York, nor to make a hotel reservation there for that night and the one following. Tracking down old Cy Friedberg at H.C.F. Television was a different matter, not least because old Cy turned out to be working for All-American Television these days. But there, after talking to six different people, one of whom turned out after some minutes to be the restaurant manager, Ronnie finally reached old Cy and invited himself and Simon to lunch with him and his wife the next day. He consciously deferred revealing what was going to be old Cy's main historical role thereafter: helping Simon to screw a new passport out of the authorities and putting her on the first possible aeroplane to London. Wishing he had some Confederate currency to do it with, Ronnie paid off the warden, who had watched him throughout his conversations as if he expected him to vanish supernaturally or die before the cost of the calls could change hands.

It was a good half-mile along the dirt road back to Cabin 8. Ronnie passed in succession the children's playground, the swimming-pool, the tennis and badminton courts, the volley-ball pitch, all deserted and as far as possible dismantled at this time of the year, regardless of the weather. Beyond them, the woods closed in on either side: horse chestnut, oak, dogwood, maple, wild magnolia. A squirrel bounded away among the fallen leaves, moving by fits and starts as though in a badly animated film. Two blue jays flew at head height across the road; another bird, of undistinguished appearance, seemed to be trying to walk up an oak sapling. An urgent rustle at ground level signalled the departure of a small snake, its shiny brown tail-end waggling furiously.

'Time you were in bed,' said Ronnie. 'It's a quarter to December.' He appreciated the show being put on for him, and thought to himself that there were times when the consensus about Nature being all balls could seem too sweeping.

Parrot's car was parked in the port at the side of the cabin. Near the veranda of this, a lot of what looked exactly like Michaelmas daisies were growing. Ronnie picked a couple of dozen of these and approached the door.

'Who's that?' called Simon from inside.

'Only me.'

'Good, I was just ... '

They met at the bedroom doorway. Simon was wearing only her underclothes. Behind her a plain green cotton dress lay on the bed.

'I was just going to change into ... What lovely flowers. Where did you get them?'

'Just outside. Growing there.'

'Oh yes, I saw them. I'll put them in ... '

'Later,' said Ronnie. He went back and turned the key in the front door, dropping the daisies on to the seat of a brand-new rocking-chair. Then he took hold of Simon. Her response was that of a girl who simply wants what is coming, a different being from the stiff, shuddering, gasping personage he had encountered that first evening. It had come to seem impossible that anything could prevent him from satisfying her, when her body suddenly became motionless beneath his. Immediately he heard what he had, in a different sense, already been hearing for a quarter of a minute or so: a motor vehicle or vehicles, within fifty yards of the cabin and approaching. 'Just other people coming to stay,' whispered Ronnie, but she did not move. Neither did he now.

The cars, seemingly two of them, came nearer, slowed and stopped. Their engines were switched off. Doors were slammed. And then—what else?—they heard voices, footfalls reaching the raised wooden floor of the veranda, and a knock at the door.

'Who is it?'

'Police. Open up.'

The reason you get a lot of talk about premonitions, Ronnie reflected, is not because they have any sort of habit of being justified, but because it is so horrible when they are. His of the previous evening had, he was certain, come true. He called 'Coming' and, as he got off the bed, murmured to Simon without knowing why, 'Bloody nuisance. Mistake or technicality, but you'd better get dressed. I'll try to hold them.'

He put on his dressing-gown and approached the front door. Another knock came at the last moment. He noticed for the first time that there were no windows in this wall. After turning the key, he had only opened the door a little way when it was pushed wide and a number of men started coming in. One was a policeman in uniform and armed, and another was Lord Baldock, but Ronnie saw nothing distinctive about the other three, the eldest of whom now said,

'This him, Lord Baldock?'

'Yes. It's him.'

Ronnie had a glimpse of the park warden staring from the middle of the road before the policeman shut the door and stood with his back to it. The others moved into a sort of semi-circle. Simon's voice came from the bedroom.

'What's it all about?'

Two of the men nodded at each other. Ronnie called, 'Good old Chummy's come visiting. With some friends he's made in the police force.'

No response. Baldock made a movement with both hands and one shoulder that showed he deplored Ronnie's tone. He was clearly in charge. Nevertheless he was master of less than his usual frenzied self-confidence. After making a high-pitched sound similar in pitch and timbre to the hee part of a donkey's bray, he said,

'This is not going to be pleasant for any of us, Appleyard, and the more sensibly you behave and the sooner we finish the better. First of all ... '

Simon walked in from the bedroom wearing the green dress. Her small nipples were faintly to be seen through it; Ronnie reasoned that she must have skipped her brassière to save time. The same two men gave her an uneasy half-bow.

'Hallo, Simon. I want you to know this is for your own good.'

'Hallo, Chummy. What is?'

'Before I go into that, let me introduce these gentlemen.

Captain Monaghan ... Sergeant Eden ... Patrolman Calloway ... and this is Mr Fields, whom you've met, Simon. Now. Your mother has sent me to bring you home.'

'I won't come.'

'I think you will. If you don't, Appleyard will be arrested. Perhaps you'd care to explain the position, Mr Fields.'

'Certainly, sir. Mr Appleyard is liable to arrest under suspicion of having removed Miss Quick from her recognized parental household, an offence under a statute of Fotheringay County, of which Fort Charles is a part. He may also be in criminality under a statute of Hardcastle County of the State of Tennessee, in which we are standing at this moment. This statute prohibits the making of a false declaration – for instance, the giving of a false name – in the furtherance of immorality. In addition, Mr Appleyard has committed a Federal offence under the Mann Act, prohibiting the conveyance of a female over a State border for an immoral purpose. In fact, Appleyard,' said Fields, who was tall, 'you can take my word for it that we have you hog-tied real nice.'

Ronnie's main feeling was still incredulity. 'But this is like something out of ... Do you expect those charges to stand up in court, you durn fool?'

'We reckon as how they will, Miss Tappleyard,' said Captain Monaghan, who was short. 'Lord and Lady Baldock are mighty respected figures all over Fotheringay County, and anybody who does them a wrong ain't going to be liked very well.'

'What about the other bloody county, the one we're in now? You're not going to tell me they're mighty respected all over here too. We're a hundred miles away from –'

'Here in the South we used to giving and receiving full

mutual police co-operation,' said Sergeant Eden, who was fat.

'I bet you are. But even so ... And this Mann Act thing is a load of crap. I know about it—it was an anti-prostitution measure. All I've done is convey a female over the age of consent here and there for a fornicatory purpose. Or is that illegal too in this county? And you'd be insane to bring the F.B.I. into this. It wouldn't take five minutes before you were the ones in bloody criminality. Unless, of course, Lord and Lady Baldock are widely respected all over Washington, D.C. I suppose all that money is bound to earn a good deal of respect wherever it goes.'

'You dare talk that way,' said Patrolman Calloway, who was thin. 'You and you goddam fancy rig. Why, you just wait'll I get—'

'Quit that, Calloway,' said Eden sharply.

Fields broke in. 'You have one point there, Mr Appleyard. No prosecution under the Mann Act would be feasible in your case. But any report of even the possibility of such a prosecution would surely bring severe damage to your good repute. Coupled with the virtual certainty of your conviction under the two County statutes, this can hardly fail to weigh with you. I understand your employers may be sensitive on such matters. Most are.'

Correct: there were enough Christers on the average TV-company Board. Not that it was really necessary to pick on Christers. Even Ronnie Appleyard himself, with all his jet-age tolerance upon him, would think several times about employing a chap who might have been a white slaver. But still ... 'I can't believe you're serious,' he said, thinking hard. 'You're all taking terrible risks.'

'What risks would they be, Mr Appleyard?'

'I'll get a lawyer, I've got friends in the Press here, I'll appeal, bring actions—everything there is.'

'Sir, you appear to be under the misapprehension that there would be something irregular or ... unconstitutional about the way our law would deal with you. This is just not so. You have provably broken ordinances which are right there in the statutes of the counties concerned. Now you may think them antiquated, absurd. Well, so they are. But they're awful darn handy, eh, boys?'

The three policemen laughed.

'When were they last invoked?'

'Once this year already—the Fotheringay County statute. Two hundred fifty dollar fine, big fuss in the papers. Oh, he had journalists going in to bat for him, complaining about our use of outdated laws for purposes they weren't designed for, but he had to quit town just the same. Couple similar last year. You'd be surprised how similar those cases were to yours.'

'This is a malicious prosecution.'

'Sure is. You bet. Real mean.'

'Would be, Mr Appleyard, would be,' said Fields earnestly. 'Would be if brought. But if Miss Quick returns with us now and you stay away from her until you leave the jurisdiction of these officers, nothing more will be heard of the matter. I beg of you to take this course.'

'I'd have some pretty bloody good things to say about all this in court, and about the Baldock set-up. The way she—'

'No doubt you would have, if the cases were ever brought to trial. Though they would not appear in the Court record or in any Press report. In any event, this use of the conditional tense is an indication of—'

'All right. Look. Will you and these cops leave the three of us alone for a bit, so that we can talk the thing over?'

After some exchange of glances, Fields asked, 'No objection, Lord Baldock?'

'No.'

As soon as the door was shut, Ronnie said to Simon, 'Who did you tell, and why?'

'Don't get mad at me. Bish. In case Mummy got really upset. She can make herself ill, you know, honestly. Heart and things. It was just until we'd really got on our way. Don't be angry, Ronnie.'

'So that was why you couldn't find your passport.'

'No. But I should have broken open the cabinet where it was.'

'Yes. Yes, that was what you should have done.'

Both of them were trembling. Baldock said,

'Believe me, this is the best way, Simon.'

'Is Lady Baldock really ill?' Ronnie asked him.

'No.'

'Bish just went and told her. As instructed, no doubt.'

'No. Bish is Simon's uncle's second wife. Widow, rather. She has no money.'

'I see. Well, that about wraps it up, doesn't it?'

'Ronnie,' said Simon, who had started crying.

'What?'

'Why don't you just be arrested? Fight them? You could kick up an awful stink. That lawyer knows you could really. I was watching him. I'd help you.'

'Thanks, but apart from anything else it would mean the end of my job, because producers don't like their people to be facing morals charges in the United States when they should be broadcasting in London, and more than likely the end of my career too.'

'Only an old job.'

'Only an old ... ' Ronnie shouted, then held his breath for five seconds or so. 'Only an old career, too. I know. Yes, there's a lot to be said against it. Not as much as there is to be said against your step-dad's career, living with a female dinosaur of hatred and self-will because he can't face the alternatives of living in shit on a couple of thousand quid a year or getting an old job ... ' After a couple of huge inhalations, he went on, 'Sure, television's a horrible career, but it's the only one I've got.'

'You write books as well. You were telling me.'

'How rich you are, Simon, aren't you? How really tremendously rich. Ronnie Appleyard was doing quite well in his career at the age of thirty-six when he suddenly lost it. So he bought himself another one and started doing well at that instead. I'm going to get myself a drink. See you around, chaps.'

When Ronnie came back into the main room with a mahogany-coloured Scotch and soda, Simon had gone, but Lord Baldock was still there, thoroughly exercising his facial muscles.

'Appleyard, I don't want you to—'

'Don't bother to say anything at all, Chummy, old chum, because whatever it is I shall hate you for the rest of my life. Yes, I know you're only acting under orders, and if it had been left to you things would have been different. Not different enough to make a difference, but different. Just a minute.'

He loaded Baldock up with Simon's white-and-gold silk dress, sweater, stockings, brassière, toothbrush, dental stimulators and other articles from the cupboard over the wash-basin. They made a double-handed bundle.

'Yes, I know she can buy herself another gross of everything whenever she feels like it, but I don't like waste any more than your wife does. That's the lot, I think.' Ronnie opened the front door. 'Now bugger off.'

Simon had bought a lot of stuff for lunch: steaks, onions, beans, carrots, parsley, an avocado pear, olive oil, vinegar, salt, garlic, a bottle of Californian burgundy, a corkscrew. The food he carried a few yards into the woods, took out of its various containers, and dumped. The condiments he put into the kitchen cupboard. The wine and corkscrew he packed in his luggage. After lunching off whisky and ice-cream, he lay down on the bottom bunk and slept for a time. When he could not sleep any more he finished the whisky, walked to the park office, paid his bill, and telephoned to Andiamo for a car to take him to the airport. Early the next morning he was in London.

Four

LONDON

'Well, what do you think?' asked Ronnie Appleyard. 'We're a democracy—or at least that's what they keep telling us. We're supposed to be responsible people, able to choose what we'll read and see on the stage and the screen without some faceless official choosing for us. Recently there's been, as we've heard, a great drive towards freedom of expression in Russia—a ferment of new ideas, the restrictions, the old conservative attitudes being swept away or at least challenged, a creative explosion. Are we in this country so stuck in our traditions that we're going to fail to rise to this challenge? I can only say ... I hope not. Well, that's all from *Insight* for today. See you Wednesday. 'Bye.'

The title music, sounding as ever like what a man in

1955 had thought music was going to sound like in 1975, began its thrice-weekly assault. Ronnie mimed some chat with his guests, a bald, plump theatrical producer with cheeks like pears and a huge, wild-eyed novelist. They had been doing an arts spot on cultural freedom. The discussion had been first-rate: animated, relevant, marked by real as opposed to worked-up disagreement, with the producer maintaining that the artist was much freer in the various Socialist countries than he was under capitalist ideology, the novelist contending, on the other hand, that he (the artist) was only a bit freer as described. With one of his thoughtful, toiling pieces of sincerity, Ronnie had suggested that here, perhaps, for once ha-ha, the truth did lie somewhere in the middle. His compromise formula, describing the Russian writer, say, as *significantly* freer than his British counterpart, was eventually accepted by both sides in the dispute.

'Well, I hope we gave them something to think about,' said the producer.

'Oh, it was ... ' said Ronnie, waving his hand and shaking his head, as if adequately commending words failed him. In fact, words of any sort were nearly failing him. They had been doing that fairly regularly ever since his return from the U.S.A. over a fortnight ago. Not while he was on—he was too much of a professional for anything short of clinical aphasia or brain damage to affect him while he was on—but a hell of a lot of the time when he was not on. After an effort, he added now, 'Done our bit to wake them up to a vital issue.'

'Isn't it?' cried the producer. 'Isn't it just that? When I think of the way these horrible little men all over TV and the Press and everywhere go on assuring us that our system is unsurpassed and unsurpassable and ... I just can't see straight. The other point of view, the minority one, simply *must* be put. I'm wondering whether a public symposium to do just that couldn't be set up, on the lines of one of the Vietnam teach-ins. I wonder, I wonder whether I might not talk the Arts Council into putting up the cash.'

'That's what they're there for,' said the novelist, driving a hand like a diving-flipper through his hair.

Ronnie lit a cigarette. 'Oh, absolutely,' he said with conviction.

The final card on the monitor screen faded. 'Okay, studio, thank you,' called the floor manager. Ronnie and the other two got to their feet. The producer—not the bald, plump theatrical producer but the bearded, pig-skin- (this time) jacketed TV producer—approached with his wrists crossed in front of his chest, palms outward. This showed a high degree of approval, well above the vampiric arm-raising and second only to the clenched fists held close to the shoulders.

'Gorgeous,' he said in a high-pitched monotone. 'Perfectly gorgeous. Above a million heads but what of it? Genuine argument. The life-blood of our poor little infant art-form. Thank you so much, David and Peter. Lovely job, Ronnie. Hey, uh, Bill Hamer phoned down to the box for you a couple of minutes ago. Wants you to join him for a drink in Hospitality A—that's the one just across the bridge in the new building.'

Ronnie said he knew the one that was meant and took his leave. He had not seen Hamer since the latter's return from Fort Charles, having been unable to bring about a casual meeting. The thought of hearing news of Simon, even stale news, made him want to swallow repeatedly. He had had none of any kind since seeing the last of her. For the first few days back in England he had not felt like inquiring after her. Then he and fat Susan had run through all possible roles in which to telephone Eaton Square. Miss Quick was not at home. She was out of the country. Where? Out of the country. No, it was impossible to say when she would be back. None of the answering voices had been that of the small red-haired butler, which among other things suggested to Ronnie that the party was indeed still abroad, if no longer at Broad Lawns then in Johannesburg or Jakarta or wherever else they went in the winter. But they must return to London before too long, if Simon were to become Mrs Student Mansfield, for that union could be solemnized nowhere but in a London church. Ronnie had been watching the Forthcoming Marriages columns with great vigilance and not much sense of what he would do when the dreaded names came up. All he knew was that he was not going to give in, not yet, and could visualize himself there on the day, ready to throw the bride a kiss and the groom a grenade. But, so far, no sign.

Hamer was at the far end of Hospitality A, a long room with a black fitted carpet and an oversized gold (-plated, presumably) model of a television transmitting aerial system on a black marble plinth, the latter heavily embossed with the L.C.M. symbol. With him was Lord Ward, whom Hamer said he did so want Ronnie to meet. But it soon emerged that what he really so wanted was not to have had to waste time waiting for Ronnie after finishing with Lord Ward. So Ronnie helped himself to a Scotch and soda and sat about while top TV artiste finished with top TV power-wielder—such, at any rate, was Lord Ward's supposed standing, though even for an ex-trade unionist his comprehension rate seemed oddly low. In the past, Ronnie would have followed the conversation closely, in the hope of picking up some crumb of information damaging to a colleague or otherwise useful. But tonight he just sat about and drank his Scotch.

'Sorry about that, Ronnie,' said Hamer finally, more cantabile than ever at having not only finished with Lord Ward but virtually sent him packing. 'Get in your hair, don't they? Well, how are you? I haven't seen you since that incredible hassle at Broad buggering Lawns. Must have taken a bit of nerve, eloping with the daughter of the house like that. Our Lady B. was beside herself, of course, and that fellow Manson or whatever his bloody name is couldn't stop asking people what he'd done to have this happen to him. When they found out she'd gone, the outside guests were all sent home without any dinner, which may appeal to you. I had to fight like hell myself for a couple of slices of turkey, I'll have you know. Anyway, what happened? The girl was back the next afternoon, in a bit of a state as I gathered. If you want to talk about it, that is.'

'I'll tell you the whole story another time, Bill, if I may. It was all rather messy and painful.'

'Of course, I can imagine. God, what a household. That Chummy character is an odd son of a bitch, isn't he?' Hamer seemed to come to a small decision. 'He couldn't not have known what was going on under that aristocratic toffee-nose of his. Yes, I gave his good lady the most frightful hammering. Not in his bed, she wouldn't stoop to that, but on practically every other horizontal surface in that ghastly house. God ... '

'What was she like?'

'On the job? Fantastic. Rather on the lines of the daughter, from what you were saying to me. Quivering like a jelly the whole time. Shoving herself against you. Panting as if she was running a marathon. What was your phrase? Bloody wild-cat, wasn't it?'

'That's right. How extraordinary. Like mother like daughter. How did she seem the next day? The daughter, I mean?'

'Old boy, I never set eyes on her the whole of the rest of the time I was there. It looked as if she was kept in her room. Meals sent up, that type of thing.'

'Where is she now, do you know? And the rest of the shower?'

'As a matter of fact I do know, yes. They're in London, staying at Claridge's. The staircase in their house hasn't finished being painted or some confounded tommy-rot of that order. Which leads—'

'Is she with them? The daughter?'

'That's what I gathered,' said Hamer seriously, defeating Ronnie's expectation that the bastard would jovially josh him along at this point for nourishing a hopeless passion, etc. 'Friend Manson, is it? Mansfield, he's certainly along. Anyway ... Look, let me freshen that for you.'

By the time they had settled themselves side by side on a low couch upholstered in white corduroy, Ronnie had the picture. He said,

'But I thought it was going to be the immigration laws tonight.'

'Ah, Mr A., you're so sharp you'll prick yourself one of these days. Yes. Advertised programme cancelled: that'll be going out in a few minutes. Instead, because some of those taking part are so important that they can't make plans ahead of time, 'The Rich'. Who are these strange people who own so much more money than you have and are so much bigger shits? Taking part will be Kyril Vassilikós, Lady Baldock, the editor of the *Financial Observer*, and, a last-minute surprise, incisive commentator Ronnie Appleyard. I owe you something for that *Insight* spot next month, Ronnie. Jolly interesting, don't you think? I was right about there being more to it than just getting that shipping laddie on the show. When I found that out, I made it clear to her that there was more to getting her on the show than being promised infinite contacts and hearing what a bloody good chap I was. But I flatter myself that that had been part of the deal from the start in her mind. Well, you know the fee as well as I do. What do you say?'

'Well, it's very nice of you, Bill, and I appreciate it, but won't she refuse to go on as soon as she sees it's me? She doesn't care much for me, as you may have noticed.'

'A fair point, and one that had actually occurred to me. But I'm sure she'll appear. She's so crazy to be on the box, and in my programme, with all her friends watching, that she'd appear with Dick Nixon or Comrade Kosygin or anybody. Also, she probably thinks in her innocence that if it came to it she could obliterate you with no trouble at all. I've got a stand-by lined up anyway. Don't you worry.'

'Who's the stand-by?'

'Oh, one of these high-powered lords who coin money out of letting the public troop through their stately homes and grounds and what-not.'

'I see. But why me?'

'Sorry?'

'I mean I'm obviously going to do the kingest-size hatchet operation I can on her. That's not going to do you any good as far as she's concerned, and she's got lots of power you could use. What's the angle? Your angle?'

'Let's just say for now that that's how I want it. I'll tell you all about it after the show. Nothing startling actually, but I don't want you bringing it out in the heat of the moment on the air, and if I'm any judge there are going to be plenty of heated moments tonight. Should be good television. And I know,' said Hamer, who did know, because he knew Ronnie knew how ready with a writ was the protagonist of the Bill Hamer Programme, 'that you'll forget all that rather indiscreet stuff I was telling you just now about the carnal joys of Broad Lawns.'

'You can certainly rely on me there. Right. What time do you want me?'

'I think just for level and cues at nine forty-five to nine fifty. Well, it should be a fun show.'

'At least that. Thanks again, Bill.'

'A pleasure, dear boy.'

A little later, Ronnie learned that not only was Miss Quick not in her room, but a paging in all public rooms had failed to discover her. He considered. Quarter to eight. Clearly the whole gang had gone out somewhere to eat. Where? There was a good chance that Lady Baldock would be throwing a considerable party to precede her television appearance, in which case there were people likely to know where. Ronnie dialled the first digit of the home number of the gossip columnist of the *Sunday Sun*, then hung up. What could he do? Gallop into the Caprice or the Mirabelle and carry Simon off across his saddle-bow? This image somehow set off the tardy realization that Simon would almost certainly be among the studio audience used by Hamer to help him show off his humility and other valuable qualities. There was a danger, Ronnie perceived, that he would start staring fixedly at Simon and dry up for the rest of the programme. Better watch that.

He went over the road to the Flower of India (Indian, Pakistani, Chinese, Malayan and English dishes a speciality). Here there was a good deal of luxury treatment and Mr-Appleyarding, but he hardly noticed. Noticing that he had hardly noticed disturbed him slightly. It went with being constantly on the verge of not being able to think of anything whatever to say to people. While he chewed Bombay duck, sipped lager and waited for his chicken biriani, Ronnie thought he saw what had happened to him. He had begun by using niceness, tenderness, what you will, as a specific aid in the Simon situation, as one of the purest means to an end in all history. And then, frighteningly soon, in fact, unknown to himself, he had started enjoying being nice to Simon, started using tenderness as an end in itself, got hooked on the bloody stuff, in fact. Then, over Scotch and dry ginger in the Duke of Marlborough down the hill, he thought he saw that he had indeed awakened the Sleeping Beauty, and now here he was not only stuck with her, but, far more alarming, wanting to be stuck with her, wishing he were stuck with her in a real sense instead of just being unable to stop thinking about her. That chap in the legend had had better luck. He too might originally have intended nothing more than a quick thrash and away, but at least he had been allowed to keep the girl he had awakened, instead of handing her over to the King of the Bastards.

Nine thirty. A mild night for the second week in December. He strolled back up the hill to the studios, not thinking or seeing anything much by this time, but savouring the glow of adrenalin at the approach of Appleyard v. Baldock. He had lost all the Aways, like a bloody fool, but this Home fixture would retrieve his honour, if nothing else.

The huge scaffolding-and-brick cylinder of Studio 3A seemed almost deserted. As usual when a live transmission is impending, those few technicians and helpers present seemed sunk in apathy or gloom, quite resigned to the futility of even attempting to get the show on the air. A lighting man shook his head wearily at some fresh arrangement of floods proposed to him; a sound man pushed a microphone boom out of his path and left the floor, apparently for ever. The half-dozen rows of audience seats, in their comfort and general style recalling a third-division football grandstand rather than anything theatrical or cinematic, were empty but for a single brown-overalled inferior, asleep or in a terminal coma. The floor manager, earphoned ears cocked for a message from on high, led Ronnie over to a number of low chairs grouped round the throne Hamer would occupy. All the seats were occupied by nonentities set there merely to have cameras lined up on them. Ronnie's substitute vacated his with perceptible ill grace, as if shabbily discriminated against. Ronnie sat down and lit a cigarette. As always, he had timed it right, was psychologically well placed to confront Lady Baldock.

Five minutes passed in conversational silence, with a few crashes and rumbles from various apparatus. Then, in a bunch, the principals appeared and approached: Hamer escorting Vassilikós and Lady Baldock, the producer of the show putting some point to Sparks, the financial journalist, Lord Ward and another director of the company bringing up the rear, presumably just to shoe-horn Lady B. into her chair. She was certainly looking at her queenliest in a pleated orange dress, with hair-do featuring a rope of coloured stones and many more of these at half a dozen other places. She saw Ronnie.

It would have taken a finely graduated stop-watch, expertly wielded, to register the interval of hostile astonishment before the gracious smile came on.

'Hallo, Ronnie. Fancy seeing you here. Though I don't know why I say that, television being your natural habitat. But nobody gave me any idea that you were going to be on the show tonight.'

'I didn't know myself until after the run-through,' said Hamer with that wonderful air of just happening to turn out to be smooth that Ronnie despaired of equalling. 'I think I mentioned that we were having trouble filling the fourth chair at short notice. Bernard couldn't do it after all, the next choice, whom I'm sure Ronnie won't mind my saying I'd rather have had than him,' and here Hamer paused to allow the little shit time to do some pretending not to mind, 'flew out to Laos yesterday, and my long-stop was so deadly dull that when I ran into Ronnie just coming out after his own show and found he was free, well, quite frankly I grabbed him. Now, Juliette, if you'll just come over this way, I'm afraid the next few minutes are going to be a bloody awful bore, but then we can relax and ... '

The two receded. Vassilikós, evidently just down from Mount Olympus in a purple velvet dinner-jacket, came amiably over to Ronnie.

'Nice to see you again, my dear Jap.'

'How are you, Mr Vassilikós?' Ronnie let him have one of the impulsive handshakes. 'You're certainly looking very well.'

'Oh, well, thank you, nothing but well. Business is good, but it's nothing but good. That's not enough in our life, I'm always saying. We must be looking for something more. But how are things with you? You seem to me a little down in the mouth, a little sad, no?'

'I'm all right. Had rather an exhausting day.'

'Jeer up, it will pass. Tell me, it's your reputation to be the great television ... hatchet-man, isn't it? That's true?'

'I suppose so, among other things, I hope.'

'Of course, of course. Then who are you hatcheting tonight? Not me, I hope?'

'Good God no, why should I? Actually this isn't really that kind of show. More of a discussion on equal terms, with—'

'Sure, sure. It seems I must go. Let's have a drink afterwards.'

'I'd love to. Good luck, Mr Vassilikós.'

'And the same to you.'

It was not until now that Ronnie had had attention to spare for the studio audience, now being driven into its seats by attendants dressed like police inspectors. At once he picked out Lord and Lady Upshot, a moment later the Saxtons, finally Mansfield, looking fatter than ever in a hospital-blue dinner-jacket. For the moment, at any rate, Simon was nowhere to be seen, neither was Lord Baldock. Perhaps they were in the box, though if Ronnie knew MacBean, the producer of the show, they would not stay there long.

Hamer leaned down from his throne. 'Chaps, could you just sort of chat about nothing for a couple of minutes, so that we can check the voice levels and so on? Don't sit stock-still. You're talking, not performing.'

'Okay, Bill,' said Ronnie loyally. 'Uh ... Lady Baldock, is your daughter going to be in the audience tonight?'

'No, I'm afraid not.' Lady Baldock spoke from Hamer's right hand, diagonally opposite Ronnie. 'She said she felt too tired, but she and my husband will be watching the programme where we're staying.'

'How is she?'

'Very well indeed, thank you.'

'Are friends of yours present here tonight, Mr Sparks?' asked Vassilikós, keeping up the conversation-class feeling.

Sparks made some reply, was asked about financial journalism, and went on in the same style with the other two while Ronnie brooded, then gave himself a five-second mute rehearsal.

'I hear your daughter's getting married, Lady Baldock,' he said.

'Always well informed, Mr Appleyard.' With this went

a splendid peaches-and-vinegar smile. 'Yes, the Tuesday before Christmas, at St Paul's, Knightsbridge, Wilton Place. A very small affair. Just the family and friends.'

'Thank you, chaps,' said Hamer, 'that's exactly what I wanted. All complete now. On the air in nine minutes. Relax until then. And stay as relaxed as you can.'

Ronnie drank water, smoked, and exchanged a remark or two with Vassilikós on his right and Sparks directly opposite. He was never nervous in the stage-fright sense, but tonight he felt that something disagreeable was going to happen. He hoped, remembering the Old Boulder affair, that he was not in for a string of justified premonitions.

Eight and a half of the nine minutes went. Everybody suddenly became military and responsible. Even Mansfield, whose bellows of inquiry or puzzlement had filled the air from time to time, was heard no more.

'Nice and quiet, studio,' said the floor manager.

'Good luck, everybody,' said Hamer, with the charming smile that told of a great load of responsibility cheerfully borne.

'Ten, nine, eight, seven ... '

A tinned voice shouted, 'London Counties and Midlands Television brings you truth and laughter, wisdom and wit, in ... the Bill Hamer Programme!' Tinned applause followed: more reliable than the fresh kind. Cameras tracked silently in under the music. This was the opening of Mendelssohn's violin concerto, shorn of its prefatory string murmur. Hamer had selected it, after careful thought and thorough sampling, as a piece many would recognize but comparatively few be able to name (and therefore acceptably intellectual), as lively but also sensitive (like him), and as featuring a soloist with a decidedly subordinate accompaniment (like his show). It began to fade and he was talking.

' ... think about that, Ronnie? After all, our civilization, rightly or wrongly, has grown up on and around the making of money, and where there's money presumably you have to have rich people. I think they're a fascinating crowd, the rich, and I suggest we just go on talking about them, who they are, what they are, what their lives are like, what part they play in our culture. The rich.'

'Of course I agree, Bill,' said Ronnie. 'I mean that under the capitalist system some people have got to be very much richer than others. But then under a feudal stysem some people, a small number of people, have got to own all the land between them, and under a fascist system some people—'

'A very good point, but before you develop it I want to tell you a bit about Tony here, Anthony Sparks to you, who though you might not think it to look at him is the editor of the *Financial Observer*, that very well-informed but also very go-ahead and entertaining journal which all investors who've got their heads screwed on right, whether they've got ten thousand pounds at their disposal or ten shillings ... '

When Ronnie had been thoroughly indoctrinated about Sparks, Hamer went on to tell Sparks about Lady Baldock, and Sparks about Vassilikós, and Vassilikós about Ronnie (no need for a lot of detail there). This was in pursuance of what Hamer called his invisible-camera method, whereby five people who just happened to be chatting about something were televised doing it with no more knowledge of the fact, at least in theory, than if they had been a family of bears going about their business in the Rocky Mountains. Introducing them in Hamer's way took much, much longer than the old, hopelessly outmoded method of closing on each character in turn while someone says who he is in a dozen words, but Hamer did not mind that, because he was on camera and talking for nine-tenths of the time. Captions, which might have been thought an obvious aid at this point, were austerely eschewed; Hamer had said that they would militate against the illusion of actuality that was the chief aim of invisible camera, without adding that they might also have helped the audience to remember who, apart from himself, had been on his show after it was over. To people who asked, as they still did occasionally, whether illusion of actuality was helped much by seating one participant three feet higher than the others, Hamer was accustomed to reply, if at all, by saying that he was afraid he had no time now to explain the concept of visual-spatial convention.

When the introductions were at last completed, Hamer got Sparks to do some stuff with figures and diagrams designed to show just how rich rich people were, how much richer they were and how many more of them there were than formerly, and things like that. Apart from Sparks himself, nobody present took the slightest genuine interest in these demonstrations, least of all Hamer, who was, of course, frequently cut to nevertheless in the act of frowning and nodding intelligently. The loss to him in personal screen time was under three minutes, and he liked to introduce these bits of head-work occasionally. To do so was the most economical way of conveying his and the programme's underlying seriousness and sense of responsibility; or, as he used to put it when he was sure of his company, a minute of maths was worth an inch in the *Guardian.*

Ronnie sat it out, his face turned towards Sparks and his eyes on Lady Baldock. Once she gave a spectacular suppressed yawn with swelling nostrils and juddering chin —adroitly scooped up by MacBean, as a quick glance at the monitor showed. Otherwise she seemed perfectly at home, reacting well and without fidgets to the rare experience of keeping quiet for so long on end, moving head or arm slowly so that the lights would catch her jewellery. She little knew what she was in for. He little knew too for the moment, but it would come to him.

Sparks finished his stuff, and the illusion of actuality, perhaps a little impaired by his activities, came back into its own when Hamer laced his fingers together and began sounding off like anybody the world over who has made the rules governing his circle.

'Very concentrated stuff, that,' he said, grinning. 'I'm afraid I'll have to be a bit more, you know, sort of informal and impressionistic. The rich ... They're not a class, are they? Are they even a group, in the way that, oh, scientists, teenagers, homosexuals if you like are a group? Ronnie, you're a literary boy, what was it that Scott Fitzgerald, that wonderful American novelist of the jazz age, said to Ernest Hemingway, that other great writer, you know, *For Whom the Bell Tolls* and all that, on this very topic oh yes of course I remember. Fitzgerald said, "You know, Ernest ..." '

It seemed to Ronnie that they were happily, or at any rate safely, set until the first commercial break, but with a couple of minutes to go Hamer startled him a little by saying,

'Well, that's all I can think of for the moment. What about you, Ronnie? Any reactions? You're not rich yourself, none of us in this damn silly profession are ever going to *get* rich that way, but like most people you've run into the rich, I mean let's face it I understand you know Lady Baldock quite well, and you've at least met Mr Vassilikós, and no doubt plenty of others. What's the word from you about this peculiar breed of human being?'

'Well, Bill, I'd say ... the first thing that strikes me is just that, that the rich are human beings like ourselves, and that's something we must all keep trying to remember in the face of all the evidence.'

Hamer looked at him as if he were a beautiful nymphomaniacal debutante. 'Could you, uh, clarify that, Ronnie?'

'With pleasure. I overstated the case, I know. Some rich people have got the strength of character it takes to be rich and remain a human being. I'm not talking about them. They're rich in the sense that they have more money that we have, Hemingway's rich. I'm talking about Fitzgerald's rich—I don't know why everybody seems to think he lost that exchange, he saw more than Hemingway did, as always—I'm talking about the rich that are different from us. They're different, and they're worse, not because they're worse by nature, but because of their opportunities. Opportunities for power without responsibility. You've got to be tough as well as decent to resist those temptations. Some people can, as I said. There are plenty of decent prison officers, and sergeant-majors, and fathers and especially stepfathers of young children. But, as we all know, there are plenty of horrible ones too. The same thing goes for the rich.' Ronnie glanced at the minute-clock which a vassal of the floor manager was holding for his benefit, holding rather affectedly away to the side of his body like a matador preparing a tricky pass. Ten to go. 'That's the first bit anyway, Bill.'

'Fine. Before you go on, there are one or two points I want to put to old Tony about those charts of his.'

This was a lie, but a large part of it never reached the viewing public, for the first commercial had begun. It was about household tools. Hamer used all the influence he had to keep the advertising material that interrruptedhis show as boring as possible, so that those at home would realize how much they wanted to get back to him. Before the latest hand-drill had finished showing off its paces, Lady Baldock left her chair, exchanged a muttered remark or two with Hamer and came over to Ronnie, who got up politely. She had a small set smile.

'Mr Appleyard, I must warn you that if you attack me I will defend myself.'

'Naturally. But what makes you think I'm going to attack you?'

'That was obviously what you were building up to in what you were saying just now. I'm not a fool, you know.'

'In that case you must have seen that I was speaking generally.'

'Don't flatter yourself you can hide behind that.'

'Zooliette, for God's sake, the sap was just putting his point of view about the Ritz, that's all. People aren't all the time having you in mind.'

The set smile set a little more firmly. 'I hope you're not going to let me down, Kyril.'

'You, you, you. Always you.'

'Thirty seconds,' said the floor manager.

Before Lady Baldock could speak again, Ronnie said, 'You'd better get to your seat in case Bill or one of the technicians has something for you before we go back on the air.'

She hated it like poison, but went. Charged up, Ronnie glanced at Vassilikós, who did a sort of snatching motion with one hand that managed to convey resignation and defiance at once. The final commercial was about something that contained up to three and a half times as much of some substance as anything else did, or perhaps as it used to itself in the old days. Mendelssohn was back, then Hamer.

'... quite clear. Thank you, Tony. Interesting how the richest men have become relatively less rich as they've increased in numbers. Now, Ronnie, you were going pretty strong when you were interrupted just now. Would you like to carry on?'

'Thank you, Bill, yes, I would. I was saying that the rich have more opportunities than most of us for behaving badly, and, being human, some of them take these opportunities whenever they occur. The exercise of power is very enjoyable to a lot of people. Ask any politician.'

'Be more specific, Ronnie,' said Hamer, smoothly cutting in. 'Behaving badly, exercising power. What have you got it mind? Telling people to go to hell whenever you feel like it, or do you mean something deeper and more ... sinister?'

'Well, there's certainly a lot of telling people to go to hell, but there is more to it. Let's take power first. There must be something infinitely enjoyable in forbidding people to smoke in your dining-room and then lighting a cigar or cigarette yourself. And having everybody move at your pace. The picnic party's due to move off at eleven sharp, but you keep seventeen people waiting about until eleven twenty-five because you couldn't find your walking-stick or your hat or you had to telephone your stock-broker. But if it does suit you to be ready at eleven and somebody less rich turns up at eleven two, then you bawl them out. Why shouldn't you? That's where the bad behaviour comes in. If you're rich, you can afford to abandon reason, justice and good manners whenever you feel like it. Take my example about smoking. You don't want other people to smoke, but you want to smoke, so you smoke. Then if someone else lights up, you can tell them to put it out. And if they dare to say, "But what about you? You're smoking," you can order them out of the house. Why shouldn't you? If you went on like that at the non-rich level, you'd soon find yourself without any friends. But the rich don't really feel at home with people who aren't rich, they're afraid they may be after their money, or a non-rich person may have some other claim to fame than just the possession of money, like being good at something, good at painting or music or science or the law or—'

Lady Baldock, not surprisingly, had been shaping up to interrupt this for some time. Hamer had used all his skill to prevent her, making faces of great but vague import, slowly mouthing incomprehensible messages, jabbing a finger at her with an expression of puzzled incredulity. They were wonderfully varied and full of conviction, but they were bound to break down in the end. She said loudly and quickly,

'Just a minute if anybody else is going to be allowed a word in edgeways. Bill, why are you letting him go on like that? I won't sit here and listen to my best friends being insulted with all this—'

By a masterly face that suggested the imminent collapse of the entire broadcast if he were not heard at once (MacBean got all but the first half-second of it), Hamer managed to shove himself in. 'Fair enough, of course. Everybody gets his chance to be heard in this discussion. And I mean everybody. You'll have your chance in a moment. Incidentally, one thing you said just now puzzles me rather.'

'Puzzles you? What do you mean?'

'As I understood him, Ronnie was describing the worst kind of rich person, the more selfish and domineering and so on. Do you mean to say that all your best friends are like that? Hard to believe, isn't it? Perhaps not.'

This was coming out into the open in a markedly non-Hamerian fashion, thought Ronnie. Lady Baldock evidently thought so too. Her high-piled head moved to and fro as if she feared that the floor manager would run up to declare his hatred.

'Kyril, are you going to stand for this? You're supposed to be an old friend of mine. These two men are insulting me. Haven't you anything to say? They're insulting you too, remember.'

'Nobody is being insulted, Zooliette, please. Nobody here present, at least. Ronnie's telling us some things about the Ritz people that I'm seeing in an awful lot of the people I know. He's very wise about them. You mustn't—'

'That's *rubbish*, Kyril, and you know it.' Juliette Baldock was moving into her oral-italics style, as experienced by Ronnie on Malakos. 'Don't be so damn *reasonable*. Can't you see that that's what they *want* you to be?'

Sparks, who looked like an inadmissibly intelligent Anglican clergyman, had been writhing about rather. Now he said, 'Look, this is supposed to be a more or less objective discussion of a fairly interesting topic. I deplore the personal element that seems to have crept into it. I suggest we discuss what we're here to discuss in a civilized way, and conduct our private differences elsewhere. Agreed?'

No. Nobody else wanted that. Lady Baldock said,

'Mr ... *Appleyard*. You're sitting there complaining about these horrible rich people you've met, people who've been good enough to invite you into their *homes* and give you their food and drink. Don't you feel a little bit *ashamed* of abusing their hospitality?'

'That's nonsense, I'm afraid,' said Ronnie, warming up slightly. 'If somebody buys me a bottle of expensive champagne and tells me while I'm drinking it that I stink and as it might be my son is a fool and ugly and hopeless, well, for me that rather cancels out the champagne. Obviously I've got to be free to–'

'A little while ago I invited you into *my* home. Not only that, I gave you a free holiday in the–'

'I'm sorry, but I rather agree with Tony's point just now,' said Hamer, rising to his feet. He was lying again, but he had come a long way in the furtherance of apparent objectivity. 'Let's by all means keep personalities out of this. Let's see what some of our friends round the place have got to say.' He began walking. 'I'm sure we can find some fruitful disagreements here.'

Actuality conversations between private persons are not normally witnessed by a couple of hundred others arranged in tiers, but Hamer had long ago decided that the studio-audience spot had to be an integral part of his show. It made him seem humble and in touch at the same time. Accepting a microphone from nobody in particular as if it were a cup of tea, he screwed up his eyes and said,

'Well, now. Hard words being exchanged. Pity. I'm sure somebody here can–'

'Uhm, would you just, uhm ... Fellow seems to, uhm ... ' Saxton leaned across and put one hand on Upshot's shoulder while beckoning Hamer with the whole of the other.

'Would you introduce yourself, sir?'

'Certainly. Upshot's the name.'

'Don't be such a damn fool, Tubby,' said Saxton, who seemed to have grasped with untypical speed both the fact that Hamer was holding a microphone and the part played by microphones in broadcasting. 'Edgar George St

Denis Wyndham Upshot, seventh Baron Upshot. Lord Upshot to you.'

'Thank you, sir. Now, would you call yourself a rich man, Lord Upshot?'

'We're modestly comfortable, my wife and I.'

'Absolute rubbish,' said Saxton. 'Fellow lives in a whacking great castle in Herefordshire and eats off silver plate every night of his life. Modest my eye.'

'It looks as if you qualify, sir,' said Hamer to Upshot. 'May I ask you, do you agree with what Mr Appleyard has been saying? Do you know rich people who behave in the way he described?'

'Certainly not. Never. The man doesn't know what he's talking about.'

'Course he does. Chap's got it to a T. You're not too bad yourself, Tubby, as long as you keep off the port, but half the people we know are like that. Take Juliette herself. Finest example of the lot. Chucking her weight about all over the shop. Moment she gets the chance she's off. You know that as well as I do, now.'

'What's he saying, Student? I can't hear,' called Lady Baldock from her seat.

'He says you're just like that Appleyard guy says we all are, Juliette,' thundered Mansfield at such volume that he might have been intending to reach at any rate the nearer viewers direct, without the intervention of electricity.

'He said … Cecil said … But that's … '

Lady B. was already halfway to her feet when Hamer arrived back at the centre of things in a hurry. He had not bargained for Saxton's intervention and its speeding-up effect. Ronnie glanced at the clock. Four and a half minutes remained before the second and last commercial break.

'Do sit down,' said Hamer, standing behind Lady Baldock with his hands on her shoulders and bearing down quite hard. He banked on her not having yet reached the stage of preparedness for physical grappling and, after a gruelling instant, proved justified. He went on immediately,

'Let's turn to a new point, and I'd like to hear from all of you on this. Patronage of the arts and sciences has always been a traditional—'

'You people are in a conspiracy against me,' said Lady Baldock in a level tone, 'and I want to know why. I want to know what I'm supposed to have done, so that I can say something in my own defence.'

'No no no. Zooliette, please. There is no conspiracy,' said Vassilikós, who might have added that a tacit understanding did not constitute a conspiracy, had he wanted to make himself perfectly plain. 'Like I told you just before, you're thinking everything is you, the world is you, everybody's only existing in the way that concerns you. It isn't—'

'Then answer me just one question, Kyril. You heard what this little ... monster here, this Appleyard, what he said about the way we're all supposed to behave. Now. According to you, Kyril, am I that kind of person?'

'Yes, Chewliette, yes, you are, I'm sorry to be saying. You behave like some tyrant whenever it seems you can get away with it. You are not humble. You don't have a feeling about our duty in this world to be good persons and to do as God has wished for us. You don't—'

'You need say no more, thank you. I can do without the uplift. I was right.' Lady Baldock looked straight into a camera and said in her level tone, 'All you people out there, at home or wherever you are, listen to me. You've heard a lot about me and the way I'm supposed to behave, though why you should be interested and what business it is of yours I can't imagine. Now I'm going to have my turn, if these people here will allow me.'

None of the other four spoke or moved.

'All right. Let me tell you something about this Mr Ronnie Appleyard who's been so devastating about me. I've been what used to be called very kind to Mr Appleyard. It may not be good manners to say so, but it seems that manners of any kind have gone by the board this evening, so I'll tell you that Mr Appleyard has eaten my food and drunk my drink, especially ... ' She checked herself, and Ronnie's slander writ evaporated before it had formed. 'He's been my house guest more than once, I've helped him make contacts, I've ... Anyway, you may wonder why Mr Appleyard accepted all these acts of hospitality of mine if he disapproves of me as much as he makes out. Let me explain. I have an unmarried daughter who will be very rich some day. Now I'm not saying that Mr Appleyard is—'

'Oh yes you are,' said Ronnie loudly. 'I'm after her money. In fact I'm not, but it's no use trying to explain that to you. I wonder when was the last time you took in a new idea or changed your mind about anything. Forty years ago?'

'How dare you, you jumped-up little con-man, you ... '

'I'll tell you how I dare. I dare because for once in your life you're not in an unassailable position. As for jumped-up little con-man, that's the best or the worst you can do, because you aren't interested in people at all, and so you just don't know what would be near enough to the bone to hurt them. All you can—'

'Ronnie,' said Hamer mildly, 'I'm not sure that all this is of much general interest. Perhaps we might move on to—'

'I don't give a damn whether it's of general interest or

not,' said Ronnie, as he had been intended to. 'And anyway, hell, it's of some general interest that we're talking to one of the most ruthless egoists in England.'

'This is wonderful,' said Lady Baldock over her lower lip. 'A moral lecture from a cynical little ... adventurer who thinks of nothing but getting his hands on to money he hasn't earned.'

'Good stuff, coming from you.'

'At least I don't tamper with people's affections for the sake of cash, which seems to me one of the worst crimes anybody can commit. Insinuating yourself, yes, making love to somebody purely and simply because they're rich and you want to be rich, not caring if you break their heart. You're the last person in the world to—'

'That's enough,' said Ronnie. Lady Baldock had got near enough to the bone after all to make him do what neither he, nor anybody who knew him professionally, would ever have predicted that he would do: forget he was on television. 'You're wrong, that's all. I want her, not the money. Listen, I wouldn't touch your bloody money with a barge-pole, not if you went down on your knees and begged me. Do you think I'd condescend to live in your world? When I see what ... '

'Time for a short break,' said Hamer.

' ... money's made of you,' said Ronnie, and stopped.

Nobody was paying any attention to him. Whether or not she knew that the programme was no longer on the air, Lady Baldock was now haranguing Hamer from the base of his throne. Vassilikós was strolling over towards them. Sparks was turning through a sheaf of papers on his lap. The studio audience were making a lot of noise, MacBean appeared and hurried towards the scene of action. Ronnie began trying to remember just what he had said.

'That was fine,' said MacBean, arriving, 'but enough is enough. That's quite as close to the wind as I care to go. So no more personalities, Bill, okay?'

'What do you *mean*?' Lady Baldock turned on him. 'I'm going to say what I like.'

'Up to a point, of course you may, but no personal attacks, please, and I'll give Mr Appleyard the same—'

'What sort of notice do you suppose he'll take of that?'

'A great deal. He works here. Now, Lady Baldock,' said MacBean, who was small and heavy and had had this sort of thing happen more than once before in fourteen years of television, 'I require your solemn assurance that you will conform to the ordinary standards of public debate for the remainder of the programme. If—'

'You'll get no assurance out of me. Be off with you.'

'I see.' MacBean spoke apart for a moment to a man in a dirty pullover, who hurried away. 'Lady Baldock, with great regret I must ask you to leave the floor of my studio.'

'I refuse. I have a right to be heard.'

'Thirty seconds,' said the floor manager.

'In that case I must have you removed, as I am authorized to do by law.'

'Don't you dare touch me. Student ... '

Ronnie sat watching it as if it were television. The man in the dirty pullover came up with two of the police inspectors. One of them put out his hand to take Lady Baldock by the arm. Student Mansfield, emerging from nowhere in particular, pulled him away. The other police inspector seized Mansfield's shoulder. Mansfield hit him and he fell over, luckily without knocking into any of the pieces of machinery that were clustered about. After that, events were difficult to follow, but by the time the floor manager said 'Ten seconds' the first police inspector was sitting down next to Hamer's throne, Mansfield was doubled up so thoroughly that he could, if he had cared to, have held a single sheet of paper securely between his thighs and abdomen, and MacBean was flexing and unflexing the fingers of his right hand and frowning. Lady Baldock, unattended, made her way towards the door.

The programme was only twenty seconds late coming back on the air. The floor manager cued Hamer, who said,

'Yes. Interesting stuff. I don't know about you, Ronnie, but the *process* of *becoming* rich has always fascinated me. Mr Vassilikós, I wonder ... '

Hamer spoke with all his usual charm, but real pleasure was showing through it.

'Of course, if she had promised to behave herself,' said Hamer the next day, 'Mac would have had to think of something else. And fast. But he'd have managed it. Got his wits about him, old Mac. Interesting chap, in a way. Came from nothing, you know. Anyway. Had much trouble from the Press?'

'They've all been on and told no comment,' said Ronnie. 'Couple of photographers outside the flat this morning. That'll be the lot.'

'Yes, this place was a madhouse for the first hour, but it's died down now. Your lady-love will have come in for a good deal of it, I'm afraid.'

'They don't know where she is. The fellow on the *Post* was telling me. By the time anybody got to Claridge's she and Chummy had taken off and Lady B. had followed them. He must have thought fast, too.'

'He can't be such a fool as he looks. Well, nobody could be that, I suppose. It isn't in nature, as Sam Johnson would have said. Mm ... '

There were sitting in Hamer's office, which was small

and full of things: magazines, newspapers, books, maps, typescripts, the Manhattan and Los Angeles telephone directories (a splendid touch), air timetables, boxes of sound tape, photographs of famous people and obscure places, gramophone records, empty bottles. Hamer had decided, probably rightly, that this scene would impress those he wanted to impress more than any amount of mahogany and marble.

Ronnie said, 'Bill, what made you do it? You knew what would happen, roughly.'

'Indeed I did, old boy, though it succeeded beyond my wildest dreams, as you might say. Good question. And, between these four walls, I don't mind answering it. Well, now. I got you along to carve her up out of what's called a mixture of motives. The first thing chronologically was her telling me, in the course of some dispute the details of which I won't bother you with, that I was a grubby little upstart. I reckoned I owed her something for that. Then, rather more important I imagine bastards like you would say, good old Vassilikós took a fancy to me, got the idea that I was an interesting sap—he doesn't half murder the English language, that boy, eh? Well, him being Greek, I wondered a bit whether it might not be something more tangible than my ideas that he admired, battered as the old charms are, but no. Anyway, one minor thing that bothered him was why a jolly good sap like me seemed to have so much time for a howling bitch like Juliette Baldock, whom he's hated for years, it seems. Evidently she tried to get into some drawing-room ahead of his mother some time in years gone by. Great on precedence, the Greeks. Well, I thought there'd be no harm in a little demonstration of where my loyalties really didn't lie, since a month on his yacht next summer was in prospect. Like some more coffee?'

'No thanks.'

'Don't blame you. Another thing was the T.A.M. ratings. Falling off rather. The word had got round that intellectually Hamer was bloody good, but a bit short on, you know, gutsy entertainment, knockabout, the kind of stuff that jams the switchboard. I think we've put paid to that mistaken viewpoint for a few weeks, don't you? And then—' Hamer did quite a long stretch of almost silent laughter—'you're in the business, Ron, so you'll understand: it was fun. Terrible thing to say, but there it is. You've got to be honest, haven't you? It was fun. God, what a decadent lot we are. All of us. In our various ways.'

Ronnie stood up. 'I'll be getting along, Bill. Thanks for the coffee.'

'You're welcome, you poor sod. I hope you didn't come in just to see me.'

'No, Eric had some film about the neo-Nazis he thought we might run some time.'

'Fascinating. Well, thank you for your co-operation.'

'Do you think she'll sue?'

'What's she got? We're having one of the lawyers in this afternoon to go over the tape, but although a hell of a lot of nasty remarks were passed I can't think of one that was actually defamatory. And we could come back on Mansfield for assault, and all that. God, that punch Mac threw was a beauty. Can't have travelled more than a couple of feet, most of it so to speak inside Mansfield. I thought his fist was going to go right through. No, Lady B. will pipe down. She won't want to remind people of a battle she lost. But see she doesn't set fire to your flat or have you tommy-gunned as you go into the studio.'

'I'll watch it. Cheers, Bill.'

Outside L.C.M. House on the edge of Soho a thin, dirty sleet was falling, eddying sharply in the cold gusts and almost at freezing-point as it lay on the pavements. The commissionaire used to hide somewhere below stairs on days like this, when he was in danger of being sent out to find a taxi, and if you telephoned for one it never came. Ronnie went and stood at the edge of the pavement, huddled into his new Italian paramilitary-style raincoat. There were plenty of taxis passing, but they all had people in them. In bad weather everybody else wanted one, and in good weather half the bastards drove to Frinton in them with the missus and kids. He would have brought the Porsche, but knew well that nothing short of a couple of pounds of T.N.T. would have provided him with a parking place.

The raincoat, which on its first outing had turned out not to exclude moisture, was now turning out not to exclude cold either. It was Italian, you see. The nearside wheel of a mail van found an invisible puddle and sent half a cupful of cold liquid mud over Ronnie's shins. He suddenly realized how tense he was feeling, strung up as though for some major ordeal. None that he knew of was in prospect. It occurred to him that he had felt like this ever since being about to go on the air the previous evening, except while his red bomb sleeping-pill was doing its stuff, and even that had, for once, lost its grip before seven a.m. Why tense? Why not just fed up?

The clocks began chiming noon and he abandoned the question. There was a case for slipping across to the Horseshoe Bar for half an hour or so, in the hope that when he came out it would be raining less, or he would mind it less. Just then a vacant taxi, skilfully keeping a Volkswagen between it and where he was standing, had a good try at slipping past. He prevented it; Mansfield could hardly have vocalized better.

In the cab he re-read the short and inaccurate newspaper account of some of last night's events, tamely headed *Hostess in TV Row*, then passed to general news. *Export Gap Widens—Britain Loses £22m. Arms Order—Textile Strike Spreads—Malta: Agreement Hopes Fade—Two Shipyards to Close—Ceylon Britons Told to Quit—England Follow-on in Sydney Test.* It looked as if the forces of progress were really gaining ground at last.

The sleet was falling faster and the wind beginning to get up. Grey swirls blew across the King's Road. Ronnie previewed the rest of his day. A sandwich at the White Lion. A couple of chapters of *Viva Fidel!—the Cuban Miracle.* A nap. Correspondence. Quick dinner at that queers' place in Sloane Square. Back in time to watch a B.B.C. programme on teachers' training colleges, which might overlap with an *Insight* item currently being planned. Then nothing. Then fat Susan? Probably.

When he paid him off, the taximan said, 'Thank you, Mr Appleyard,' and did not go on to ask him if he knew Bill Hamer. Well, that was something. Not much, though. Descending the steps to his front door, Ronnie wondered why it should be that not knowing where Simon was, after having known where she was for just a few hours, should make everything seem so much worse.

It was dark in the flat, so much so that Ronnie suddenly decided he must start looking for somewhere else straight away. This afternoon. No, tomorrow morning, if the *Insight* conference finished in time. He went to the lavatory. As he was coming out again, somebody started coming down the steps outside, moving irregularly, as if drunk or infirm. He could not see who it was. Opening the door, he found Lord Baldock standing there in a green plastic mackintosh, his forefinger outstretched towards the bell-push.

'What the devil do you want?' asked Ronnie.

Baldock frowned, then started blinking and shaking his head, evidently trying to suggest visually that Ronnie's approach to the situation was ill considered. He kept his forefinger where it was for a time. Finally he found speech. 'Have you got a bird in here or anything?'

'No. Why? What do you want?'

'Is there a pub near here or anything?'

'Yes, just over the road. Why?'

'Come on, you're not safe here.'

'What the hell are you talking about? What do you want?'

'Come on, I tell you.'

Baldock turned and made his way back up the steps. Ronnie hesitated, but not for long. He took his wet raincoat from the back of the door and followed.

On the pavement, Baldock stood in the falling sleet with his hands on his hips. His expression indicated that he would not rest until the row of houses opposite was torn down.

'What's going on?' asked Ronnie.

After further delay, Lord Baldock said, 'I've got Simon here in the car. Now, Appleyard, you're to be gentle with her. She's in a very—'

'Here? Where?'

'In the *car*.' Baldock plunged into a rapid walk along the street.

Ronnie caught him up and continued at his side. 'What for?'

'I'd have thought that that was rather up to you. And her, of course. She's scared stiff of seeing you after what you said to her at that log cabin place. I had to practically carry her downstairs. So, as I say, you've got to be decent to her. Is that understood? And I take it you do want to marry her?'

'Yes. Yes.'

'Right. I'll just tell her.'

Baldock halted at the kerb where a red Mini-minor was parked and put his face close to the window, which slid aside. Ronnie saw part of Simon's face and a hand.

'He's not angry,' shouted Baldock, as if she were much farther off than ten inches or so. 'He says he's not cross and he wants to marry you.'

The door opened and Simon, wearing a white riding-mack, got out and stood facing Ronnie. Here at last was a fact. They put their arms round each other and stood like that until Baldock, now carrying a suitcase with one hand, tapped Ronnie on the shoulder with the other.

'Come along. Where's that pub?'

'This way. Are you letting me have her after all?'

'I'm delivering her to you. Sorry about that business at the log cabin. I was wrong, but at that stage I still thought you were after her money, you see, so Student would be better for her. Just about better. Probably wrong there too. Anyway, I could keep an eye on her: I thought she was probably in love with you, yes. But that would only have made things worse. Student would never have broken her heart. In here? What are you going to have? I suggest whisky. Keep the cold out.'

In the saloon of the White Lion, Lord Baldock's manner lost a good deal of its habitual fuzz. Rather against the odds, he proved more than capable of finding his way to the bar. The landlord, today wearing yellow corduroy trousers and what looked like a cut-down towelling bathrobe, leaned towards him with pretended deference. Ronnie and Simon sat down in an alcove where there were post-horns and a table with a very inaccurate map of Europe under its glass top.

'I'm sorry I told Bish where we'd gone, and I'm sorry I

was such a fool about your job,' said Simon, who had not let go of Ronnie's hand since their embrace in the street.

'That's all right. Look, fill me in a bit, for Christ's sake. Where's Mummy?'

'Buying curtains with some designer chap. She thinks I'm shopping too. I'm supposed to be meeting her for lunch at one. Ten minutes from now.'

'What did Chummy mean about me not being safe in my flat?'

'Well, you won't be as soon as Mummy realizes I'm not going to turn up and then finds that a lot of my clothes have gone.'

'That'll be some time yet.'

'Don't be too sure. That woman's got a sixth sense.'

'That woman, eh? We are making progress. Look, if you want to take your mack off you'll have to leave go of me for just a second. I'll still be here.'

Simon turned out to be wearing a knitted white Chanel suit with coffee-coloured ribbon round the edges. Before sitting down again she took his hand again.

'We are getting married, are we?' she asked.

'Yes.' He leaned across the table and kissed her. This naturally coincided with the reappearance of Lord Baldock, carrying the drinks and a pseudo-Georgian jug of water on a tin tray that bore a jeering pop-art picture of Britannia.

'Plenty of time for that later,' he said. 'Got to be off soon to establish my alibi at White's. Here's what you do. As soon as I've gone, you scoot across to your flat, Ronnie, and pack a bag. Then out, the two of you. Vanish. Poof. Get a special licence and bribe the registrar to keep his mouth shut. Keep away from your usual haunts until you're married.'

'But what can she do? Simon's not a minor or anything.'

'If you'd sooner hang about waiting to see what she can do, I can't stop you, I suppose. She can be an irritant, to put it no higher. Can't she? Eh? And don't keep telling yourself you're not in Tennessee now.'

'Yeah, I know,' said Ronnie grimly, 'a little-known unrepealed ordinance of 1519 prohibiting those below the degree of esquire from marrying daughters or step-daughters of peers of the realm unless the chap's presented a fully-rigged three-master to the King's navy. You're right. Cheers.'

'Good luck to you. Actually you've had a fair slice of it already, me old sport. You only just got your message across in time last night, didn't you?'

'Message?'

'Sorry, assumed you realized. Assumed you realized. That bit about your not taking Juliette's money even if she begged you to. That did it. Up to that point, do you follow, there was still a chance that if you ever did succeed in running away with Simon, even perhaps after she'd married Student, then Juliette would come round in the end. Millionairess Lady Baldock, whose daughter is teaching at a comprehensive school in Battersea ... Wouldn't do, would it? Anyway, it's different now. Now you've told her to stuff her money in front of however many million people it was, pigs'll be flying to the moon before you ever see a bean of hers. Did you know that at the time you said it?'

'No, it took me a minute or two. I was in a bit of a state.'

'Yes, thought you were. Not like you at all. I mean not your old self at all.' Baldock's stare at Ronnie focused for a moment, then went vague again. 'So. Ronnie doesn't want Simon's money. Says he wants Simon. Of course, if you'd told me a few minutes back that I could keep Simon now you'd said goodbye to her money, I should have looked a proper charlie. Didn't think you would, though. The other half of the thing was Simon wants Ronnie. The last couple of weeks convinced me of that. So. Bang! Here we are. Oh. Before I forget.'

He took a slim wad of pound notes out of his breast pocket and gave them to Ronnie. 'Wedding present. Only twenty-five, I'm afraid. As much as I'm allowed to draw out at one time. Still, better than a ram up the duff.'

'Thank you very much, Chummy,' said Ronnie, putting the money away.

Simon, speaking up unexpectedly, said, 'Yes, Chummy, that's awfully sweet of you.'

'What's she going to do to you?' Ronnie asked him.

'Something, undoubtedly. Undoubtedly something. Even on the most charitable view, her most charitable, I've been guilty of criminal negligence in not reading Simon's mind and locking her up in the hotel.'

'She'll guess you did more than just not do that,' said Simon.

'Yes yes, but she can't prove it. She'll be pretty sure that you would never have done this on your own, you'd have to have had a shove from somewhere, but no surer than that much, mm?'

'That much is quite enough to make her cut up good,' said Simon.

'Good Lord, I know. But it's not a, you know, fully attested act of defiance in public, such as our Ron goes in for. She doesn't like those, does she? Do you know, I think I might start going in for some of those myself. Often wanted to.'

'With what object?' asked Ronnie.

'Oh. Object. I've been getting fed up. Really fed up. And now that Simon's settled ... There's a pink woollen dinner-jacket she wants me to wear. Might kick off with that, eh? You know, when you're doing exactly what she wants you to do, she's the warmest and most affectionate and loving person in the world. But that's rather like saying how marvellous that tiger looked when he jumped on to the antelope and sank his teeth in. Not worth it. Right, I'm off. When you're settled you can drop me a message at White's. Enjoy yourselves.'

Baldock shook hands with Ronnie, kissed Simon, and left.

'I told you so,' said Ronnie. 'In the office at Broad Lawns.'

'I remember. It was just my mother not wanting him and me to get on. I knew all the time, really. I'm hungry.'

'We'll go over the road and I'll pack a case and stick it in the car and then we'll go somewhere where the rich would die rather than go. And then we'll drive out somewhere and find a non-rich hotel and have a nap.'

She smiled at him with faint complacency: another of her new expressions. He noticed for the first time that there was some very dark blue or purple somewhere in her eyes. She looked precariously grown-up, like a senior schoolgirl in her first thoroughly adult get-up. Helping her on with her mack, he said,

'Very odd, this whole thing. I was a shit when I met you. I still am in lots of ways. But because of you I've had to give up trying to be a dedicated, full-time shit. I couldn't make it, hadn't the strength of character. Which is a pity in a way, because when you fall back into the ranks of the failed shits or amateur shits or incidental shits you start taking on responsibility for other people.'

'You're not a shit in the least. Well, not now. I've been a terrible fool all my life and I still am. I haven't changed. Well, perhaps a bit.'

'A hell of a lot. And nobody could blame you for what you were.'

'Oh, I could. I do. No sense at all. Silly all the time. Awful.'

'Perhaps we'll have to work on each other.'

'Helping each other not to be as bad as we would be on our own.'

'That's it.'

He picked up the suitcase. They went out and in a diagonal shuffle, arms about shoulders, made their way across the road.